"To pursu[...]
be better if we marry.

Rowena's voice gained a bitter edge. "If you are asking me to be your wife, you ought to at least have the courtesy of looking at me."

Marshal Hunter pivoted on his boot heels, and Rowena could feel the scrutiny of those cold green eyes. "What I'm proposing is a business arrangement," he informed her. "You said you wanted to go back to Twin Springs, settle there. If we marry, I can make that possible. Do we have a deal?"

Such a cold, businesslike approach. Rowena controlled a frisson and brushed aside the fleeting regret. She'd had a proposal that came with kisses and declarations of love, and those had turned out to be false.

"Yes," she replied. "I have no objection to marrying you. So far you have treated me with courtesy, acted with honor and shown remarkable generosity. I believe my chances of finding happiness with you are as great as they are with any other man."

The marshal's jaw tightened. "Don't expect too much from me."

Author Note

The Old West is a fascinating time and place to write about. Wild, lawless, lacking in organized social structures, it was the land of opportunity for some, and a place of heartache and suffering for many.

I have enjoyed doing the research to create authentic, detailed settings for my stories, and writing about typical Western heroes—outsiders; loners; men who seek a new start, perhaps due to lack of opportunities, to escape some personal trauma or out of necessity after being on the wrong side of the law.

Dale Hunter, the hero of *The Marshal's Wyoming Bride*, is such a man. Born to wealth, he has seen the war between the states tear his family apart and destroy his home. Now he needs to find a new place to belong.

The heroine, Rowena McKenzie, is running away from trouble. The West was hard on a woman alone. There were limited employment opportunities, property records could be patchy and law enforcement inconsistent. When Rowena inherits a ranch already embroiled in a range war, she lacks the strength to defend the land on her own.

The two of them join forces. What begins as a marriage of convenience grows—through some twists and turns—into a union that gives them the security and belonging they yearn for.

I hope you'll enjoy Dale and Rowena's story.

TATIANA MARCH

The Marshal's Wyoming Bride

HARLEQUIN HISTORICAL

Recycling programs
for this product may
not exist in your area.

ISBN-13: 978-1-335-05184-4

The Marshal's Wyoming Bride

Copyright © 2018 by Tatiana March

Printed in U.S.A.

Before becoming a novelist, **Tatiana March** tried out various occupations—including being a chambermaid and an accountant. Now she loves writing Western historical romance. In the course of her research Tatiana has been detained by the United States border guards, had a skirmish with the Mexican army and stumbled upon a rattlesnake. This has not diminished her determination to create authentic settings for her stories.

Books by Tatiana March

Harlequin Historical

The Outlaw and the Runaway
The Marshal's Wyoming Bride

The Fairfax Brides

His Mail-Order Bride
The Bride Lottery
From Runaway to Pregnant Bride

Harlequin Historical *Undone!* ebooks

The Virgin's Debt
Submit to the Warrior
Surrender to the Knight
The Drifter's Bride

Visit the Author Profile page at Harlequin.com.

Chapter One

Chicago, early spring, 1886

Dale Hunter sat in the office of US Marshal William J. Arnold and met the older man's scrutiny without a flinch.

"Sure I can't change your mind, Hunter?"

"No."

"I could transfer you back to the Eastern Louisiana District."

Dale shook his head. He didn't belong anywhere anymore. Not in the South of his mother's birth. Not in the North of his father's. The only place he belonged was some remote piece of land where he could live alone, bothered by no one.

"I'm sorry, sir." His tone was calm but implacable. "I'm tired of chasing moonshiners for the whiskey tax they haven't paid, and I'm tired of arguing with local officials who resent federal intervention. In my three years as a deputy US Marshal I've saved most of the fees I've been paid. By now, I have enough for a down payment on a ranch where I can retire and live out my days in peace."

Marshal Arnold's broad face clouded. "Don't give me that garbage. It sticks in my craw to hear a rich man talk about scraping together a few dollars."

Dale spoke sharply. "My mother's money is not mine." He gritted his teeth, controlling the flare of guilt. He knew his mother had suffered more than any woman should. The War Between the States had destroyed her family—husband dead, daughter murdered, son's quest for vengeance turning him into an outlaw at eighteen.

After eleven years outside the law, Dale had gained a pardon. His mother had expected him to take over the family business and find a suitable young woman to marry. Only he couldn't do it. The nightmares stamped on his scarred face, the horrors that kept him awake at night made it impossible for him to fit into such a genteel lifestyle, and his refusal to follow his mother's wishes had come between them.

"My mother's money is not mine," Dale said again, quietly this time.

Marshal Arnold cleared his throat. "Perhaps so. And I am grateful for the contribution you have made to the Marshals Service. Before I accept your resignation, I have one more assignment for you."

"Thank you, sir, but I'm done." Dale got to his feet, unpinned the tin star within a circle from the lapel of his suit coat and placed it on the desk between them.

Marshal Arnold gestured for him to sit down again. "Hold on a mite, Hunter. Where is this ranch you plan to buy?"

Dale shuffled on his feet. "California."

At his reply, Marshal Arnold gave a satisfied smirk. "California? That is very convenient. The assignment is in the Arizona Territory, only a stone's throw away.

You could travel at the government's expense and continue to your ranch after you have finished the job."

Dale considered the suggestion. Train fares were expensive, and his savings were barely enough to cover the down payment on the property he wished to buy.

"What is the assignment?" he asked.

"It's about a woman called Rowena McKenzie." Marshal Arnold leaned forward in his seat. "A lady, I'm told. She's been indicted for murder and refuses to speak up in her own defense. The local sheriff is reluctant to hang a woman, and the federal marshal for the territory is newly appointed, not yet confirmed by the senate. He is wary of stringing up a lady and making a mistake. I'd like you to go over and figure it out."

"That's it?" Dale frowned. "I'll review the evidence, make sure they haven't overlooked anything, and if the judge decides she's guilty, the local law will take care of the hanging?"

Marshal Arnold nodded.

Dale reached down, picked up the badge from the desk and pinned it on again. "I'll wire my report to you."

When he was halfway toward the door, Marshal Arnold called out after him. "The appointment of the United States Marshal for the Arizona Territory is pending confirmation and it wouldn't be the first time the senate has rejected a candidate. If a promotion would persuade you to remain with the Marshals Service, the position could be yours."

Dale pretended not to hear. In the three years since his pardon, he had avoided going back to the western territories. He'd lived in the steamy South, in the cold and damp North, but he had never had the courage to face the dusty desert landscape where coyotes barked at night and buzzards feasted on carcasses. And he doubted the wisdom of doing so now.

There was no mistaking the look of relief on the face of Sheriff Macklin in Pinares when Dale walked into the ramshackle office and introduced himself. A big, burly man in his fifties, with graying hair in a military cut, the sheriff barely glanced at the official papers Dale held out to him.

"You've come to take the prisoner away?"

"No," Dale replied. "I'm here to help you decide if she should hang or not."

He took off his long canvas duster and shook away the droplets from the drizzle outside. To his relief, Pinares was on high ground, surrounded by pine-covered hills instead of the red, dusty desert of his nightmares.

He'd taken the train as far as Holbrook, a lawless Arizona ranching town, where he'd bought a horse from the livery stable and ridden the remaining thirty miles south. Preferring to arrive in the morning, he'd camped overnight outside town.

Like always, his legs ached after a day on horseback. He didn't walk with a limp, for after he'd been injured in the gunfight to break away from the outlaw gang, the best surgeons in the country had pieced together the broken bones. Even more important, his arms had healed well enough for him to draw a gun or throw a punch with the same skill and accuracy as before. When fully clothed, the only visible legacy of his lawless past was the crescent-shaped scar on his left cheek and the slightly uneven sound of his footsteps.

Sheriff Macklin scrambled to his feet behind his battered desk. "No time like the present."

Dale hesitated. Although he no longer wore his jet-black hair down to his shoulders, it could do with a cut. He ran the palm of one hand along his jaw and felt the roughness of stubble. A lady, Marshal Arnold had told him. He brushed aside his scruples. A disreputable look might be helpful in persuading a gently bred female to provide answers.

"Is there a medical report on the victim?" Dale asked.

The sheriff extracted a bunch of iron keys from his desk, shut the drawer with a bang and halted, eyebrows raised, keys dangling in his hand. "You don't know the details?"

"Only that you have a female prisoner who goes by the name Rowena McKenzie indicted for murder."

The burly sheriff nodded. "That's the gist of it. There is no medical report on the victim, for the body can't be retrieved. Miss Rowena shot a conman who was trying to flee after being caught selling shares in a phony mining claim. The conman, Elroy Revery, was whipping his wagon horse into speed when Miss Rowena fired a pistol at him. The horse bolted and the wagon took off with the body."

"Didn't anyone give chase?"

"Not right away. One of the men who'd lost money in the swindle suffered a mental fit, screaming and yelling, scaring the women. By the time we'd dealt with him and rode after Revery, we found his wagon tracks leading to the edge of Dead Man's Gully. It's a ravine a mile outside town, too steep to climb down. With a pair of field glasses you can see the smashed-up wagon and the dead horse at the bottom."

"And the body?"

"Can't pinpoint the location. Must be beneath the

wagon, or thrown off and fallen between the boulders at the bottom of the gully. But there's no doubt Miss Rowena killed him. She snatched Kurt Lonergan's pistol from the holster and fired. Elroy Revery clutched his chest and toppled into the wagon. Before he fell, a dozen people saw blood spurting out between his fingers, staining the front of his shirt."

With each word, Dale's skepticism grew. He'd seen it before, a staged killing to facilitate a getaway after a swindle. He expected the ladylike qualities of the prisoner to be as phony as the mining claim her partners had been peddling.

"Is this Miss Rowena new in town?" he asked.

Sheriff Macklin shook his head, looking troubled. "I know what you're thinking, but it can't be. Miss Rowena came into Pinares two years ago and she's been working in Alice Meek's café ever since. Whatever her reasons, she shot Revery. I had to arrest her." The sheriff jangled the bunch of keys in his hand and jerked his head toward the jail. "I'm counting on you to straighten this out. No one wants to see Miss Rowena hang."

Dale's first glimpse of the prisoner was her back. She was seated on the narrow cot in the nearest of the three jail cells, gazing up at the patch of overcast sky visible between the iron bars that covered the small window high up on the far wall. Dale halted midstep, nearly stumbled. Memories of his sister, Laurel, flooded his mind.

It wasn't so much the slender body, or the glossy dark brown hair, the color of polished mahogany, although they were the same. It was the elegant line of her neck, exposed by the simple upsweep. It was the way she wore the faded blue cotton dress, as if it had been made for a queen. Instantly, Dale recognized the stamp of an expensive academy for young ladies, the kind that put emphasis on deportment and etiquette instead of practical skills.

Sheriff Macklin unlocked the iron grille and rattled it aside. "Miss Rowena, you have a visitor."

The girl—she looked barely over twenty—rose to her feet and whirled around, every motion graceful. Dale felt his breath catch. He had to clench his hands into fists to hide the impact she had on him. He wanted to ignore her beauty, wanted to treat her just like any other prisoner, but he couldn't help the way his eyes swept over her features, taking in every detail.

Her face was not dainty, like Laurel's had been. Her features were fuller, with a square chin and a bold line of dark, almost straight eyebrows. From this distance, Dale guessed her eyes were a deep blue, an unusual combination with the dark hair.

As he stared at the girl, he could see a blush fan across her cheeks. If possible, her posture grew even straighter. He wondered if she could feel the pull of attraction, the way he did, and was reacting to him as a man, or if her discomfort was due to a guilty conscience and the fear of consequences of her criminal acts, or if she was merely embarrassed by the boldness of his inspection.

Dale stepped into the cell, oddly reluctant to get anywhere near her, to expose himself to the power of that beauty. "How are you, Miss McKenzie?"

She inclined her head to acknowledge his greeting. Dale turned to the sheriff. "I'll take it from here."

He waited for the man to lumber down the corridor. When Dale was alone with the lady, he turned toward her and sought refuge in his experience, relying on a hundred similar situations. And yet no other situation of stepping into a prisoner's cell had ever been the same as this.

"My name is Dale Hunter, and I'm a deputy US Marshal. I've been tasked with…helping you to prepare for your defense." He'd been planning to say *tasked with finding out if you're guilty or not*, but somehow the words came out different.

Again, she gave him that regal nod. Dale felt irritation join the mix of his confused emotions. As foolish as it might sound, he wanted Rowena McKenzie to seek help from him. But it was clear that instead of seeing him as a white knight, she regarded him as the enemy.

"Why did you shoot Elroy Revery?" he asked.

"I have nothing to say."

Dale nodded, as if to accept the challenge. "Why don't we sit down?"

Miss McKenzie's eyes flickered to the cot covered with a rumpled blanket.

"Well?" Dale gestured. "Please, be seated."

Her mouth flattened into a line before easing back to its plump fullness again. "If you want both of us to sit down, you'll have to get a chair."

A lady. No doubt about it. Even while locked up in a jail cell, she clung to the constraints of her upbringing and she would refuse to sit on a bed beside a man, for it had been drilled into her that such behavior might taint her reputation beyond repair.

Dale retreated into the corridor. When out of sight, he closed his eyes for a few seconds. The past, Laurel, and all the guilt and shame that went with her memory washed over him. He knew it wasn't just Rowena McKenzie's beauty that had affected him so. It was the echoes of the past, of how he had failed to save Laurel, and those echoes made him want to save Rowena McKenzie, as if preserving one woman's life might balance out the loss of another.

But the past could never be changed. Only accepted. Perhaps even forgiven, although never forgotten.

With a tired shake of his head, Dale pushed aside the grim thoughts. He picked up a rickety wooden chair from the corridor, carried it into Miss McKenzie's cell and propped it against the wall. Cautiously, he lowered himself onto the seat. The chair creaked but held his weight. Only when he was safely seated did the lady perch on the edge of the cot, wriggling her backside to find a comfortable position on the lumpy mattress.

"So," Dale said, closing his mind to everything but the facts of the case. "Why did you shoot Elroy Revery?"

"I have nothing to say."

"Did you know him from before?"

"I have nothing to say."

Oh, but you're saying plenty, ma cherie, Dale thought. *The flicker in your eyes just revealed that you knew him in the past.*

"So, why would you want to kill an old acquaintance?"

"I have..." She was halfway through her stock answer before the question fully registered. Her lips pressed together, as if to trap any unwise words inside. She quickly regained her composure and finished in a mutter, "...nothing to say."

Dale found himself staring at her full, wide mouth.

Heat rose beneath his collar. He'd succeeded in blocking out the tragic memories of Laurel, but he didn't have the same success in steeling himself against Rowena McKenzie. She'd ruined his concentration. A twist of shame at the lack of professional discipline tightened in his gut. Never before had inappropriate thoughts about a female prisoner taken hold of his mind.

Bristling, he scowled at her. "This is a hanging town, and Judge Williams is a hanging judge. With a Democrat taking over the White House, the judge has been tied up with administration, but he is riding circuit again and will be here within a week. Do you really want to be strung up? A rope round your neck, a trapdoor beneath your feet and a hangman to pull the lever and let you drop?"

"I have nothing to say."

Angry at himself, angry at her, Dale pushed up to his feet. The flimsy wooden chair gave an ominous creak. On an impulse, he curled his hand over the top of the backrest, lifted the chair a few inches from the floor and slammed it down again, breaking it into pieces.

"It's that quick," he warned her. "Once you are standing on the gallows, it will be too late to change your mind and decide that you would rather live, after all."

From the way her nostrils flared and her breathing quickened, Dale knew she wanted to talk, had to fight to hold back the words that might save her life, but her willpower was greater than her fear.

"I have nothing to say."

"Are you afraid of someone? Afraid to talk?"

She pressed her fingertips together in a gesture Dale

recognized from his mother, from Laurel—a means by which a lady stopped herself from fiddling with her clothing or her jewelry.

"I am waiting for a telegram."

"A telegram? Will that prove your innocence?"

She considered a moment, and then she spoke very carefully, weighing up each word. "It will *allow* me to prove my innocence."

Dale frowned. "It will not prove your innocence, but it will *allow* you to do so. How will you be able to do that? What information will the telegram bring?"

"I have nothing to say." The firm tone of her voice made Dale suspect she feared she had already said too much, so he chose another line of attack.

"Is Rowena McKenzie your real name?"

"It is the name I was born with and expect to die with."

Despite the tension in the air, a smile tugged at the corners of Dale's mouth. "Not if you marry. Then you'll die with your husband's name."

Miss McKenzie's expression grew pinched, hinting at some past hurt. "Some women never marry but live out their days as spinsters."

His smile deepened. "I doubt you'll be one of those."

But as soon as he had spoken Dale realized it might be difficult for a lady fallen on hard times to find a suitable husband. Affluent, educated men sought wives who could boost their fortunes and increase their social status. A café waitress could expect to be courted by ranch hands and storekeepers, and a gently bred female might consider such men too rough, too lacking in culture. It occurred to him that he and Rowena McKenzie had something in common. Both of them were caught between the world they grew up in and their present circumstances, not fully fitting in either world.

The rain had ceased and a cold, clear night was falling outside. Rowena huddled on the cot in her jail cell, her attention focused on the small square of starlit sky she could see through the iron-barred window.

Was she afraid? No, she was not. At least not afraid of the noose.

But she had once been afraid. Alone and afraid. And she had taken the route of a coward and fled from her father's house, from her father's grave, unwilling to take over the fight that had killed him, unwilling to stay on the land that had killed both her parents.

Only four years old when her mother died, Rowena could barely remember her. All she could remember was the distant chanting of the Shoshone by the stream where her mother had gone to do the laundry. They had killed her with a blow to the head and taken her scalp. Flaming red hair, it would now be a prized possession in some brave's lodge.

And her father—she didn't know who had killed him. Just over two years ago, she'd returned home from school in Boston, to see her father's coffin lowered into a grave. He'd been gunned down, but no one could—or would—tell her who had fired the bullet.

Reese, the man in charge of the ranch, Twin Springs, had been a stranger to her. He'd claimed that her father had employed him and his band of gunfighters to defend the property. But Reese had been living openly in the house, as if he owned the place. Unable to tell enemy from friend, Rowena had fled into the night, leaving

Twin Springs for others to fight over, like a pack of hungry dogs might fight over a bone.

Her thoughts drifted to the marshal who had come to interrogate her. Even now, in the privacy of her jail cell, Rowena could feel her pulse accelerating. She didn't know what it was about him that disturbed her so. He wasn't the most attractive man she'd met, but there was power about him, and determination and intelligence.

The marshal's comments about a husband had stirred up unwelcome memories. Only two men had ever proposed to her. Freddy Livingston was rich and handsome, and she had imagined herself in love with him. He had courted her, believing her to be an heiress to a ranching empire, but the moment he had discovered the modest nature of her father's holdings he had cast her aside. Had he broken her heart? No, Rowena decided. The shame of a public rejection had hurt more than the loss of Freddy as a future mate.

And the other proposal had hardly been a proposal at all. It had been Reese pointing at a young man in the crowd of men at her father's graveside. "We'll hold the ranch for you. It would make things easier if you married Luke here. My son, and as good a man as any."

She'd barely caught a glimpse of this Luke Reese, a shadow among shadows in the twilight of a winter evening. She'd had some idea of a lithe man of medium height, with high cheekbones and jet-black hair. Part Shoshone, if she wasn't mistaken, and the grief of growing up without a mother had caused her to speak up too sharply.

"How dare you talk to me about marriage?"

That night, she had walked off into the frozen darkness. Maybe one day she would find the courage to go back and claim Twin Springs, the ranch that was hers by law. However, she might have to fight for the property, and a woman could not win such a fight alone.

To claim Twin Springs, she needed help from a man, a fighting man. She would have to employ a man as unyielding and capable as the marshal with cold green eyes and a crescent-shaped scar on his face. The imprint of fangs was clear to see, as if some wild beast had taken a bite out of him and found him too tough to chew. What was it her father used to say?

"Make a deal with the devil and you might end up in hell."

With a sigh, Rowena burrowed deeper into the blanket, trying to ward off the night chill. Of course, it was just an empty dream. She had no money to employ a gunman of any stature, not even the cheapest whiskey-soaked old-timer, and she was not brave enough to simply ride up to Twin Springs and claim ownership.

She directed her attention to the more pressing problems. What had happened to the two conmen who had rescued her from a snowdrift after she'd walked away from her father's funeral? Eugene Richards and Claude Desmond—or Elroy Revery and Robert Smith, as they were calling themselves for this particular caper. Had they become stranded after their circus-trained horse, the faithful Scrooge, met his end at the bottom of the gully? Were they trying to make their escape on foot, lost in the desert?

Doubt and worry dulled her vision, dimming the stars visible between the iron bars. She had made her choices, but guilt ate away at her. Why did it have to be so hard to do the right thing? Why did it have to be so hard to *know* what was the right thing to do?

Claude and Eugene had found her nearly frozen to death, and had put their business activities on hold while they nursed her through the fever that followed. She'd known that they earned their living by dishonest means, but she had never seen it done. They had laughed about it, making it sound like an amusing escapade, a gambling game.

When she was well again, the pair had dropped her off at a stagecoach depot with enough money to last until she found a place to settle down. And now, two years later, fate had brought them to Pinares, and the cruelty and selfishness of their actions had become evident, leaving her with an impossible choice.

The people in Pinares were her friends. And by not exposing the scam she had failed to protect them. But what could she do? While she'd been close to death, Claude and Eugene had confided in her, shared their traumatic past. Claude, a slender man with delicate features, had been abused as a boy, hired out to men who gained pleasure from hurting children. And Eugene, a giant of a man, had been locked into a broom cupboard by his father, to stop the teenage boy from sneaking into the pantry and stealing food to nourish his growing body.

The history of incarceration in a closet barely big enough to accommodate the breadth of his shoulders had left Eugene terrified of enclosed spaces. And Claude would rather die than relive his childhood torment. Prison would be the end of them.

So, she had chosen to protect those two. But soon she'd have to tell the truth, even if no telegram arrived to let her know that Eugene and Claude had escaped to where the law couldn't reach them. The pair of fraudsters might have once saved her life, but her loyalty didn't extend as far as dying at the end of a rope to keep them out of prison. However, until the circuit judge arrived, she would have to remain silent, waiting for the right moment to reveal that she could not be guilty of murder, because there had been no murder at all.

The hotel room was quiet, the mattress firm, the sheets clean, but none of it improved Dale's mood. He'd made a dog's dinner of it. He'd barged into the jail, expecting to coax the facts out of the accused and be done with his assignment within a day.

Restless, he rolled over, the sheets tangling around him. He could always tell when a nightmare hovered at the gates of his mind. Sometimes he preferred to stay awake all night instead of letting the past horrors intrude. But tonight the long ride from the railroad took its toll. As Dale slipped into the shadowed world of slumber, Rowena McKenzie seemed to accompany him, her elegant beauty like a ghost of a life he had once expected to lead—the life of a gentleman, with a gentleman's manners, a gentleman's house, and a gentleman's wife.

When the nightmare came, it was not the rancid breath of a coyote in his nostrils and the fangs tearing into his cheek. Neither was it bullets slamming into his flesh and the ground rising up to meet him as he tumbled down to the canyon floor. Those restless dreams were a legacy of the gunfight to break out of the lawless life.

This nightmare was from deeper into his past. He was twelve years old, the summer hot, Spanish moss hanging from the trees, the river low and sluggish as he and Laurel—already a young woman at sixteen—sat fishing on the bank. He could hear the sound of heavy boots crashing through the undergrowth. Coarse voices. Laurel's whisper.

"Hide. Hide. Let me take care of them. Whatever happens, don't come out. Promise me... Promise... promise."

The images jumbled, flashed before his eyes. Soldiers holding Laurel down. One of them had his trousers pulled down all the way to his ankles. Bare buttocks rising and falling, rising and falling. Throughout the assault, Laurel made no sound at all but the soldiers joshed each other.

"Hey, Krieger, hurry up, it's my turn."

"Shut up, Ives, you idiot."

Dale watched from his hiding place behind a tree, fraught with despair. He'd promised to Laurel not to come out. But the guilt, the sense of helplessness felt like a rock crushing his chest. Tears of shame stung his eyes. At twelve years old he regarded himself a man, and now he was behaving like a little boy, too frightened to intervene while the soldiers did those terrible things to his sister.

Craning forward so he could study the men waiting for their turn, Dale memorized the name of each man, and their features. Fisting his hands, he gave himself over to the hatred, his little boy's mind striving for that grown-up feeling again.

When it was over, when all four men had sated their lust, they buttoned up their trousers and shared a smoke. Laurel lay on the ground, her dress torn, blood on her thighs, one arm slung across her face to keep her suffering private. But she was alive.

Not daring to move for the fear that the snap of a twig or the rustle of leaves might alert the men to his presence, Dale blinked away the tears of pity and shame and waited for the soldiers to be off on their way again.

"The little bitch, we have to do something."

"No, leave her be."

The one wearing a sergeant's stripes dug out a few coins, tossed them down.

"Buy yourself a new dress, sweetheart."

Heavy boots crashed past Dale's hiding place. He counted the men passing. One. Two. Three. Only one more, and they'd be gone. He could go to Laurel. Help her. Comfort her.

A gunshot.

"Hey, Krieger, what did you do that for?"

"Couldn't leave the little bitch telling tales."

Dale woke up, the sheets soaked with perspiration, his body trembling, the nightmare still holding him in its grip. Two sets of patrician beauty, one merely a promise at sixteen, the other fully blossomed in her early twenties, merged in his mind. And it became clear to him that whatever the outcome of his investigation—whether Rowena McKenzie was guilty of murder or not—he could not let her die at the end of a rope.

Chapter Two

Tired and bleary-eyed, Dale ate breakfast in the hotel dining room. Sitting alone at a corner table, he fished a pencil stub from his pocket, tore a piece of paper from an old copy of the *Arizona Weekly Citizen*, and jotted down a list of questions:

1. Who was the man who caused a commotion when Revery was shot?
2. When did that man come into town and where was he now?
3. Had anyone seen Rowena McKenzie talking with Revery?
4. Who owned the wagon Revery crashed into the gully?
5. Who owned the wagon horse that ended the same way?
6. Had Rowena McKenzie lost any money in the swindle?
7. Who else had lost money and how much?

Not wasting any time, Dale tossed down his napkin, finished his coffee and set off to conduct his interviews.

Outside, the street was quiet. Clouds had gathered in the sky again, and yesterday's drizzle was turning into a few flakes of snow, the final gasp of winter. *Good*, Dale thought. The bad weather would keep people indoors and the storekeepers would have more time to talk.

He started with the barbershop. The small, dapper man with an oiled mustache gave him an assessing glance. "A haircut, sir?"

Dale nodded, took down his hat and settled in the reclining leather chair. Might as well use the time productively while he went about his business.

By early afternoon, he'd had his boots polished, his coat pressed, the fraying cartridge loops on his gun belt restored. He'd tasted three different kinds of angel cake, sipped whiskey and beer and tea and coffee. He'd listened to voices that ranged from shrilly female to the croak of an adolescent boy to the raspy cough of a man who smoked too much.

Everyone had good things to say about Rowena McKenzie. Pinares had been founded by Quakers, and although no one used *thou* or *thee* anymore, the abhorrence of violence that went with the religion was deeply ingrained in the community. In some other town, Rowena McKenzie might not even have been arrested for what she had done, but instead the citizens might have taken up a collection to reward her for so efficiently dispatching the conman who had taken advantage of their trust.

Dale's best source of information was Alice Meek, the sturdy proprietor of the café where Rowena McKenzie worked. Needing little prompting, the woman talked in a breezy monologue while she chopped meat and vegetables for a stew, the only item on the lunch menu chalked to the blackboard by the entrance.

"The man that caused the commotion were a feller by the name of Robert Smith. New to town, he was. A small man, quiet and well spoken. A good customer at lunchtime. The first one to lay his money down for this mining claim. Kept telling everyone what a good investment it was. Went right off his head, poor soul. Don't know what became of him. Rode off that very night. I reckon he took to hiding, too afraid to let his wife know he'd lost the money he was meant to use to bring his family out here. He were from Pennsylvania."

"Did Miss Rowena get taken in by the swindlers, too?"

Carrot slices tumbled into the cauldron. "Miss Rowena? Invest? Poor lamb, she ain't got a penny to spare. I'd like to pay her more but times are tough." Mrs. Meek shook her head. "She'd been ill with a fever, Miss Rowena, but when she got to her feet again she went round warning people against parting with their money. Nobody listened to her, though, even though she has more book learning than any of them, of course excepting Mr. Carpenter—that's the lawyer—and Reverend Poole."

"Did you ever see her engage in private conversation with Revery?"

Mrs. Meek slammed the meat cleaver over a chunk of beef, mouth pursed, mental struggle evident on her rounded features. "Might as well tell you. Things usually come out anyway. Minna Tellerman—that's the hotel owner's wife—seen her come out of Revery's room one night. Now, if it were any other woman, I'd think she been doing a bit of trade, if you take my meaning. But not Miss Rowena. She's a lady, a real lady. Not a lady of the night."

At his next stop, the livery stable, Dale discovered

the wagon used in the escape had been rented but the horse, a big chestnut thoroughbred, had belonged to Revery, and he had ridden the animal into town. It was uncommon to have a horse trained for both harness and saddle, a detail which added to Dale's suspicions.

A telegram to the Claims Recorder in the Warren Mining District received the surprising reply that the mining claim the swindlers had been peddling did in fact exist and had been legally filed, but the land had been sampled and was deemed worthless. However, the presence of the nearby Copper Queen mine in Bisbee, valued at nearly two million dollars, allowed even plain gravel to be marketed as if it were solid copper.

Dale returned to his room, compiled a list of the victims and the amounts they had lost. No one had been swindled out of more than one hundred dollars, a relatively modest amount in such an affluent town, and the majority of the victims had lost fifty or twenty-five dollars. It seemed the fraudsters were skilled in estimating what people could afford, and only allowed them to invest accordingly, using the excuse that they had a limited number of shares in the claim available and needed to give everyone an opportunity to profit.

When the list of investors was complete, Dale added up the total. Altogether, Revery and his accomplice, Robert Smith, had taken just over three thousand dollars.

Of course, Revery and Smith were unlikely to be their real names. Frowning, Dale searched his memory. He could recall reading about a similar case in Colorado a year earlier. On that occasion, the perpetrators had called themselves Edmond Rawlins and Billy Jones. One name with matching initials, the other so common it wouldn't trigger any alarm bells. Everything tied together neatly. The only thing Dale couldn't figure out was how Rowena McKenzie fitted into the setup. He got to his feet, glimpsed at his new haircut in the mirror and pulled on his freshly pressed coat. Time to find out.

It was not lonely in the jail. Women came to visit, delivering clean clothes and gossip. As long as the other two cells remained unoccupied, the nights were calm. The meals were adequate and the sheriff provided hot water to wash and the privacy to benefit from it.

If it hadn't been for the worry about Claude and Eugene, and the guilt over having betrayed the people in Pinares that constantly chafed at her, like a pair of ill-fitting shoes, Rowena might have regarded her incarceration as a holiday. She harbored no fears about her own fate, for she took it for granted that the judge would believe her when the time came to reveal the truth. But today she felt restless. When her ears picked out a slightly uneven cadence of footsteps in the corridor, her heartbeat quickened.

She bounced up from the cot. Turning her back to hide her efforts, she fluffed up the wispy curls at her temples and adjusted the collar of her sage-green wool dress, a worn but good quality garment which Permelia Jenkins, the tailor's daughter, had only just that morning returned after cleaning and pressing it with an expert touch.

Today the sheriff must have dispensed with his guardian duty, for the marshal with a crescent-shaped scar on his cheek walked up to the cell unaccompanied. A jolt went through Rowena at the sight of him. He'd had a haircut. And he'd tidied up his clothing. Although the difference was subtle, it emphasized the combination of violence and elegance that would surely have sent all her old school friends into a swoon.

The marshal unlocked the iron grille with one hand, while dangling a sturdy captain's chair from the other. Not making a sound—not even a muffled clunk, as if to compensate for his angry outburst the day before—he lowered the chair to the floor, settled onto the wooden seat and fired a question at her.

"How do you know the men called Elroy Revery and Robert Smith?"

Rowena controlled a flinch. So, the marshal had already figured out the connection between her and the fraudsters. She sank to sit on the cot. "I have nothing to say."

"What are their real names?"

"I have nothing to say."

"Why did you help them escape?"

She clamped her lips together. *I have nothing to say* no longer seemed an adequate response, so she chose to meet a question with a question.

"How did you get your scar?"

"Do they have some kind of hold on you?"

"How did you become a federal marshal?"

That last question hit its mark. She could tell from the slight narrowing of those cool green eyes that watched her every move. "I have a deal for you," Marshal Hunter said. "I shall answer one of your questions if you answer one of mine."

Rowena mulled it over. In the back of her mind, she could hear her father's voice, raspy from a lifetime of herding cattle in the harsh Wyoming climate. *"Make a deal with the devil and you might end up in hell."* He'd quoted those words about using violence to defend the ranch, and the memory of his reluctance had made her doubt the word of Reese, the gunman who claimed her father had employed him.

But now, as Rowena met the sharp scrutiny of Marshal Hunter, an odd tingle of anticipation and daring skittered along her skin. Such a bargain could be used to provide misdirection, confuse the marshal's train of thought. And, in truth, she wanted to learn more about him. What harm could there be, if she posed her questions wisely and gave her replies with caution.

"Can I choose which questions to answer?"

Marshal Hunter nodded his assent.

"How did you get your scar?"

"I was left for dead and a coyote tried to have me for his supper." He paused and gave her a speculative look. "How did you end up in Pinares?"

Rowena suppressed a smile. So, he had accepted she wouldn't talk about the shooting. He would lead her round and round the topic, attempting to trip her up. Sitting straighter on the cot, she curled her hands around the rough timber edge and sharpened her concentration. "I came here soon after I left school. How did you become a federal marshal?"

"I had nothing better to do. Where did you go to school?"

"Boston. Where did you grow up?"

"Louisiana. Are you running away from something?"

"I…" She was wearing thick socks and no shoes, and she lifted her heels, balancing the balls of her feet against the cold cement floor, the nervous movement hidden by the folds of her green wool skirt. "I was running away…when I came here…" Rowena lowered her lashes, but she could not resist glancing up again. She studied the crescent-shaped scar on the marshal's face—a scar that bore the fang marks of a coyote. "And you… when you became a United States Marshal…were *you* running away from something?"

To her surprise, Marshal Hunter broke into a smile. It transformed his face, making him look young and carefree. The green eyes sparkled with humor. "I *was* running away from something," he admitted. "And that something was an overbearing, determined mother who had her own ideas about how I should live." The smile lingered. "My turn. Who were *you* running away from?"

She hesitated, then spoke quietly. "Myself."

"Never an easy thing to do," the marshal replied with a note of empathy in his tone.

Rowena nodded. "My turn."

She intended to fire out another question, but her mind went blank. She had asked about his home, about his choice of career. What about his family? Before her brain caught up with the implications of the question, she blurted out, "Are you married?"

Slowly, the marshal's expression sharpened and those green eyes fastened on her, so bold and direct Rowena believed they could see to the very core of her. But when the marshal replied, his voice was bland, perhaps a little impatient. "Why do you want to know?"

Up to now, she'd been enjoying the sparring. It had been like bantering with her suitors in Boston—not that she'd had many, for unlike some of her school friends she possessed neither great wealth nor important family connections—but what she felt now was not the girlish, superficial fluster of those occasions. What she felt now was deep and dark and laced with undertones of danger.

She inhaled a fortifying breath and refused to contemplate why the question about the marshal's marital status might be of interest to her. "No particular reason," she replied with a casual air. "I was just making conversation. And that was your question. My turn."

She racked her brain, but her concentration was in tatters. She couldn't think of anything that would allow an emotional retreat, could come up with no casual question that would draw them back from the dangerous waters of exchanging intimacies, of confessing hidden thoughts.

"Will you come back tomorrow?" she asked finally.

"Yes." Like a gentleman who has been given a hint that his allotted visiting time had come to an end, the marshal rose to his feet. "Good night, Miss McKenzie."

He retreated with those strangely deliberate footsteps she'd noticed before, not because of any visible quality in how he walked, but because her musician's ear had picked out the distinctive cadence of his boot heels against the cement floor.

As the marshal turned around to slide the iron bars back in place, Rowena couldn't stop herself from staring at him. One by one, she registered every part of his appearance—the coal-black hair, freshly cut, the gaunt face with high cheekbones, the green eyes framed with dark lashes, the hard slash of a mouth, the lean yet powerful body. Marshal Hunter stood still, aware of her scrutiny. For a while, it appeared to Rowena that time had stopped turning.

After what seemed like an eternity, the marshal dipped his head in a curt nod of farewell and vanished out of sight, leaving her alone with an avalanche of confused thoughts that ran the gamut from past failings into future possibilities.

Dale finished his morning shave and studied his reflection in the gilt-framed mirror hanging above the cracked porcelain washbasin in his hotel room. What had Rowena McKenzie seen when she'd stared at him with such intensity? Had she been repelled by his scar?

Are you married? Are you married? Are you married?

The question seemed to whisper at him from every corner of the shabby, well-worn hotel room. Dale shook his head, as if to dislodge the soft feminine voice that appeared to be stuck inside his mind. The attempt proved as futile as swatting at a fly with a piece of string.

He'd never considered that marriage might be an option for him. And yet, he could not stop his thoughts from reeling back to Roy Hagan, a friend he used to ride with in his outlaw years. Born with different colored eyes, Roy had been an outcast all his life. He'd been an outlaw when he met Celia, a bank clerk's daughter, and escorted her on a trail through the Arizona Territory. They had fallen in love, and despite Roy's lawless background, Celia had accepted him. She'd given herself to him, had fought to have a future with him. Their love had seemed so perfect, so complete, even with death looming over them, for at that time Roy had not yet broken free from the Red Bluff Gang, or been granted a presidential pardon. But Celia had loved him anyway, had been prepared to risk her life and sacrifice her reputation to be with him.

Could it happen to him? Could a woman love him like that?

Dale scowled at his image in the mirror. Of course it couldn't happen to him. Rowena McKenzie had stared at him because she'd been repelled by his scar. He had done his duty. He had uncovered the facts, at least enough to piece together a clear picture of the situation.

Number one: he knew that Robert Smith and Elroy Revery were professional fraudsters who had perpetrated the same scam on many occasions. On at least one such occasion Revery—or whatever was his real name—had been shot and carted away by a bolting horse. As Revery had since reappeared, it was evident that he had not died, and the same was likely to apply on this occasion. The lack of a body supported that assumption, although this time Revery had been forced to sacrifice his horse.

Number two: Rowena McKenzie was an honorable person—Dale trusted his lawman's instinct on that—and she had lived in Pinares for two years, during which time Revery and Smith had been operating elsewhere. During those two years Miss McKenzie had not sent or received any letters or telegrams. She could not have been in contact with the fraudsters. It must be a coincidence that they had come to Pinares.

Number three: Rowena McKenzie had done her best to stop people from investing in the worthless mining shares, and hence it appeared that she was not part of the fraud. However, she had secretly visited Revery in his hotel room, which was evidence of a bond between them. The bond did not seem sinister, with the conmen having some kind of a hold over her, for Miss McKenzie seemed confident that once she revealed the truth about the shooting her troubles would be over. Further, she did not appear to have any dark secrets that could be used to blackmail her.

Number four: Rowena McKenzie had grabbed Kurt Lonergan's pistol from the holster and fired the shot that allowed Revery to escape. She had done this after Smith, masquerading as one of the disgruntled investors, fell over in the crowd and was unable to use his gun. Clearly, she had facilitated the escape of the conmen, but it appeared to have been an impulse, dictated by the occasion. Had it been premeditated she would have arranged to be carrying a gun.

Number five: Rowena McKenzie was refusing to defend herself against a murder charge. She was waiting for a telegram that would allow her to reveal the truth. The telegram must be to let her know that Revery and Smith were safely out of the territory, and any other territory or state where there might be a warrant out on them.

This information, part fact, part speculation, ought to be enough to convince any judge that Rowena McKenzie should not hang, but should instead remain in custody until she was prepared to talk. He could relay his findings to Sheriff Macklin and be on his way to California. He ought to hurry, sign the agreement to buy his ranch before anyone else discovered the place and pushed the price beyond his reach by offering more.

Are you married? Are you married?

Ignoring the voice that whispered inside his head, Dale pulled his suit coat on. His task was *not* completed. He understood the chain of events, could be almost certain that Rowena McKenzie had not committed murder. However, she had aided and abetted fraudsters, and he couldn't consider his job finished until he had discovered what had caused her to do that. It would then be up to the judge to decide if Miss McKenzie was guilty of participating in a fraud, or had merely acted unwisely out of misplaced loyalties.

Outside, the sky was laden, the ground white with a layer of frost. Steeling himself against the icy wind, Dale hurried down the street to the small brick building that housed the jail and the sheriff's office.

Sheriff Macklin sat at his desk, feet propped on top, a steaming mug of coffee balanced between his hands. "Go right in," he told Dale. "She's between visitors. The cell door is unlocked."

Dale walked down the corridor, keeping his footsteps quiet. He found Rowena McKenzie in her jail cell, squatting on all fours beneath the window, peering at something on the floor. Like yesterday, she was dressed in a green gown, with a shapeless man's sweater worn on top to provide an extra layer of warmth.

"Miss McKenzie."

Even though she ignored his greeting, her body seemed to stiffen. Then she sighed, loud enough for the sound to carry out to him, and hard enough for her shoulders to slump. She scampered up to her feet and turned to him, a frown of dismay on her face.

"I almost had him," she complained. "Or her. I don't know which."

He stepped into the cell. "Had what?"

"Mousie." Her expression softened. "He—or she—is a tiny mouse. A field mouse, I think. I've been feeding him with bread crumbs. He's been letting me get very close. I was hoping that today he would let me pick him up, but you scared him away."

"I have that effect on small children and mice."

Miss McKenzie glanced at him, but either she missed the reference to his damaged looks or chose to pay no attention. Once again, Dale speculated about her past. She must have been brought up wealthy. However, he could sense no bitterness in her, no resentment over her loss of status in life. To the contrary, she seemed to possess the ability to find joy in little things, even having a rodent for a pet.

"Try it," she urged him now, gesturing toward the floor beneath the window. "Mousie knows she didn't get all the bread crumbs. She'll be back."

Dale edged closer and dropped to his haunches where he could see a scattering of bread crumbs. He wondered if Miss McKenzie realized she had just made her little mouse into a female, presumably for his benefit. He kept still, his attention on the floor. Silence settled over the jail cell. Just as well, Dale thought, for he seemed at a loss for words.

Seconds ticked by, turned into minutes. Rowena McKenzie crouched beside him. Their bodies seemed very close to each other in the confines of the narrow space. Dale could feel the sleeve of that shapeless sweater brushing against his arm, adding to his awareness of her presence.

"Listen," she whispered. "Mousie has returned."

The slight rustling sound grew louder, and then a tiny gray-brown mouse emerged from a crack in the brickwork. Scurrying, the creature hurried over to the pile of crumbs and began to feast on them.

"See," Miss McKenzie said. "She is not afraid of you at all."

Side by side, they watched the mouse, until the clatter of footsteps along the corridor sent the tiny creature into a frantic flight back into the safety of the hole in the brick wall. Instinctively, Dale curled his hand around Miss McKenzie's elbow to help her up. She accepted the gesture with practiced ease, which added to his certainty that she'd been brought up a lady, accustomed to men who performed such courtesies.

By the time a sturdy woman wrapped in a long wool cape came to a halt by the open iron grille, they were facing the entrance, however Dale's hand remained curled around Miss McKenzie's arm.

"Good morning, Miss Rowena."

"Good morning, Mrs. Powell."

The woman held out a basket. "Brought you lunch."

The visitor's face was red from the cold, her nose dripping, but she managed to give Dale a haughty look. "I trust you to do your job, Marshal. None of us understand what's going on, but we know Miss Rowena is no murderer. We don't need no badge and gun to figure that out."

Rowena flapped her hand. "Oh, don't be so grumpy, Mrs. Powell. We were just feeding my pet mouse. The marshal wasn't beating me up so I'll sign a confession."

"I'm not cooking lunch for no mouse," the woman muttered. She pulled out a handkerchief and blew her nose. "Well, I'd best be going. The chicken coop won't clean itself and the firewood don't fall into a pile on its own. I'll see you on Tuesday, Miss Rowena." With a curt nod of farewell, the visitor turned around and strode off, her bulky cape flaring behind her.

"I apologize for Mrs. Powell," Rowena whispered after the woman's footsteps had faded away. "She likes to gossip, and being stuck in a jail cell makes me a captive audience. You being here deprived her of spreading what little scandal she has managed to stir up since her last visit."

Not pausing to ask if he wished to eat, Rowena stuck her head into the corridor and yelled, "Can I come out, Sheriff Macklin? I need plates and cutlery."

"Prisoner transit approved," the sheriff called back.

Bemused, Dale watched as Miss McKenzie marched out, graceful even with the shapeless man's sweater covering her dress. Her feet were encased in thick socks that made her footsteps soundless. Her glossy mahogany hair was piled into an upsweep that her mouse-taming must have caused to unravel, allowing strands to flutter free around her face.

As Dale followed her with his eyes, he felt a tug in his chest. There was a gentleness about Rowena McKenzie that touched some sore spot inside him. He'd known ladies in his childhood, and many of them had been haughty and conceited. Lacking concern for the welfare of others, taking masculine admiration as their birthright, they had only shown friendship to those they considered their social equals. Rowena McKenzie was different, and that, combined with her beauty, fascinated him.

When she came back, she bustled about. Using the edge of the bunk as a table and the floor for seating, she served him a lunch of spicy stew. While they ate, they talked. Nothing personal, merely lighthearted observations about the town and its inhabitants. Two more times they were interrupted by visitors, a blushing teenage girl who came to lend Miss McKenzie a book, and an elderly woman who brought her another pair of thick wool socks.

"Why not tell the truth, Miss McKenzie?" Dale asked after the woman left. "The people in town worry about you."

She stacked the empty plates, ready to return them to the sheriff's office. "I will…eventually…when I have to…"

Dale didn't press it. It might be something to do with her background, perhaps the events that had brought about her reduced circumstances. Most likely, she owed a debt of gratitude to the men she'd helped to escape, and her silence was to protect them. But did she understand the gamble she was taking with her life? She expected that once she decided to reveal the truth, everyone would believe her and the charges would be withdrawn. However, sometimes the wheels of law took a wrong turn, and being innocent might not be enough.

Dale shuffled the pack of cards and dealt two hands of five-card draw on the table fashioned from an overturned crate. Despite the bare brick walls, the jail cell appeared homely now. Books jostled for space with newspapers in the small bookcase he'd knocked together from a piece of waste lumber, and a coal burner in the corner provided a source of heat.

Rowena picked up her cards, studied them with a notch between her straight, dark brows. Unable to hide the flicker of excitement, she rearranged the cards in her hand, extracted three and laid them facedown on the table.

"Three," she said.

Dale gave his own hand a cursory study. Two eights,

two kings, a queen. Why did luck favor him now that he would have preferred it to remain absent? He discarded one of the kings and dealt the replacements.

"Three for the lady. One for the dealer."

Rowena picked up her cards. Her face clouded with disappointment. Dale gathered his own hand. Damn. Another eight. He kept his features impassive while he waited for Rowena to open the betting. Maybe he could scare her into folding.

"Bet one hundred thousand," she said.

"Call your hundred thousand…and raise five hundred thousand."

"Call your five hundred thousand…and raise another hundred thousand."

Like the eager novice that she was, Rowena kept raising her bet. Between rounds of adding more imaginary money into the pot, she stared at her cards and tapped her forefinger against her pursed lips, a sure sign she was bluffing. Dale decided to rein her in, limit her losses. "Call your million."

"Raise…" Rowena darted him a questioning glance. Dale replied with an imperceptible shake of his head, and to his relief Rowena had the good sense to stop.

With excruciating slowness, like tasting a foul-flavored medicine, Rowena spread her cards on the table. A pair of jacks. Dale revealed his own hand and jotted the entry to the exercise book they used for their score keeping. "You owe me seventeen million four hundred thousand dollars."

Rowena rolled her eyes. "You'll bankrupt me yet, you cardsharp."

Smiling, Dale gathered the deck, passed it over to her. "Your turn to deal."

Inexpertly, she shuffled the cards, talking at the same time. "I'm surprised the Marshals Service lets you stay in Pinares until the trial. You're not doing much to earn your pay. It's not as if I'm a dangerous criminal who needs constant guarding."

"Marshals don't get a salary. They get paid a fee for each assignment." In truth, Dale knew he might be overstepping the boundaries with his visits, but he enjoyed her company. Every afternoon he arrived a little earlier and left a little later. Her feminine presence, her laughter, her beauty and her carefree manner seemed like a summer breeze that dispelled some of the darkness inside him. He was even regaining his sense of humor.

It seemed that for the first time since his genteel world of Southern aristocracy had vanished into cannon fire and flames, he was experiencing the social niceties he'd missed out on. From the age of twelve to eighteen he'd been consumed with tracking down and killing the soldiers who'd murdered Laurel. The next eleven years he'd lived in an outlaw hideout, isolated from the world, surrounded by cruel, coarse men.

When he'd gained a pardon, he could have re-entered the world he'd been born into, the world of ballrooms and parties, of plays and music, of culture and refinement, of money and comfort. However, although a pardon made him an honest man in the eyes of the law, it couldn't restore his peace of mind. It couldn't heal the guilt and shame over Laurel's death. It couldn't make his scars disappear. It couldn't keep away the nightmares that forced him to relive the horrors of his past, time and time again.

The legacy of his outlaw years held him back from attempting to rebuild his life as a gentleman, a gentleman of high birth and affluent means. Instead, he had sought some measure of restitution by becoming a federal marshal, a man who upheld the law instead of flouting it.

Because of his past, Dale had never courted a girl. Sure, he'd paid for a whore in his outlaw years. But in the last three years he'd lived celibate. Not because of a moral conversion of some sort, but because he couldn't tolerate the prospect that when faced with the sight of his scarred body a whore might demand extra payment.

But now, in Rowena's company, he felt as if he was getting a glimpse into what he'd missed out on, all those parties and balls, the pleasure of a woman's voice, her laughter. Although Rowena's gentleness and her impish sense of humor appealed to him, he couldn't deny there was a carnal element to his fascination. All too often, his eyes strayed to the curve of her breasts, the dip of her waist, the fullness of her mouth, but he possessed enough discipline to keep her from becoming aware of it.

He could see no harm in it, so he allowed the feeling to grow, safe in the knowledge it couldn't lead to anything. Rowena McKenzie was not the kind a woman a man could trifle with. Perhaps it was curiosity more than anything, a new experience, attraction that was more than just physical. And, to start with, spending his nights racked with unfulfilled desire had seemed preferable to nightmares. As Rowena McKenzie got deeper and deeper under his skin, Dale had begun to doubt the wisdom of that assumption.

"Anyway," he went on, "I am retiring from the Marshals Service."

"Retiring? Aren't you a bit young for a rocking chair on the porch?"

"I'm thirty-two. And I don't plan to be idle. There is this place, this valley over in California...the prettiest place you ever saw, with a stream running through it... I stumbled upon the property by chance a year ago, when my horse went lame..."

Half resenting the words as they spilled out, he went on nonetheless, telling her of the ranch, of the old man who wished to sell. He told her how he'd saved every penny of his fees and could now just about afford the down payment, with a bank lending the rest.

As he talked, Dale felt a tension coil within him, like the anticipation before a gunfight. He had never shared his dreams with anyone, except perhaps the dream of breaking away from the outlaw life, a dream he'd once shared with his friend Roy Hagan.

When he stopped, emotionally drained, silence fell. Rowena clutched the pack of cards in her hands. "I once knew such a place, too." Although her tone was wistful, she cast him an odd, speculative look. Dale had noticed it once or twice before, as if she were somehow assessing him, measuring his mettle. And then, with a visible effort to regain the lighthearted mood, Rowena dealt the cards, placing them on the table with an exaggerated flourish.

A pair of tens for him. When Rowena saw her own hand, her face lit up. To keep things simple, they skipped the initial rounds of betting and went straight to replacement cards. She took only one. He asked for three, failed to improve on the pair.

Rowena opened, forefinger tapping at her lips, her attention riveted on the cards. Dale suppressed a sigh. Another bluff. The pot grew until they had fifteen million of imaginary money on the table. Rowena laid down her cards. "Ace high."

Dale revealed his own hand. "When will you learn that a busted straight is worth nothing?"

"You ought to have folded when I kept raising."

"Never expect to control what the other players do." He updated the scorecard. "You owe me thirty-two million and change." With a rueful smile, he looked up at her. "*Cherie*, promise me you'll never gamble with real money."

She laughed, that light, sunny sound that touched something inside him. He spoke quietly. "Don't gamble with your life either, Miss Rowena. The judge arrived a few hours ago. He is reviewing his docket today. He'll hear the criminal cases first, before the civil disputes, and yours is the only one. Your trial will take place tomorrow morning."

Dale knew he could have revealed the truth by now—that there had been no murder, merely an elaborate charade to facilitate the escape of the two conmen who'd been selling shares in a worthless mining claim—but he also knew that Sheriff Macklin wouldn't accept his findings without the prisoner's own testimony.

Every day, the postmaster's boy came by to tell Miss Rowena there had been no telegram. Dale didn't know what information the telegram would contain, only that Rowena was determined not to disclose her innocence until it arrived. He hoped she wouldn't take her obstinacy too far. Judge Williams could be like a bear, easily riled, and the judge's verdict, however misguided if handed down in a fit of anger, would become the law.

Chapter Three

Dale surveyed the packed courtroom. Traveling theater shows were rare and not everybody could read, which added to the value of court hearings as entertainment. Feet shuffled, cigar smoke curled in the air. The stove in the corner radiated heat, raising the temperature in the room. Women fanned their flushed faces and men tugged at their shirt collars, until someone had the good sense to prop the door open and let in a cool draft.

Sheriff Macklin rose to his feet and called out in a formal tone, "The court is in session, the Honorable Judge Williams presiding."

The crowd hushed into silence. The judge flapped his meaty hand to wave away the preliminaries. Squat like a frog, with a jowly face and florid complexion, his every gesture spoke of impatience. He shuffled his papers. "The Territory of Arizona versus Miss Rowena McKenzie. What is this? A deputy US Marshal will testify for the defense?"

Dale had entered himself on the record and was seated in the front row with the other witnesses. He stood up. Before he had a chance to speak, the rapid clatter of footsteps and a childish voice disturbed the silence.

"It came, Miss Ro! It came! Your telegram!"

A boy of about eight, swamped in his older brother's hand-me-downs, charged into the room and scrambled to a halt in front of Miss Rowena. He thrust a folded telegram at her. "It came just now on the wire, *clackety-clack*. Pa wrote it down and I brung it over as fast as me feet carried me."

Rowena folded open the telegram, gave the message a cursory glance and threw her arms around the boy. "Oh, Clarence, you are wonderful. I'll pay you later. A dollar. Remind me."

Blushing, the boy extracted himself. "I don't need no money, Miss Ro."

"But you shall have it anyway." Relief evident upon her features, Miss Rowena turned to the judge. "May I take the stand first, Your Honor? I think it will save time."

Sheriff Macklin swore her in, her hand on the Bible that must have been handled by more criminals than clergymen. While Miss Rowena gave the oath, a smile hovered around her mouth. She sat down in the witness chair and turned to the judge. "I plead innocent, Your Honor, due to the simple fact that there was no killing."

A startled intake of breath hissed around the court-room. Everyone kept their eyes riveted on the witness stand. Still coasting on the rush of relief, Miss Rowena burst into rapid talk. "You see, I know these two men— Elroy Revery and Robert Smith—from the past. They operate a swindle, and they have an emergency measure that allows them to escape, should the need arise."

Gesturing, she went on with her explanation. "Revery leaps onto his horse—or onto the wagon bench if the horse is in harness—and Smith, who is pretending to be one of the disgruntled investors, fires his pistol. The horse is trained to bolt at the sound. Revery has a pouch of red ink hidden beneath his shirt. He makes the pouch burst and slumps down, clutching at his chest, as if mortally wounded. The horse canters away, carting Revery to safety. Smith behaves like a madman, to create a diversion that stops anyone from setting after Revery."

Rowena paused, to allow the judge to review the details in his mind. "See?" she said brightly. "It's a simple plan, but it works. No one realizes Smith is part of the swindle, and he quietly slips out of town. He has never been arrested for doing the shooting, because everyone believes Revery got what he deserved. And, because everyone believes that Revery will die from the bullet wound, they don't worry too much about chasing after him. Only on this occasion Smith fell over in the crowd, and he couldn't fire his pistol, so I had to do it instead of him."

Stop smiling, Dale berated in his mind. *Don't look so damn pleased.*

But, just like she lacked a poker face, Miss Rowena lacked the skill to hide her emotions, and now her entire demeanor reflected the easing of fear, the joy of finally being able to tell the truth.

The judge scowled at her. "You helped your accomplices to commit fraud?"

"No." Furiously, she shook her head. "No! I don't work with them. I've never participated in a swindle in my life, never cheated anyone. It is simply that I owed these men a debt of gratitude, for they once saved my life. I had to help them escape."

"Fifty dollars I lost," someone shouted.

"They took twenty-five from me!"

The judge banged his gavel. "Silence! Silence in my courtroom."

The angry voices faded to a mutter.

"I tried to stop the swindle." Alarmed now, Rowena faced the crowd, flinching at the angry stares directed at her. "I'd been laid down with a fever, and by the time I recovered and learned Revery and Smith were in town, the fraud had already been perpetrated. I went to see Revery, begged him to give back the money, but he said it would be too dangerous, that he would be prosecuted anyway. I tried to warn people, told them not to invest, but nobody would listen to me…"

The judge made a stabbing motion with his gavel, pointing at her. "You could have gone to the sheriff."

"I thought of it…of course I did… For days, I was fraught with indecision, torn between conflicting loyalties… But the sums they took were not significant…" Rowena nodded at the crowd, picking out some of the victims. "Mr. Timmerman, I know you spent much more than that on the new furniture for your living room…and Mr. Hoskins, I've heard you boasting that you gamble far greater amounts in the saloon every Saturday…and Mr. Silver, everyone knows that your new breeding bull cost at least three times as much." Rowena spread her hands, looking contrite. "I feel bad for your losses, of course I do, but I know they will not have a lasting impact on your welfare. But these two men…" She shook her head and spoke with a plea in her tone. "I couldn't have them arrested… I owe them my life…"

Gavel pointing, the judge addressed his words to

Dale. "Marshal Hunter, you've entered yourself on record as a witness. Am I to believe this fancy tale?"

Dale got to his feet. "It's not a fancy tale, Your Honor. My findings support what Miss McKenzie has testified. I believe these two conmen have been operating the same swindle throughout the western territories. They have escaped the attention of the law because they are careful to keep the amounts small, and I believe the mining claims they sell are genuine. They just happen to be worthless."

The judge turned to Sheriff Macklin. "How much did the victims in this town lose? Has someone tallied it up?"

The sheriff handed over a sheet of paper. Head bent, eyes on the document, the judge announced his verdict. "The territory versus Miss Rowena McKenzie. The accused has been found guilty of participating in a fraud and has to make restitution to the amount of…" A pudgy finger traced down the column. "The amount of three thousand two hundred dollars, which allows everyone to be reimbursed and adds something for the court expenses. If the accused fails to make restitution within thirty days, she is sentenced to three years in the territorial penitentiary."

The crowd gasped.

The gavel banged.

The judge called, "Next case."

The sounds of the courtroom faded away in Rowena's ears, as if she'd been trapped inside a bubble, isolated from her surroundings. She felt someone tugging at her arm. She turned to look and saw Sheriff Macklin frowning down at her.

"Miss Rowena, I've got to escort you back to the jail."

Her eyes darted about, searching for Marshal Hunter. He was over by the judge's desk, huddled in conversation. Of course, she was no longer his responsibility.

On legs that nearly buckled beneath her, Rowena rose from the witness chair and followed Sheriff Macklin out, past the rows of seats. People were staring. She clung to the deportment drilled into her by her expensive education and held her head high, but she knew the terrified look in her eyes betrayed her panic.

By the exit, she paused and turned around to face the crowd. "I'm sorry for what I have done. But I felt I had no choice. It is my firm belief that these men wouldn't have survived a prison sentence. Not even for a year or two."

Not pausing to evaluate if her apology had any impact on the hostile crowd, Rowena allowed the sheriff to escort her away. At the jail, the iron grille that had previously given her a sense of safety and privacy took on a sinister quality. She listened to it clunk shut and curled her hands around the solid iron bars.

"Sheriff Macklin, please… Yuma prison…do they take women…?"

"There's been female felons incarcerated there."

Felons. She was a felon. "Are they kept separate from the men?"

"I have no time for this, Miss Rowena. Not now. I've got to go back to the courthouse. We can talk in the evening."

She watched him go, listened to his footsteps fade away, each muted thud stirring up guilt and doubt within her. *"You can't have your cake and eat it,"* her father used to say. When she'd asked him to explain, he'd told her it meant that when a person faced two divergent paths, they could only follow one.

She'd chosen to protect Claude and Eugene. And in doing so she had betrayed her friends and neighbors. *Don't fall for those lies*, she had wanted to yell at everyone. *They are conmen. Fraudsters.* But a greater loyalty had sealed her lips. She'd told herself it didn't matter if people lost money, because the sums were small, easily afforded by the victims.

And then, when the angry mob had surrounded Eugene, and Claude had stumbled and fallen, unable to fire the shot required to make the charade complete, it had been no choice at all. She had acted upon instinct, the way one might jump into a river to save someone about to drown, and had assisted her friends in their escape.

And now she would have to face the consequences of her actions. What was Yuma penitentiary like? Horrors reeled through Rowena's mind. Convicts, including murderers and rapists, gaining access to the female prisoners. Male guards taking liberties. Beatings. Poor food. Lack of medical care. Intrusive physical examinations.

She'd be twenty-six when she came out, and she might look like an old woman. Feel like an old woman, too—no future, no hope, nothing to look forward to. She couldn't let it happen. Deftly, bursting into action, Rowena bent over, rummaged beneath her skirts and extracted a tightly rolled document from a narrow pocket sewn into her petticoat.

Her father's will, leaving Twin Springs to her. She had treasured the document, believing one day she would go back, find a way to fight for what was hers. Now those dreams had to be swept aside in the face of greater necessity.

She would ask the attorney, Mr. Carpenter, to sell the land on her behalf. He would come to see her if the sheriff sent out word. Slowly, her panic subsided. Everything would turn out all right. Claude and Eugene would be safe. Everyone would get their money back. She would have lost any chance of reclaiming Twin Springs, but those chances had been slim anyway.

Pacing the cell, Rowena waited for the sheriff to return. Outside, the light gained midday brightness and then dimmed again. No visitors came. No one brought her food. Either everyone was too busy at the courthouse, or they had turned their backs on her.

Finally, voices. She rushed to the iron grille, pressed her face between the bars and yelled into the corridor. "Sheriff Macklin! Sheriff Macklin!"

The burly lawman appeared, keys dangling in his hand.

"Sheriff Macklin, can you please fetch Mr. Carpenter for me? I have a property I can sell. I can reimburse everyone." She was babbling, the words tumbling out like grains in a mill. "I meant no harm. I will make restitution, just as the judge ordered."

The key rattled in the lock. The grille slid open with a screech. Sheriff Macklin stepped aside and gestured for her to come out. "You're free to go, Miss Rowena. Your fine has been paid."

"Paid?" Her brows drew into a baffled frown. The telegram had said: *Safe in San Francisco. Catching boat immediately.*

The message had been to inform her that Claude and Eugene were beyond the reach of the law, and it would be safe for her to reveal the truth. There was no way the conmen could have found out about her plight, could have wired the money to pay her fine. She made a small, helpless gesture with her hand. "But how...who...?"

"Marshal Hunter had a bank draft for three thousand and the rest in cash."

Stunned, Rowena blinked. She could clearly recall the marshal telling her that he could only just afford the down payment on the property he wished to buy, that he carried a bank draft for the exact amount. In settling her fine, he had not only given up the land he coveted, he had also spent most of his traveling cash. In her mind, she could hear his voice, the way it had softened when he described the land, and she recalled how his gaunt features had lit up with pleasure, how his wistful expression had revealed a longing for a place to call his own, a place to lay down roots.

Guilty conscience stalking like a ghost by her side, Rowena walked out of the jail. It was not her dream that had been sacrificed, but Marshal Hunter's dream. As she made her way through the evening chill to the boardinghouse, the rolled-up document hidden beneath her skirts tapped against her leg, like the finger of fate pointing out that she possessed the means to make restitution, to help the marshal resurrect his dream of land of his own.

There was no time to waste, for Marshal Hunter might be planning to ride out at first light. Barely pausing at the boardinghouse to make sure her room and her belongings remained undisturbed, Rowena hurried over to the hotel.

Minna Tellerman was sitting behind the reception counter, busy with a needle and an embroidery hoop. Rowena walked up to the frail woman and managed a shaky smile. "Hello, Mrs. Tellerman. Could you tell me where I can find Marshal Hunter?"

Minna Tellerman—whose husband had bought a share in the worthless mining claim—refused to meet Rowena's eyes. "Room four. Turn left at the top of the stairs."

So, restitution might not buy forgiveness. Rowena turned to go, then spun back and spoke softly. "I'm sorry for not having revealed the truth sooner, Mrs. Tellerman. I hope you have heard that everyone will be reimbursed in full?"

Minna Tellerman's chin dipped in a reluctant nod that confirmed she had indeed heard the news but was not allowing the recovery of her husband's investment to blunt her resentment. Pointedly ignoring Rowena, she focused on her embroidery.

Ill at ease, Rowena gathered her skirts and set off up the stairs. Some of the men waiting to enter the dining room followed her path with sly, disrespectful looks. Puzzled, Rowena averted her face. Then it struck her, another blow to her already battered armor. Gossip must have gone around that Marshal Hunter had paid her fine, and people believed that for a man who barely knew her to spend such a large amount for her benefit, she must have given him something in return.

Shame burned on her cheeks, but she soldiered on, located the correct room, raised her hand and rapped on the door. "Marshal Hunter. It's Rowena McKenzie."

That familiar, uneven trail of footsteps crossed the room. The door sprang open and Marshal Hunter stood in front of her, hair mussed, the tails of his shirt hanging free. Rowena hesitated. The rules of social propriety seemed inconsistent—it had never crossed her mind there might be something improper about the marshal visiting her in jail, but entering a man's hotel room seemed out of the question.

"I need to talk to you," she informed him, a pointless comment since there could hardly be any other reason for her to appear at his doorstep.

The marshal stepped out into the corridor and left the door ajar behind him.

Rowena gathered every bit of courage, every aspect of ladylike decorum she could muster. "I understand you settled my fine. Why did you do it?"

When they first met, Marshal Hunter had hidden all his emotions behind a blank mask, and now he put on the same neutral expression. "Had some money on me. Seemed as good a way to spend it as any."

Exasperated, Rowena flapped her hand in the air. Why did men think it made difficult situations easier if they pretended it didn't matter? "What about your land?" she demanded to know. "That ranch in California you said was the prettiest piece of property you'd ever laid eyes on."

"There'll be other parcels of land."

"Maybe. But we both know what you have given up." She met his guarded gaze with a fraught look that implored him to stop belittling his sacrifice. Being denied the opportunity to express her gratitude wouldn't lighten the burden, but instead add to it. "Thank you," she said. "Thank you from the bottom of my heart. And please don't do me the discourtesy of saying something trivial, like 'You're welcome' or 'Don't mention it'."

Marshal Hunter said nothing, merely nodded.

Rowena went on, "I know explanations and excuses won't change anything, but please don't think ill of me.

I was faced with a choice. The people who invested were only losing modest amounts of money, something they could easily afford. Claude and Eugene—those are their real names—would have lost their freedom. Both of them had a tragic childhood, filled with neglect and abuse. I feared prison might destroy the last of their humanity. And I owed them a debt of gratitude."

"It is not my forgiveness you should seek. I'll be gone tomorrow. Address your apologies to the townspeople."

"I've tried." Rowena expelled a sigh. "I fear they may be unwilling to listen."

"What did you expect? You had to choose sides, and you chose against them. They have been campaigning on your behalf, proclaiming your innocence. They'll feel foolish and angry now to discover that you were deceiving them."

Fighting spirit rallied within Rowena. She adjusted the folds of her skirts and lifted her chin. "I felt an obligation to protect those who would have lost the most."

"The law does not recognize compassion. It only recognizes right and wrong." The marshal's voice lost its challenging tone. "I don't judge you for what you did. I figured out the way of it from the start—that you knew those two men from the past and were protecting them. If I wanted to judge you, I would have done it by now."

"Yes. Well, anyway…" Rowena let her shoulders slump. "You are absolutely right. The people in town, although foolish, were acting honestly. Claude and Eugene were crooks. I shielded them, and I can see why a judge might consider that a crime, and why people who lost money might resent me."

Marshal Hunter lifted his brows with a hint of mockery, as if to remind her that the judge and the tricked investors had a point. "You came to thank me and you've done it." His tone was wry. "Don't torture yourself by worrying about me. I can remain with the Marshals Service, save up again. Like I said, there'll be other pieces of land."

"That's just it." Rowena held the rolled-up document out to him. "I can give you a ranch. Twin Springs, Wyoming Territory. My father left it to me in his will."

Marshal Hunter took the document from her, unrolled it and studied the pages in silence.

Her nerves rioting, Rowena kept talking. "I told you, I was running away from something when I came to Pinares. When I returned from school in Boston, I arrived in the middle of my father's funeral. He had been killed in a range war."

She blinked to keep the sad memories at bay. "My mother died in an Indian raid when I was small, and now my father… It felt as if the ranch had killed them both. Something inside me snapped. I just walked off into the night and didn't stop walking until I collapsed. If Claude and Eugene hadn't found me, I'd have frozen to death in a snowdrift."

Marshal Hunter glanced up from the document. "Do you ever think of going back?"

"Every day," Rowena admitted. "But I have no idea what's been happening. The house might have been burned down. There may be squatters. I don't possess the strength and courage it takes to fight for the ranch. But *you* do. I was going to sell the land anyway, so I could reimburse everyone for their losses and avoid going to prison. Giving Twin Springs to you achieves the same result. If it turns out the property is worth more than the fine you settled on my behalf, the excess will compensate for any risk you might face when claiming the land."

She waited. From their poker lessons she knew Marshal Hunter's features wouldn't reveal his thoughts, but she stared at him anyway, her eyes traveling over his scar, the sharp blade of a cheekbone, the line of his jaw, the curve of his mouth.

Finally, he spoke. "Do you have the title deed?"

"No." She shook her head, relieved to hear the silence broken. "My father kept it in a strongbox in his study. Unless someone has stolen it, it might still be there. I know the deed was filed at the courthouse in Cheyenne. If the original has been lost or destroyed, you should be able to get a certified copy there."

Marshal Hunter held out the will, but Rowena refused to accept the document. "Please. Don't add to my burden by rejecting the offer. I don't have the fighting skills to assert my ownership, which means the ranch is worthless to me. But it might be worth something to you."

"Perhaps." Marshal Hunter shrugged his shoulders in a gesture of doubt. The collar of his shirt was undone, and the movement made the front fall partly open, revealing bronzed skin with a sprinkling of dark hair. Before he adjusted the garment to cover the bare skin, Rowena could see a puckered white line that could only be another scar, although not as jagged as the one on his cheek.

"I'll talk to a lawyer," the marshal said. "Without the deed it might be impossible to prove ownership. I don't want to add to my losses by resigning from my post and then finding out some other man has a stronger claim on your land." He raked his free hand through his hair.

"Good night, Miss Rowena. It has been a long day. Get some sleep and I'll do the same. I'll seek legal advice tomorrow and let you know the outcome."

"Thank you. I'd appreciate it."

The marshal reached behind him and pushed the door open. When he was about to disappear out of sight, Rowena spoke to his back. "Why did you do it, Mr. Hunter?" Addressing him as mister instead of marshal somehow made the question more personal. "Why did you sacrifice your savings to help me?"

Without turning around, he replied, "I once had a sister. She came to a bad end. I didn't want the same to happen to you."

The door closed with a soft thud. No sound of footsteps followed, and Rowena could picture the marshal standing still, fighting the memories. In that instant it became clear to her that just like she had been, he, too, was running away from his past.

The short journey back to the boardinghouse had the potential to turn into a gauntlet. People might not actually pelt her with rotten eggs, but angry looks could hurt just as much. The sun had set, leaving the street in shadows. Keeping her head down, Rowena hurried along, the rapid click of her heels on the boardwalk betraying her unease.

Oh, no. A group of men loitered outside the tobacconist. She edged past. No one called out angry remarks. No one intercepted her. No one voiced accusations. To the contrary, a few of the men touched their hat brims as she passed, and some muttered a greeting.

Her heart lurched with hope. Perhaps there was forgiveness, after all. Increasing her pace, she darted down the steps at the end of the boardwalk—and nearly collided with a tall, thin woman rounding the corner.

"I'm sorry," Rowena said. "I wasn't looking ahead."

She recognized Mrs. Moreton, the butcher's wife. Quiet and timid, Mrs. Moreton suffered from ailments that confined her into the upstairs apartment she shared with her belligerent husband. When she eventually recovered and resumed her duties behind the store counter, not even a thick coat of rice powder could hide the fading bruises on her face.

"Miss McKenzie..." Mrs. Moreton spoke so quietly Rowena had to bend closer to make out the words. "That man, Smith...he had a hangdog look about him that I could relate to... I understand why you wanted to protect him, and I admire your courage. I don't mind that my husband lost money. Not even if he takes his anger out on me."

Before Rowena could reply, Mrs. Moreton slipped past and vanished into the store. Stunned, Rowena stood still. Tears of pity for the poor battered wife pricked behind her eyelids. The law might not recognize compassion, only right and wrong, but the weak needed the strong to protect them, and a fierce surge of pride filled her at the thought that she could count herself among the strong. She didn't regret what she had done. She might have been foolish not to realize there would be a price to pay, but she would pay it. Pay it gladly, and make no more excuses for having put protecting life before protecting wealth.

The lawyer, Carpenter, was a neatly dressed man in his fifties, so cautious he appeared to mistrust even himself. The air in his office smelled of alcohol but it could have been the yeast vapors from the bakery below. Nevertheless, Dale kept a close eye on the lawyer. The advice of an intoxicated man might be worthless.

Carpenter slid the will back across his immaculate desk. "Difficult," he said, shaking his head. "Someone could have used the title deed to record a transfer of ownership."

"But I could dispute that, could I not, if I have a bill of sale from Miss McKenzie?"

"The bill of sale could be dismissed as a forgery. Or, the other party could claim that Miss McKenzie sold the ranch to them prior to selling it to you. If they find out about her criminal conviction for participating in a fraud, they could use the information to support a suggestion that she might have sold the same property twice."

The lawyer cast a longing glance toward a cabinet by the wall, making Dale suspect he kept a bottle there. "I could do with a drink," Dale said.

"I can accommodate you." Carpenter bounced up, as eager as a grasshopper, and hurried to the cabinet. "I keep this for the benefit of clients," he said as he returned to his desk with a bottle and two glasses. "Whiskey can ease the sting of bad news."

He poured, and they lifted their glasses and downed their drinks. Making no offer of a refill, the lawyer put the bottle aside. "Let me see the will again."

Dale slid the document over. Carpenter shuffled the pages, read out loud. "To my daughter Rowena McKenzie or to her husband…"

"There is no husband, as far as I know," Dale pointed out.

Animated now, Carpenter leaned forward across the

desk. "And that is the key to making the most of the situation. The best way for you to pursue your claim is to marry Miss McKenzie and make sure she travels to Wyoming with you. A legal marriage will give you a right by inheritance that cannot be disputed, and Miss McKenzie can prove that her signature on any document claiming a prior sale is not genuine. Of course, that is assuming she is telling the truth and there has been no prior sale." The lawyer paused to let the idea of Rowena McKenzie as a habitual fraudster stew for a moment.

"However, even if you managed to prove ownership, the ranch could be occupied by squatters. You might then have to fight them to gain possession." A note of warning entered Carpenter's tone. "I have to stress that there are a number of risks involved in pursuing your claim. Is Miss McKenzie being honest with you? Will you be able to disprove any competing claims? Can you evict any potential squatters already in residence?"

The lawyer sat straight again, adjusted his silk tie and gave a discreet cough. "Should you decide to accept those risks, and go ahead and marry Miss McKenzie, I would advise you to make sure the marriage becomes binding. Otherwise, after you've secured the ownership of the ranch, Miss McKenzie could file for an annulment and send you off on your way. You'd have done everything, perhaps even risked your life, for nothing."

Dale thanked the lawyer, collected his papers, paid the bill and left. His mind seemed to have seized up, refusing to process the information. The clearest thought in his head was that Carpenter was not an alcoholic. He was a skilled lawyer who lacked confidence. The shot of whiskey had merely served to sharpen his wits and loosen his tongue.

Outside, the sky was gray. Gusts of wind whipped along the street, chasing litter and making shop signs clatter. He set off and kept walking, all the way to the end of Main Street and beyond, where the town petered out. Turning left, he took a winding path up into the pine forest. The chill in the air bit through his clothing, but he liked it. It was dry cold, unlike the damp winters of the northeast. Wyoming would be like that, too.

Like the wind stirring in the trees, the lawyer's words whispered through his mind.

"Marry Miss McKenzie... I would advise you to make sure the marriage becomes binding..."

Would she do it? Would she marry him? Even if she refused to consummate the marriage and they settled on a union which was nothing more than a business arrangement, he'd have the pleasure of her company. He could enjoy her warmth, her laughter, her serene presence that dispelled some of the darkness inside him.

And if she did agree to make the marriage binding, as the lawyer had so cunningly advised, he could have her. Perhaps just the once. Perhaps more than once. Would she touch him without horror when she felt the scars that covered his body? If she managed that, if she could tolerate him, the physical side of their relationship might create a basis on which friendship and affection could grow. His hands clenched into fists, as if he were already fighting not to touch her, not to demand more than she might be willing to give.

Chapter Four

*B*oom, *boom, boom.*

Rowena flinched at the sound. No one had ever pounded on her door like that before. Then again, she'd never been late with her rent before. In her haste to put down her mending, she pricked her fingertip with the needle. She muttered an unladylike word, sucked away the drop of blood and hurried across the cluttered boardinghouse room to the door.

On the landing outside, Marshal Hunter stood on the hooked rug, looming as tall and straight as one of the pines in the forest. The sight of him robbed Rowena of speech. His features reflected the winter chill outdoors, and a gun belt circled his lean hips. She'd never seen him armed before, but the ease with which he wore the pair of heavy pistols told her he was more used to being with them than without.

He must have noticed her wide-eyed stare, for he said, "They don't allow guns in the courthouse. And the sheriff refused to let me carry firearms when I visited you."

"Quite right, too," she muttered. "I'm a dangerous felon and I might have tried to escape."

Marshal Hunter's mouth quirked into a smile. "You did snatch Lonergan's pistol from the holster. That gives you a prior record."

Rowena rolled her eyes, a habit her teachers had never quite managed to stamp out. She inspected her finger but conquered the urge to ease the sting by licking the tip. Her nerves rioted. *"I'll be riding out tomorrow,"* the marshal had said yesterday. Only now did she realize how much those words had been weighing on her mind.

"How did you get on with Mr. Carpenter?" she asked.

"We need to talk."

She made a vague gesture, meant to usher him away from her doorstep. "There's a parlor downstairs for receiving guests."

Ignoring her comment—and the requirements of propriety—Marshal Hunter edged into the room. The air of determination about him made Rowena scoot backward, granting him clear passage. Once inside, he lifted one booted foot a few inches from the floor and used the heel to kick the door shut. He surveyed her private domain. "It's preferable we talk in here."

Had he changed his mind about paying her fine? In terrified silence, Rowena watched him negotiate his way across the room to the window. She'd been overhauling her wardrobe, assessing the damage caused by sleeping fully clothed in the jail. Items of female clothing lay scattered upon every surface—a chemise on the back of a chair, drawers in a tangle on the small bureau, stockings draped over the nightstand.

The marshal halted by the window. Not turning around, he spoke with his back toward her. "According to Carpenter, to best pursue the claim for Twin

Springs, we both need to travel to Wyoming. You may need to prove who you are, and you will need to refute any claims that you or your father had previously sold the property to someone else. And, instead of giving me a bill of sale, it will be better if we marry and I make my claim as your husband. That way, we don't have to prove the validity of the sale from you to me, but I can simply file my ownership based on our marriage certificate and your father's will."

An ugly, unreasonable wave of anger surged in Rowena. Nothing to do with Marshal Hunter, but the memory of Freddy Livingston, and the callous way in which he had rejected her after their engagement had already been publicly announced. Since she'd left Boston, she'd never told anyone about the heartache and humiliation she'd suffered.

Her voice gained a bitter edge. "If you are asking me to be your wife, you ought to at least have the courtesy of looking at me."

Marshal Hunter pivoted on his boot heels. The daylight through the window silhouetted him, leaving his face in shadows, but Rowena could feel the scrutiny of those cold green eyes.

"What I'm proposing is a business arrangement," he informed her. "You said you wanted to go back to Twin Springs, settle there. If we marry, I can make that possible. We could share the property."

With both her anger and her fear of going to prison after all finally ebbing, Rowena felt a stab of shame at her outburst. She'd been on edge all night, barely sleeping. She'd told herself it was the uncertainty over her future, but now she admitted to herself it had been the sense of unfinished business between herself and Marshal Hunter. Not just about Twin Springs, but the friendship they had forged during their afternoons in her jail cell. Somehow, that closeness needed to be acknowledged. And perhaps now it had been, in the form of a marriage proposal, albeit one of a very practical nature.

She tried to make up for her sharp comment with honesty. "I'll...I'll not deny that I've dreamed of going back to Twin Springs. And I need a man to help me fight for the land. The right kind of man, one capable of winning such a fight. And I admit that from the moment I first saw you I believed you might possess the required qualities."

Marshal Hunter spoke with amusement. "I did wonder why you gave me those assessing looks, like a drill sergeant inspecting a new recruit."

Rowena ignored the flash of humor and went on, "Since I possess no money to hire a gunfighter, perhaps I've known all along that my only chance to get a man to help me fight for the land is by marrying him. I am even prepared to admit that when I offered you Twin Springs, it might have crossed my mind that such an arrangement could benefit the both of us. But I want you to be absolutely clear on the nature of the property."

She knew she was talking like a land agent, prattling out facts, but she had to contain the confusing emotions that whirled inside her head, push them aside until she could understand them. Barely pausing to draw a breath, she ticked off the facts with her fingers. "The land is not the best. It is at the top end of the valley, on high ground, and the grass is thin. The house is neither large nor elegant. My father built it with his own hands, and his main concern was to keep the heat in and the enemies out. The cattle—if any remain—are not great in number. However, the water is good. The two springs that feed the stream through the valley are on my father's land. That is why the neighbors covet the property."

While she'd been talking, the marshal had been looking around the room, as if bored by her speech. Now he returned his attention to her. "The details were in your father's will. I don't have any illusions about the ranch. And I hope you have no illusions about me as the kind of husband you might find in a Boston ballroom. Do we have a deal?"

Such a cold, businesslike approach. Rowena controlled a frisson and brushed aside the fleeting regret. She'd had a proposal that came with kisses and declarations of love, and those had turned out to be false.

"Yes," she replied. She wanted to maintain the businesslike tone by enumerating the benefits a marriage brought to her, now that she most likely had lost her job and had no money to pay her rent. But instead, she found herself talking softly. "I have no objection to marrying you. So far, you have treated me with courtesy, acted with honor and shown remarkable generosity. I believe that my chances of finding happiness with you are as great as they are with any other man."

The marshal's jaw tightened. At first, Rowena thought he was going to avoid meeting her eyes, but he ceased his restless movements and contemplated her squarely. The starkness of his features seemed to deepen, like a storm cloud settling over the landscape. His voice was gruff. "Don't expect too much of me."

It hurt, not to have even a pretense of romance, but Rowena hid her disappointment behind a flippant comment. "I have a right to a few expectations. To start with, marriage makes supporting me your responsibility, which removes one of my worries. Further, there is gossip in town that I sacrificed my virtue in order to lure you into paying my fine, and marriage is an excellent way to restore my reputation." She gave a careless shrug, as if discussing an afternoon outing instead of the rest of her life. "How could I not agree?"

The marshal was fiddling with the frill of a chemise slung over the back of a chair. "What kind of marriage do you want?"

The married kind, she wanted to yell at him. *The loving kind.*

But she didn't say it. Didn't say anything. She had an inkling of which particular aspect of their union the marshal wished to negotiate, and she reined in her tongue. He was hiding all his emotions while drawing out hers. If he wanted to strike another deal, this time he had to put his cards on the table before she revealed hers.

"What do you mean?" she prompted him when she could no longer tolerate the silence. "Are there many kinds of marriages, like the selection of cakes on the bakery counter?"

She could see a flicker of emotion in his eyes, but couldn't tell if it was anger or amusement. He kept his attention on the frills of the chemise he was toying with. "Even though it is a business arrangement, I want to consummate the marriage."

It was unfair that the light fell on her, revealing her blush. She had anticipated the topic, but had not been prepared for such bluntness. Rowena started to say something, not quite sure what, but the marshal held up a hand to silence her. She expected him to launch into a sermon about men and their carnal needs, but instead he explained how Mr. Carpenter had advised him to take the precaution, to stop her from engaging in a devious female ploy of using a man to gain something and then proceeding to discard him.

She spoke in a low voice. "Don't you trust me?"

"The people in Pinares trusted you."

"I—" She took a deep breath, started again. "I may have failed my fellow citizens but in doing so I proved my loyalty to the men who once saved my life. I believe I did the right thing, and so far no one has convinced me otherwise. However," she went on, "I have no objection to consummating the marriage. According to my limited knowledge, it is what one must do if one wishes to have children."

The marshal's fingers tightened around the chemise in a convulsive grip that threatened to snap the lace. When he spoke, his words came out strained. "Let's go and find the judge. He has cleared his docket and will ride out this afternoon. There isn't much time."

He didn't offer her an opportunity to change into her best dress, not that she really had one. But she might have liked to comb her hair and pinch a bit of color to her cheeks, instead of simply hurrying after him, like a dog following its master.

Out in the street, several people called out a greeting to the marshal. It occurred to Rowena that although he'd spent his afternoons visiting her at the jail, he must have done something else with his mornings and evenings—settled local disputes, gambled in the saloon, chased light-skirted ladies, helped the elderly, contributed to a barn raising.

She had no idea what. And that drove home how little she knew about the man she was about to marry. He was born in Louisiana, a coyote had once tried to have him for supper, he had a sister who had come to a bad end, and he had joined the Marshals Service because he had nothing better to do. That was the sum total of information he had revealed about his background, and the last item she suspected to be a lie.

At the thought, her feet grew heavier and heavier. The marshal, a step ahead of her, halted to wait for her to catch up. "Second thoughts?"

"I…" She met his eyes, and all those secret hopes, all those feelings she hadn't admitted even to herself, washed over her. Somewhere in the back of her mind the image of Freddy seemed to fade away, like an old newspaper cutting. She felt a physical pull, as if her body obeyed the will of the man standing in front of her instead of her own.

"No," she said, and set into motion again. "No second thoughts."

They found the portly judge alone in the deserted courtroom. Hunched over the vast desk, he was turning over the pages in a ledger with one hand while eating from a meal tray with the other.

Upon hearing their footsteps, he looked up. "There are no refunds for fines."

"I'm not here for a refund," Dale replied. "I'm here to be married."

The judge tore off a piece from a chicken leg with his teeth while using his free hand to gesture them closer. When they were standing in front of his desk—and when his mouth was empty again—he contemplated Rowena with a notch of concern between his bushy eyebrows. "Miss McKenzie, are you entering into a marriage out of your own free will or are you taken into bonded servitude to pay a debt?"

Baffled, she faltered for a moment. The judge took another bite of his chicken and spoke through the mouthful. "It is only noon, but I have already had a dozen people barging into my courtroom, interrupting my work, to tell me that they are happy to forgo reimbursement for their losses if it means that Miss McKenzie will avoid going to prison." The judge swallowed, patted his mouth with a linen napkin. "So, you do have a choice."

The surge of delight and gratitude nearly made Rowena's knees buckle. They had forgiven her. They didn't hate her for what she had done. She could feel the judge's probing eyes upon her. Fearing he might have misunderstood her relief, Rowena hurried to speak. "No, no, Your Honor. Thank you for your concern, but everything is perfectly fine. Marshal Hunter didn't buy himself a bond woman. I am entering into this marriage of my own free will because it is an arrangement that suits both of us."

Appearing to be satisfied with her answer, the judge nodded, and intoned in a mechanical voice, "Do you, Marshal Hunter, take this woman, Miss McKenzie, to be your wife?"

"I do."

"Do you, Miss McKenzie, take Marshal Hunter to be your husband?"

Disappointment over the lack of ceremony made Rowena hesitate. The judge, always in a hurry, hadn't even bothered to find out their given names. And, instead of looking at them as they spoke their vows, he had dipped his pen in the inkwell and was scribbling on a piece of paper.

"Do you or don't you?" the judge prompted her. "I haven't got all day."

"I do," Rowena replied with a touch of annoyance in her tone.

"Sign here." The judge slid the piece of paper across the desk and offered the pen to her. That careless scribbling had been their marriage license. Rowena bent down and signed her name. Her hand was unsteady, and the signature didn't come out anything like her usual even letters. *It looks like a forgery*, she thought with a touch of hysteria.

When it was Marshal Hunter's turn to sign, the pen was almost dry of ink and she could hear the nib rasping against the paper. She leaned to peek over his shoulder. On the bold curve of the capital D of his first name, the ink had smudged, making a blot. She fought to hold back a nervous groan. Her marriage was starting with a forgery and a blot, and what looked like a stain of chicken grease from the judge's lunch.

Judge Williams inspected the completed document, made an entry in his ledger and handed the marriage license to Marshal Hunter. "One dollar," he said. "Another dollar if you want the marriage to be entered in the courthouse records."

Marshal Hunter dropped two silver coins on the table. Rowena tugged at his sleeve. She wanted to get out of there. Out of the courtroom where she'd been declared a criminal. Away from the judge who'd wanted to send her to Yuma prison, to mingle with hardened criminals. She wished she'd insisted on a church wedding, on being married by Reverend Poole, anything but this.

When they were halfway to the door, the judge called out, "Mrs. Hunter?"

It took Rowena a moment to realize he was addressing her. Her feet rooted to the floor. Not because she wanted to halt and listen to whatever further chastisement the judge might see fit to deliver, but because her married name had suddenly put a stamp of reality on the proceedings that up to now had seemed like a scene from a poorly enacted play.

She curled her fingers over Marshal Hunter's arm for balance and craned her neck to look back. The judge was bent over the ledger, talking quietly, as if to himself. "I know what you're thinking, Mrs. Hunter. That I'm a monster. A cruel man, willing to send you to prison and ruin any chance you might have of a decent future."

"I'm—"

The judge cut her off. "It is my duty to administer the law. I send men to prison, or to their death. I break up families. I leave behind grieving widows and orphans. I can't afford to see them as people. If I did, in every man's life I could find an excuse for the evil they have done, for the crimes they have committed. I must uphold the law, and the law allows no pity."

Judge Williams stopped talking and looked up. In his eyes Rowena could see the humanity and compassion he had just denied he possessed. "I understand," she told him quietly. "Wrong is wrong, even when it is done for the right reasons. I allowed a fraud to go ahead, and I take full responsibility for my actions and I accept that you were fair in passing your sentence."

Dale ushered his bride along the busy street. He felt on edge, the way he did when preparing to arrest a dangerous criminal. It made no sense to feel that way about marriage. But he did, and the town, the people covertly observing them, the residue of a week of hanging around in enforced idleness, suddenly felt suffocating.

He tugged Rowena to a halt. "Could you be ready to leave at once?"

"Leave? Now?" Her eyes darted about, taking in the curious glances of the ladies going about their shopping, of the men loitering outside the saloon. She straightened her spine. "Yes. I can be ready. I don't have many possessions."

"Good." He took her by the elbow and steered her along.

She dragged her feet. "I don't have a horse and the stage only goes once a day, first thing in the morning. How do you expect me to get to the railroad?"

"I'm not expecting you to sprout wings and fly, if that's what's worrying you." He directed her toward the hardware store.

Inside, the short and stocky owner, Mr. Atkinson, was stacking kegs of nails, muscles bulging beneath his rolled-up shirtsleeves. He straightened and walked over to them. "Marshal Hunter. What can I do for you?"

"We just got married, and I'm eager to take my bride home. Are you by any chance headed out to Holbrook to pick up a delivery from the railroad depot?"

Mr. Atkinson wiped his brow with a brawny forearm and swept a shrewd look over Rowena. "Married? Well, now, that is news, good news indeed." His heavy features eased into a smile. "Congratulations. Congratulations to you both."

He rolled down his shirtsleeves, all friendliness now. "I'm not going this week, but Mr. Wheaton told me he has ten barrels of grain coming tonight on the west-bound train." The storekeeper peered at the grandfather clock ticking in the corner. "By my reckoning, he should be leaving right about now. You need to hurry."

Dale nodded his thanks and tugged his bride along. She was half running to keep up with him. "Are we going to catch a ride to the railroad in Mr. Wheaton's wagon?" she asked.

"*You* are going in the wagon. I'll ride ahead. I need to return the horse to the livery stable in Holbrook and take care of a few errands."

He bundled her into the feed store and explained the situation to Mr. Wheaton, a lively man with ready laughter and an endless supply of jokes. "Married?" Mr. Wheaton said. "Oh, my…oh, my. Don't that just about beat everything?" Shaking his head, he called to the back of the store. "Pete!"

His son, a fair-haired boy of around eighteen, sauntered out of the storeroom. "What is it, Pa?"

"You'll have a passenger to the railroad. Mrs. Hunter. The marshal's wife. You mind your manners around her, son." Wheaton turned to Rowena. "I'm right pleased for you, Miss Rowena. I mean, Mrs. Hunter. Right pleased."

They arranged for the boy to collect Rowena outside the boardinghouse, and Dale escorted his wife back to her lodgings. In the room, he surveyed the feminine disarray. All those flimsy garments. They tied his gut in knots.

"I don't understand…" Conscious of the need to make haste, Rowena was snatching up undergarments draped around the room and stuffing them into a leather traveling bag, while talking to him at the same time. "I thought people had forgiven me, but they seem pleased that I'm leaving town."

"Some of them will be glad to see the back of you."
At her stricken expression, Dale tried to soften his comment. "You tried to counsel them against making a bad investment, but they failed to listen. Seeing you reminds them of their lack of judgment. And having you around creates a conflict between those who have forgiven you and those who still want to blame you. If you are gone, it is easier for everyone to put the incident in the past and move on."

"I see," Rowena replied in a forlorn mutter. Her movements slowed down, no longer swift and agile. Dale cursed himself. Despite her plucky spirit, Rowena was sensitive. She needed harmony around her. Needed everyone to be friends, at peace with each other. No wonder she'd run away from a fight over her father's ranch. His mood sank at the thought of the hardships ahead. What business did he have taking her back to a place that might turn into a battleground?

Dale held on to the bridle of the stocky Clydesdale harnessed to the feed store wagon to keep the horse steady while young Peter Wheaton secured Rowena's leather bag. Up on the bench, Rowena sat in ladylike calm, dressed in her green wool dress and a matching fitted jacket.

A cold wind swept along the street, biting through Dale's clothing. He looked up at his wife. "Don't you have a warm coat?"

"I'll be fine."

Fine, my ass, Dale thought. *You're already shivering.*

He waited for Peter Wheaton to climb up beside Rowena and pick up the reins. The boy looked young for eighteen, not quite a man yet, but with a man's instincts, and right now he was staring at his traveling companion with knightly chivalry shining in his eyes.

Dressed in a warm sheepskin coat, the boy would soon feel compelled to take off the garment and wrap it around Rowena's shoulders. Stripped to his shirtsleeves, young Wheaton would damn near freeze to death. And if he failed to offer the coat to Rowena, *she* would be cold. Whichever way it went, one of them might end up with pneumonia.

"Wait here," Dale ordered. "Don't go yet."

From the look of respect on young Wheaton's face Dale surmised the boy would obey the command. He strode off along the boardwalk, went into a dress shop. "Do you have an overcoat? Thick and bulky. Sheepskin or wool."

The pretty brunette, almost cut in two by a tightly laced corset, looked aghast. "We sell fine gowns for ladies. Not outdoor garments for farm wives. Try the general store."

"I have no time to go trawling through every shop in town. Don't you have anything warm for a woman to wear?"

"Well…" The woman surveyed the racks of satin and silk and lace. Her expression brightened. "A shawl. I have a selection of shawls. Ladies use them with low-cut evening gowns, to cover their arms and shoulders against the night chill."

"Give me one of those."

The woman flounced off into the rear and came back with a shawl in bright orange. Dale smirked. The store-keeper was clearly trying to use his hurry to get rid of the least attractive merchandise.

"You said a selection," he pointed out. "Show me other colors."

With a huff of frustration, the woman whirled around, fetched a stack of soft wool shawls and dumped them on the counter. Dale rifled through the colors, chose one in dark red, another one in pale cream, and a third in forest green to match Rowena's gown. After paying for his purchases, he hurried back to the wagon. "They didn't have any overcoats but these should keep you warm."

Upon his insistence, Rowena wrapped all three shawls around her shoulders right away. "Knot them up tight at the front, so they don't fall off," Dale instructed. With satisfaction, he watched his wife's slender figure disappear beneath layers of wool thick enough to protect her even from the fiercest of winds. "Have a safe journey," he said and stood back from the wagon. "I'll see you in Holbrook."

Dusk had fallen over Holbrook and there was still no sign of the feed store wagon. Dale buttoned up his duster against the evening chill and paced the railroad station platform, the urgent beat of his boots on the timber planks betraying his concern.

He should have ridden in with Rowena and young Wheaton. But he'd had business to take care of, telegrams to send. One to his friend Roy Hagan, now settled down with a wife and child in a nearby town called Rock Springs, to let them know that he needed to postpone his planned visit. The other to the elderly rancher in California, to advise the old man that the sale could not go ahead.

Of course he could have sent the telegrams from Pinares. However, some deeply ingrained sense of privacy had stopped him from doing so, even if it meant a day's delay in getting out the messages. There was no need for the townspeople to learn of his shattered dream, to know how dearly it had cost him to pay Rowena's fine.

His ears picked out a new sound. Dale halted his pacing, cocked his head to listen. His senses had not deceived him. Over the tinny music streaming out from the saloons he could hear the rattle of wheels and the steady thud of a large, lumbering horse.

Dale curbed the urge to run down the street. As he stood still and waited, a wagon emerged into the sphere of the gaslights that illuminated the platform. Relief poured over him. Up on the wagon bench, Rowena sat beside Peter Wheaton, wrapped up in her shawls, appearing completely at ease. When she spotted him, she smiled and gave him a jaunty wave.

Dale strode over, waited for young Wheaton to rein in the big Clydesdale and apply the brake. Only when the wagon was securely halted did Dale reach up with his arms, locate his wife's narrow waist beneath the layers of shawls and swing her down to her feet.

"Did you have a good journey?" he asked, studying her face.

"Lovely. Peter has a wonderful voice. He entertained me with songs."

His hands still curled around Rowena's waist, Dale turned toward young Wheaton and spoke with the respect of equals. "Thank you for taking care of Mrs. Hunter. It is easier for a man to go about his business if he knows his wife is safe."

At the remark, the boy appeared to grow in stature. "It was no trouble. It was nice to have company."

For a few moments longer, they exchanged the polite

pleasantries of acquaintances about to part. Squirming a little at revealing his ignorance, young Wheaton asked, "Will there be anyone to unlock the depot so I can load the wagon?"

Dale stepped closer and lowered his voice, so the men who had arrived to wait for the eastbound train would not overhear. "A word of advice, if I may. Once you load your wagon the goods become your responsibility. It is better to leave them overnight at the railroad depot and return to get them in the morning."

The boy nodded and muttered his thanks.

"Where do you plan to stay the night?" Dale asked.

"Pa gave me money for the boardinghouse." The way young Wheaton's eyes flickered toward the nearest saloon revealed where those funds would likely be spent. The boy would end up sleeping under a tarpaulin in his wagon.

Dale dipped into his pocket, pulled out a silver dollar. "Perhaps I could buy you a drink to thank you for taking such good care of my wife. I'd join you, but we're taking the night train."

The boy hesitated, wanting to be gallant but he also wanted to sleep indoors. He accepted the money.

"Do you have a gun?" Dale asked.

"No. Should I?"

"No. And when you go into the saloon, keep aloof. Some men like to make a game of riling strangers, trying to pick a fight. If someone shoves you, apologize. If anyone calls you a coward, ignore them. It takes more courage to avoid a fight than it takes to lose one."

After young Wheaton had rattled away to park his wagon in a safer place before hurrying to taste the delights of the saloons, Dale turned his attention to his wife. Her cheeks were pink, her eyes sparkling. She looked happy. *Like a bride should on her wedding day*, a thought crossed his mind.

"What has put you in such high spirits?"

"To be truthful, it was a relief to get out of Pinares. And I am eager to see Twin Springs again. And…" She paused, looked down at her toes, looked up again and met his eyes with a disconcerting directness. In a low voice, she went on, "I'd like you to know that I don't face the start of our married life with reluctance. Our circumstances might be unusual, but the apprehension I feel is the same as any other woman might feel on their wedding night. No more. No less."

The platform was filling with people, the eastbound train due soon. Dale glanced around. No one appeared to be eavesdropping. He sought for the right words but could find none. Tension coiled within him. A hundred times he'd faced death. He'd killed, had almost been killed, but he'd never felt so exposed, so defenseless. He cleared his throat. "About the wedding night… It needs to be postponed. The journey is complicated… Atchison, Topeka and Santa Fe Railroad to Santa Fe… change there to Denver, Rio Grande and Santa Fe Railroad…then take the Denver Pacific to Cheyenne…"

Blue eyes searched his. "Can't we stop here for the night?"

"This town is a rough, lawless place. I don't want to…" He gave a small, awkward shrug. "Not here."

"Are there no sleeping cars on the train?"

"They only put in enough sleeping cars for passengers who've booked all the way through and have paid in advance. There may be a few berths left free but we won't know until we get on the train. I'll go and buy the tickets now. I didn't want to get them earlier, in case you arrived too late. Will you be all right for a few minutes on your own?"

Her eyes darted about the crowd. "Oh, yes. I like to watch people."

Dale pivoted on his boots and stalked into the ticket office. His heart was beating too fast and his hands were so unsteady he dropped a coin when he paid. Despite the extra cost, he bought first-class tickets, since only first-class passengers had access to the sleeping cars.

Never in his life had he been torn with such conflicting forces. His body ached to take what Rowena was offering. He'd give anything to taste her sweetness, to gain a moment of oblivion in her arms. But doubt held him back. How would Rowena react when she saw the scars that marred his body—if she ran her hands down his chest and felt the puckered lines on his skin—if her feet tangled with his and she could feel the ridged, uneven shape of his lower legs? Would she recoil? Would she shudder in disgust, pull away? Pretend not to notice? Go through the act anyway, despite her revulsion, because it was her duty?

The truth of it was that he was a coward. The longer he put off consummating the marriage, the longer he could avoid facing Rowena's reaction, could cling to the belief that his scars wouldn't matter. That she would accept him as he was, a man with a damaged body that bore evidence of the violence and lawlessness in his past.

Chapter Five

Despite the rocking of the train, sleep eluded Rowena. The reclining seats in the parlor car allowed her to rest in comfort, and the three shawls kept her warm while she dozed and watched the world roll by. Night fell outside. Stars appeared in the sky. The plume of steam from the engine fluttered like a bridal veil in the darkness.

She stole a glance at Marshal Hunter stretched out on an identical seat next to her. He lay still, eyes closed, his head slightly turned toward her. She studied his features. The lean, almost gaunt cheeks were covered with dark stubble, except for the puckered red-and-white line that formed the lower curve of his scar. Even in repose, the grim set of his features hinted at some inner turmoil. She leaned closer, listened to the sound of his breathing. Was he asleep? She thought not, and the instant the assumption formed in her head, the marshal opened his eyes.

He didn't move, didn't fidget. He showed no sign of transition from slumber to full wakefulness. He merely contemplated her with those green eyes, the most alert eyes she had ever seen. After a moment of silence when time seemed suspended, he asked, "Can't you sleep?"

She shook her head in reply.

"Me neither." In one smooth motion, he rose from the reclining seat. "I'll see if I can rustle up a cup of coffee. Would you like me to bring you one?"

She shook her head again. "Coffee keeps you awake."

"I know." Although one corner of his mouth kicked up in a crooked smile, the look in his eyes was bleak. *He wants to stay awake. He dislikes sleep. Even fears sleep.* The knowledge came to Rowena in a flash of certainty.

Puzzled, she watched the man who was now her husband walk away in the dull illumination of the gas lamps mounted in brackets along the wall. Broad-shouldered, lean at the hip, he moved with grace, and yet she could hear that strange, determined cadence of his footsteps, even though he was treading softly in order not to disturb their fellow passengers.

After he'd vanished through the glass-paneled door into the gangway in search of the restaurant car, her thoughts returned to the topic, which she had introduced with such unaccustomed boldness at the railroad station—their wedding night.

When she'd been engaged to Freddy, she had looked forward to it, the way one might look forward to a summer picnic—the expectation of calm, carefree pleasures. Thinking of Marshal Hunter in the same way filled her with an edgy tension, the way one might look forward to cantering on a horse at breakneck speed, or sneaking out of the schoolhouse for a secret outing after curfew hours. Surely, Marshal Hunter would be eager to enjoy the physical aspects of marriage. And yet, something was making him reluctant. As if, contrary to what he had claimed earlier, he hesitated to make the marriage binding.

What if...? What if...?

She almost bolted up on the seat as Freddy's scowling, angry features formed in her mind. What if Marshal Hunter would feel the same as Freddy had when he discovered that she was no great heiress? Marshal Hunter was marrying her for her father's land, after all. What if, once they reached Twin Springs, they found a worthless ruin? Would Marshal Hunter be like Freddy, and cast her aside in anger and disgust? If he did, she couldn't bear it. She simply couldn't bear the thought of another humiliation, couldn't bear the thought of being alone again, deemed worthless as a woman simply because she was lacking in wealth.

The sound of those familiar footsteps alerted her before the door at the end of the car swung open. Reining in her panic, Rowena looked up. The marshal sauntered through, coffee cup in one hand. She followed him with her eyes as he walked up to her.

"What's wrong?" he asked. "You look as if you've seen a ghost."

Helpless, bound by the hurtful memory, she merely shook her head, unwilling to trust her voice. With a flash of wry humor she told herself she was turning into a marionette on strings, only able to gesture, and not to speak.

"Are you cold?" her husband asked.

She nodded. Marshal Hunter settled into his seat, not spilling a drop while he stretched out his long legs and leaned back. He held the coffee cup with his right hand and extended his left arm toward her in invitation. Without thinking, without hesitation, Rowena scooted closer, leaning over the gap between the seats. She curled up against his side, and he wrapped his arm around her, anchoring her in place.

"Go to sleep," he said. "I'll watch over you."

"I'll watch over you." When had anyone last offered to do that for her? With a sigh of contentment, Rowena relaxed against the man beside her. The heat of his body enveloped her. She could smell the rich aroma from his coffee, and the scents of horse and leather on him. With a small wriggle to get more comfortable where his pistol butted into her side, she closed her eyes and drifted off to sleep.

They changed trains in Santa Fe, and again in Denver. Rowena could not have asked for a more attentive husband. He kept her warm, made sure she had enough to eat, and did his best to ensure her comfort. And yet, the easy camaraderie of their afternoons in her jail cell never returned. The fact that she still addressed him as Marshal Hunter summed up the lack of closeness between them.

On the Denver Pacific train that rocked through the cold, clear night, they had first-class seats again, in a parlor car with gas lamps mounted on the wall, between narrow mirrors that reflected the light. The car was nearly empty, the half-dozen passengers sitting with their heads drooping. Behind them, a man snored. The wood-burning stove at the rear of the car filled the air with a smoky scent but did not emit enough heat to keep the chill at bay.

The conductor, a small, dapper man with a neatly trimmed black beard, strode down the aisle and paused next to them. Marshal Hunter looked up, instantly alert. The conductor bent to him and whispered something. Marshal Hunter nodded and pressed a gold coin into the conductor's palm before the man hurried off again.

What is it? Rowena wanted to ask, but the nervous tension kept her silent.

The marshal turned toward her and spoke in a low voice. "A sleeping compartment has become free. A passenger who had paid all the way to Cheyenne stopped off in Denver. The conductor is making a bit of extra money by letting us take over the compartment for the rest of the journey."

Rowena felt a jolt, like the sensation she had once experienced when she had touched an electricity making machine in Boston. And, just like then, her heartbeat quickened, with a mix of fear and excitement at the prospect of something unknown but fascinating. Without a word, she rose and followed Marshal Hunter, who had picked up his saddlebags and her leather valise and was leading the way down the corridor.

But the sleeping car was not as she had expected. Instead of a single wide bed, it had two narrow bunks, one above the other. "You take the top one," her husband said. "I'll wait outside while you undress and settle down." And with a soft thud of the door, he left her alone.

Torn by a confusing mix of disappointment and relief, Rowena quickly changed into a nightgown and clambered up to the top bunk. She intended to lie awake and wait for the marshal to return, but as she stretched out beneath the warm blanket on the comfortable mattress, the rocking of the train allowed fatigue to take over, and she went straight to sleep.

* * *

A sound woke Rowena. She felt no motion of the train, and she guessed they must be stopped at a station or at a water tower. It came again, that harsh sound, something between a growl and a wail. At first, Rowena thought it might be a wild animal outside, but then she got her bearings and realized the sound had come from within the compartment.

Cautiously, she eased to a sitting position on the bunk, swung her feet over the edge and climbed down. The carpeted floor was soft beneath her toes but she could feel an icy draft that fluttered the hem of her nightgown.

That terrible sound came again. *"Arrgghh..."*

The gas lamps had been turned off, and Rowena did not wish to fumble about, relighting them. Instead, she swept the curtain at the window aside, as quietly as she could. Through the dusty pane of glass she could see the tall structure of a water tower, the timber skeleton revealed in a stark silhouette by the light of the full moon. As she waited, standing still, letting her eyes adjust to the darkness, she heard a clank and a muffled shout outside, and the train jerked into motion again.

They picked up speed and rounded a curve that lined up the moon with the window, cutting a stronger beam of light into the compartment. On the lower bunk, Rowena could see Marshal Hunter fling his arm in a wide circle. He made that tortured sound again.

Rowena sank to her knees in the narrow space between the bed and the wall. Even in the darkness, she could see how pale Marshal Hunter's face was. Beads of perspiration glinted on his brow. He twisted about, and the blanket slid aside, revealing his naked chest.

Rowena had to bite back a cry. Such scars. She'd caught
a peek at them once before, when his collar fell open,
but the top end of the scar had been a neat white line.
Lower down along his chest the scars grew to a web
of jagged, intersecting lines. She could only guess, but
they might have been caused by a large hunting knife,
the kind with a serrated edge.

And the sound…it was coming almost constantly
now, a guttural moan so full of agony that in a theater
play it would signify the torment of a lost soul in pur-
gatory. She couldn't bear to listen to it a second longer.
Reaching out with one trembling hand, Rowena gently
touched Marshal Hunter's stubble-shadowed cheek.

Instantly, he became awake, but in the fraction of
a second before his vision cleared, Rowena could see
a look of grief and terror in his eyes that stunned her.
How he must have suffered, to be left with such scars,
to be haunted by such nightmares.

She spoke very softly, as if her voice might have the
capacity to ease the marshal out of his distressed state.
"You had a bad dream."

He merely nodded, a matter-of-fact gesture that told
Rowena nightmares were a frequent visitor in his nights.
Now she understood why he preferred to avoid sleep.

"Is there anything I can do?" she asked.

"Go back to sleep." Shadows of past torment lingered
on his gaunt features. The marshal did not lack emotion,
it occurred to Rowena. He was just very good at hiding
his feelings. Perhaps also denying them.

"Did I say anything?" he went on. "Perhaps call out
a name?"

Rowena shook her head. "You spoke no words. You

just made an angry sound, kind of a growl. And you swung your arm in a big circle."

"Ah." Marshal Hunter's lips curled into a wry smile. "That particular one."

"Are there others?" she asked.

"Yes," he replied quietly. "I have a whole repertoire of nightmares. And before you ask, the answer is no. I don't want to hash out my troubled dreams. Talking about them will not make them stop. Forget what you saw, and the next time you hear me moan in my sleep, just turn away. Or throw something at me, to make me wake up."

Despite the effort Marshal Hunter made to hide his pain—or perhaps exactly because it was evident how much effort it took for him to act casual—Rowena could sense the depth of his grief. What tragedies could there be in his past that held him in such a vicious grip? She couldn't even begin to imagine them, but to witness his suffering stirred her compassion. And, with the deep feminine conviction, misguided or not, that comforting can ease every kind of hurt, she wanted to offer him the balm of that comfort.

She let a shiver ripple over her body and made a sound. *"Brrr."*

"Are you cold?" the marshal asked at once, just as she had expected he would.

Always gallant. Always concerned to ensure her welfare and comfort. What harm was a small lie, when told for the right cause?

"I'm freezing," she replied. "Can I get in with you?"

Dale stared at his wife, unwilling to let his brain accept the words she had just spoken, unable to compre-

hend the suggestion she had just made. Illuminated only
by moonlight, she crouched in the narrow gap between
the bed and the wall, her hair cascading down her shoulders, her eyes full of compassion, the prim nightgown
hiding the contours of her body but clinging here and
there in a manner that fired up his imagination.

She had never looked more beautiful. And he had the
right. Every right. Right by marriage. Right by agreement. Right by consent. Right by mutual attraction.
Right by lust, if you will. Right because life owed him.
Owed him something good and unsullied.

And therein lay the problem.

He could not. Could not. Must not. Not now, with
his blood burning like molten acid in his veins, with
his heart hammering like the grim reaper knocking
at the door. He was too keyed up, too frantic after the
dark abyss of the nightmare. If he touched her now, he
might end up releasing all those demons he kept locked
up inside him and take her roughly. And no matter the
practical nature of their marriage, he wanted to be gentle with her. She deserved nothing less than the best he
could be. And that meant *not now*.

But there she was, his beautiful wife, not waiting for
an invitation, instead simply climbing in between the
worn sheets and wriggling to fit herself beside him on
the narrow railroad bunk. Dale could feel his control
slipping. She was warm and vibrant, with a woman's
allure…a woman's scent…a woman's shape…a woman's softness…

Not now, Dale reminded himself. *For God's sake,
not now.*

His tone was gruff. "There's not enough space for
two."

"We'll manage." Rowena eased closer to him and gave another wriggle of her hips. Right where it drew the maximum response from him. Dale gritted his teeth. He could feel his entire body quivering with the effort of restraint. He hoped she would mistake his restless tremors for the aftermath of the nightmare she had just witnessed.

"Why don't you turn around, face the other way?" he suggested. Not allowing Rowena the opportunity to consider his request, he gently rolled her around so that their bodies spooned together, her back to his chest. He wrapped one arm around her waist to hold her still, but not even his firm hold could stop her backside from butting into his groin.

To distract himself, as much as to focus Rowena's mind away from his nightmares and any speculation over what might have caused such terrible dreams, he introduced a practical topic.

"This range war that got your father killed—could you tell me everything you know about it? I need to understand the situation, learn as much as possible about the enemies."

He could feel her body tense and cursed his thoughtlessness. In directing her thoughts away from his troubles he had steered them right into her own. "Sorry," he said quietly. "I know it will trigger painful memories. However, it is a conversation we need to have, and I doubt either one of us is capable of sleep right now."

Rowena expelled a long sigh and relaxed within the circle of his arm. Dale tightened his hold a fraction, pulling her more snugly against him. It felt good to hold her. In some odd way, having her so near to him made him feel safe from the nightmares. As if her frail woman's body possessed some magical powers of protection. And perhaps in some indirect way it did, guiding his thoughts to the future instead of the past.

"It's not exactly a range war," she explained. "It's more like a feud."

"Who was your father feuding against, and why?"

"It was not his feud. He just happened to be caught up in it."

Rowena fell silent, and Dale waited, allowing her time to arrange her thoughts. All his senses were alert now, attuned to the woman in his arms. Surely, there could be no harm in enjoying her nearness, just a little, right now, tonight. He bent his head a fraction so he could nuzzle her neck. She smelled good. And yet she had benefited from no more opportunities to bathe than he had.

"What's that smell?" he asked.

She made a sniffing sound. "What smell?"

"You. The way you smell. I like it."

"Oh." He felt her body rock with suppressed laughter. "It's not me. It's the nightgown. While I was in jail, the women in town did my laundry. Orla Jones, who washed my nightgown and undergarments, said she was going to put a few drops of rose essence into the final rinse but her little boy barged into the room and crashed into her. She dropped the whole bottle into the wash pail. She apologized, saying she didn't mean my smalls to reek like a whore's boudoir."

"A whore's boudoir, huh?" Dale inhaled another deep breath of the floral fragrance. "You smell much better than any whore I've ever known." As soon as the words were out, he regretted them. Regretted letting his past intrude.

"Have you…known many…such women?" The hesitation in Rowena's tone made it clear to Dale that the answer mattered to her. It gave him pleasure to be able to be truthful.

"Not many," he replied. "And none at all in recent years."

"I'm glad."

He pressed a fleeting kiss to the back of her neck, where the nightgown had pulled aside, and wondered if she could feel the intimate touch. There wasn't much he could give her. If she valued his celibate existence, the abstinence had been worth the sacrifice.

He spoke with his lips grazing her skin. "This feud… Who is feuding…and how did your father get caught in it?"

"I like what you're doing."

"I like it, too." He made his kisses bolder, his mouth traveling along her neck, tasting, teasing, nibbling. She squirmed a little, her rear end rubbing against his erection.

"Are you going to answer my question?" he prompted her.

"What question?"

"The feud."

"Oh, yes." She sounded breathless now. "The feud… there are three ranches in the valley. My father's land is a small section at the north end. The rest of the valley belongs to two wealthy men. Mr. Spencer owns the land to the east of the river and Mr. Faraday owns the land to the west. They hate each other. On the day my father was shot their hired hands had a confrontation. My father stepped in, trying to calm the situation. Someone shot him. No one confessed to having fired and no one saw who it was. The killer went unpunished."

Dale could hear the bitter edge in her words. So, despite her gentle nature Rowena was capable of holding a grudge. He filed the information away in his mind.

"How come your father got the best land if the two other properties are bigger?"

"It wasn't always like that. My father arrived first, and he claimed the best land. A dozen small ranchers followed. Then, when the War Between the States broke out and beef prices fell, the others went bankrupt or sold out. Mr. Spencer bought one side of the valley. He is an educated man. A Southerner, like you."

"I'm only part Southerner. The other half of me is New England Yankee."

Rowena craned around and gave him an impish smile. "You're a Southerner through and through, at least in how you treat a lady. And you are a Southerner in how you handle a deck of cards."

"I'm a Yankee in how I do business."

"I'll reserve judgment until I see evidence."

"You'll see it soon enough." He rose up on one elbow, balancing against the rocking of the train, so he could study her expression in the moonlight through the window. "What about this other man, Faraday?"

Rowena frowned. "He bought the other side of the valley, and he is as uncouth as Mr. Spencer is refined. His great ambition is to rise in social standing and breed a family of gentlemen. That desire stands at the heart of the feud."

Her tone grew serious, foreshadowing a tragedy. "Mr. Spencer is liberal minded. In defiance to public opinion, he married a full-blooded Native woman. They had one child. A girl, Lucille. Her mother died when she was small, and Lucille was educated in a convent in New Orleans. I was perhaps ten years old when she returned home. I can still remember how awestruck I was by her. She was a vision. Willow slim, with long coal-black hair and dark eyes that seemed to hold a million secrets."

Dale shook his head, a rueful gesture that mocked the ways of the world. "Let me guess. Did Mr. Faraday have a son?"

"Three of them, in fact. The youngest, Edward, fell in love with Lucille, and she with him. They wanted to marry, but Mr. Faraday put a stop to any such plans. He wanted to breed a dynasty of gentlemen, and a part-Indian daughter-in-law did not fit in."

Dale could see a shadow of anguish on Rowena's face as she went on with her story. "So, the lovers decided to elope. On one moonlit night, Edward drove over in the fancy buggy his father had bought for him, and Lucille snuck out of her father's house to join him. Only Mr. Spencer spotted them and set off in chase. Not because he had anything against the marriage, but because he didn't trust Edward to marry Lucille. He wanted to protect his daughter."

"Did he catch the eloping couple?"

"In a way." Rowena spoke quietly. "When Edward realized they were being chased, he whipped his horse into speed. They hit a gully and the buggy overturned. They were both killed instantly. That's how the feud started. Mr. Spencer and Mr. Faraday blame each other for killing their child. Mr. Spencer thinks Mr. Faraday is at fault because he did not allow his son to marry Lucille. Mr. Faraday thinks Mr. Spencer is to blame because he chased the eloping couple and brought about the accident. Neither can forget their loss. Neither can forgive. Their burning goal in life has become to destroy each other. That's how my father became involved. Whoever owns Twin Springs controls the water. If one of the feuding pair can take over my father's land, they can dam the stream and ruin the other."

Rowena wriggled around again, this time to face him. Dale could see the sheen of tears in her eyes, could hear the anguish in her voice. "They didn't bury them together. Edward and Lucille. They are each buried alone, on their father's land. Can you believe the cruelty of it? Not even in death did they allow them to be together."

Not making any comment, Dale wrapped his arms around Rowena and cradled her to his chest. So, his wife was a romantic at heart. Why would a woman who so clearly believed in love agree to a marriage of convenience?

He had given her little in the way of courtship, and he might never be able to give her the devotion she deserved, but he could give her a small taste of romance, a tiny bit of the kind of cherishing every bride had the right to expect at the start of their marriage.

"Listen," he said, talking in haste before the impulse faded. "What do you say, when we get to Cheyenne, we find a nice hotel and stop there for a night or two? Have ourselves a little honeymoon?"

"But I thought…" She tipped her head back, and her eyes darted about his face, searching his expression. "…I thought we… Don't you want to…?" Her voice fell to a whisper. "Don't you want me?"

Dale had noticed it before, that strange uncertainty,

as if Rowena needed confirmation of her feminine appeal. It puzzled him. She had to know that she was beautiful, and she did not suffer from an excess of vanity. The way she appeared not to mind her plain, threadbare dresses attested to that.

"Of course I want you," he told her quietly. "But not here. Not now, while we're traveling. I don't want to have to worry about a conductor barging in, or some other interruption. And I don't want us to be tossed about on the narrow bunk as the train slows down and speeds up again. You deserve better on your wedding night. You deserve comfort and privacy. A soft bed and a lock on the door and enough time for us not to have to hurry. A hotel in Cheyenne will offer those, and more, if we find the right kind of place."

Chapter Six

They alighted in Cheyenne as the sun reached its zenith in the sky, but despite the bright spring day the air still held a winter chill. Here and there, Rowena could see soot-stained heaps of snow, and the chimneys belched out thick columns of smoke.

"Are you up to walking?" Marshal Hunter asked. "It's not far."

Color flared to her cheeks. It had been like that all morning, since they'd woken up and untangled their entwined bodies. Every glance, every word, made her acutely aware of him. But even though she looked forward to her wedding night, she could not ignore the warnings that rattled inside her head.

After consummating their marriage there would be no turning back. They would be bound to each other, whether they were satisfied with their bargain or not.

"Is something wrong?"

The question cut through her troubled thoughts, and Rowena realized they were standing at the station platform while the crowd around them was dispersing with joyful reunions and polite greetings. She fumbled, attempted to gather her wits.

"It's just… It's just that it's all so big…"

He gave her a puzzled look. "But you've spent time in Boston. You're used to much bigger cities. Cheyenne has five thousand people. Boston has nearly half a million."

"I know… I know…" She inhaled a deep breath. "It's just that I don't remember *this* Cheyenne. When I left for school I boarded the train in Rawlins and went straight through. And when I came back I was too much in a hurry to get home because my father had written about the troubles…"

The marshal spoke in a low voice. "What do you say, today we forget everything about our troubles. About *anyone's* troubles. Today the world is perfect. Just for this one day. No child goes hungry, no country is at war, no one gets sick, the homeless find shelter, the lonely find a friend, the unhappy find a reason to smile…"

"We pretend?"

"We believe. Believe the world could be like that."

From the marshal's bitter tone Rowena could tell he'd seen too much misery and cruelty to ever truly believe such a thing, but the idea appealed to her. "All right," she said. "The world is perfect. Just for tonight."

"Tonight," the marshal replied, and they set off walking.

As they made their way along the grand streets, the mood grew strangely light between them. The marshal was carrying both their bags, and he pointed out the sights. The Opera House. The Millionaires Row with more than two dozen mansions, built by the cattle barons and the mining magnates. A site where they would soon start building a State Capitol, in anticipation of statehood for Wyoming. The fine boutiques and dress shops, attesting to the wealth that in recent years had made Cheyenne the richest city in the world.

Instead of admiring the buildings and inspecting the store windows, Rowena found her attention drawn to Marshal Hunter. He hadn't shaved in the morning, and the stubble on his jaw emphasized the starkness of his lean features. She'd gotten used to the crescent-shaped scar on his cheek and barely noticed it anymore, but now she looked at him through the eyes of a stranger, through the eyes of a woman. The hint of violence, combined with his good looks and casual elegance, sent a frisson of attraction through her, and it occurred to her that other women might feel the same. The prospect stirred an uncomfortable sensation in the pit of her belly.

The marshal came to a halt outside a whitewashed stone mansion. "I thought this place might suit." He gestured at the front steps leading up to a canopied entrance.

"But…" Rowena stared at the turreted building. "Can we afford it?"

"Remember?" He smiled at her, carefree and easy. "Tonight the world is perfect." His lips curled into a wry grin. "And from the way you keep pulling your shawls tighter around your shoulders and mincing your steps I gather you're freezing all the way down to your toes."

"Oh? Oh…? Of course…" She remembered the odd, hesitant rhythm of his walk and stole a glance at his booted feet.

He must have noticed, for he shook his head and spoke quietly. "I am able to walk as far as any man. Farther than most. I have scars on my legs and I step in a certain way to keep the boot leather from chafing against my skin, but my strength and stamina are unimpaired." His voice fell lower still. "But we agreed that tonight everything will be perfect. I hope you'll extend the benefit of such thinking to me."

Quickly, not pausing to observe her reaction to his comment, the marshal set off again and carried their bags up the hotel steps, leaving Rowena to follow.

The grandeur of the entrance hall made her gasp. Not even in the Boston home of Freddy Livingston's family had she seen such luxury. Black-veined marble floor, softened by hand-knotted Oriental rugs. Crystal chandeliers with a hundred candles burning, despite the daylight. In a big stone fireplace, a log fire crackled, filling the room with forest scents. To the left, the archway to a dining room gave a glimpse of tables topped with white linen and gleaming silverware, arranged in readiness for guests.

Marshal Hunter strode over to a reception desk discreetly tucked into a corner. Behind the counter, a slender, well-dressed blonde in her forties gave him a bland, impersonal smile.

"We'd like a room for one night," the marshal said. "Perhaps two nights."

The woman's smile remained in place while her pale gray eyes took stock of their appearance. Rowena felt a blush flare up to her cheeks. Despite his handsome features, Marshal Hunter looked disreputable in his long canvas duster and mud-spattered boots, unshaven, with a scar on his face. The twin bulges of concealed firearms, evident at his hips, added to the aura of danger around him.

Aware that she herself presented a no more elegant

picture, Rowena adjusted the shawls around her shoulders. With her upsweep nearly collapsed, and one button missing from her scuffed half boots, she must look little better than a tavern slut. She quickly tugged off her gloves to hide the fact that they were worn through at the fingertips, but when she noticed the woman's gaze home in on her left hand, her blush deepened to crimson. In the eyes of a stranger the lack of a wedding ring might brand her just that—a slut.

"We only have a suite with a private bathing room," the woman said. Her smile faded and a frosty note entered her tone. "That will be ten dollars a night."

"A suite?" Marshal Hunter spoke calmly, but Rowena detected an undertone of warning in his quiet voice. "That is most fitting. We're on our honeymoon."

The woman frowned. Her ploy of scaring them away with a high price had failed. "Payment in advance," she added tartly.

"That's fine," Marshal Hunter replied.

Rowena had only seen him act in anger once before, when he'd smashed up the chair in her jail cell. However, instinct warned her that he had the capacity for cold fury, the kind that wielded destruction without remorse. Alarmed, she watched as he unbuttoned the front of his long duster. Slowly, dragging out the motion, he pulled apart the edges of the garment to reveal his pair of pistols.

The woman's attention fell on the tin star within a circle pinned to his chest. "A marshal? A federal marshal?"

Marshal Hunter nodded. "Deputy US Marshal Dale Hunter at your service, ma'am. But I'm not on duty right now. We're newlyweds, and I'm on my way to inspect my wife's land holdings in Wyoming. A ranch called Twin Springs—you may have heard of it, if you have any dealings with cattlemen?"

The woman flustered. "We do not cater to such trade here at High Meadows. Our establishment is a peaceful haven in a turbulent world. An oasis of culture, if you like. We mostly attract tourists from the East, and local customers for the dining room. Today, we have a ladies' luncheon at two o'clock, and a fiftieth birthday party in the evening."

"Peace and quiet is just what we like." Marshal Hunter made a show of patting the pockets of his suit coat. "Ten dollars, you mentioned, and I assume you would prefer hard cash. I believe I have a few gold eagles tucked away somewhere."

The woman smiled with a hint of genuine warmth. She swung the register book around, dipped a pen in the inkwell and handed the pen to Marshal Hunter. "Eight dollars. We give a discount to lawmen. And there is no need to pay in advance."

When they were climbing up the stairs to their second-floor room, Rowena couldn't resist craning closer to Marshal Hunter and asking in a hissed whisper, "Did you have the money, or were you bluffing?"

The corners of his mouth tugged into a grin. "Bluffing."

"But how can we... We can't stay here without paying!"

"Hush. Don't spoil our chances."

Rowena halted her ascent and stared aghast at her husband.

He gave her a gentle pat on the rear to get her moving again. "Don't look so scandalized. I'll go and find a Western Union office. I can collect my expenses, and I'm owed a fee for saving you from the gallows. You can try out that private bathing room while I'll go out and restore our finances. I'll order hot water for you before I go."

It was bliss to be clean, even though she had only been able to air her dress instead of getting it cleaned and pressed. Rowena tucked an escaped strand of hair into her upsweep and watched the uniformed waiter set a plate of roast beef and duchess potatoes in front of her. It was also bliss to be waited upon. Normally, in a restaurant, she'd been the one doing the serving.

She glanced at Marshal Hunter seated across the small, square table. He'd taken his turn to freshen up while she dried her hair. The close shave revealed the vivid crescent of the scar more clearly, but without the guns at his hip and the long duster to hide the good cut of his broadcloth suit, he looked every inch the gentleman she suspected he had once been.

What had he said? *"A mother who wishes me to enter a different lifestyle."* With a frisson of unease, Rowena realized how little she knew about her husband's background. She might have gained a mother-in-law who would dislike her if they ever met, just the way Freddy's mother had been frank with her disapproval.

It was almost four o'clock, late for lunch. At the long table next to them, the ladies' social club had progressed to dessert, a huge concoction of meringue and whipped cream and strawberries that must have been grown in a hothouse. Like a flock of chattering magpies, the ladies were going *ooh* and *ahh* over the delicacy, while complaining about the havoc it caused with their tightly laced corsets.

"You can go shopping, buy a new dress."

Startled by the quietly spoken comment, Rowena turned her attention to Marshal Hunter. He made a covert gesture with his chin toward the crowd of women. "I've noticed the looks they give you, as if you don't belong in the same room with them. If it bothers you, I can afford to buy you a silk dress, the fashionable kind they are wearing."

Rowena clamped down on the flare of shame and anger. Didn't men understand anything? He thought those looks of disdain were about her clothing. When she spoke, she held her head high, although she avoided meeting the marshal's eyes. "It is not my threadbare gown they are looking at. They are looking at my left hand."

"Your hand?"

"The third finger of it, to be precise. What is missing from it." Finally, she found the courage to look straight at him. "They think I'm your mistress. A fancy piece."

She saw his eyes flicker to her empty ring finger, then back up to her face. Then to the group of ladies chattering away at the next table. She sensed his anger, sensed his movement even before he pushed up to his feet.

"Don't," she pleaded in a whisper. "Please, don't cause a scene."

He made a small, stalling gesture at her. She couldn't tell if it was meant for reassurance, or if it was an order for her to keep out of the way. Her heart pounding with apprehension, Rowena sank deeper into her padded chair and waited for the storm to break.

Marshal Hunter took a step toward the party of women. "Ladies, might I have your attention for a moment?"

The chattering voices petered into silence. The woman seated at the head of the table, formidable in orange satin and frothy lace, diamonds sparkling beneath her double chin, looked up at him through a pair of lorgnette spectacles. "What is it, young man?"

"I was hoping you might offer me some assistance."

"I very much doubt it."

A frail, silver-haired lady cut in, "Vera, let the gentleman make his inquiry."

The matron in orange huffed but yielded to the frail lady's superior rank.

"I'm a stranger to Cheyenne," Marshal Hunter said, with a charming hint of a smile. "We got married a few days ago, in a small town where there was no jeweler. I have an engagement ring for my bride in a New York bank vault, a family heirloom—square-cut diamond that once belonged to the Countess of Clairmont—but I need to buy her a wedding ring. I was hoping you ladies could recommend a suitable store."

Rowena could feel it, the collective easing of tension that flowed over the group of women, like ripples expanding in a pond. Some of the younger ones called out recommendations. A few of them glanced over at her with envy. The frail, silver-haired lady held up her hand. Instantly, the others fell silent, attesting to her elevated status.

"Young man, as far as I know the last Countess of Clairmont came to a sticky end during the French revolution almost a hundred years ago. How did you acquire her ring?"

"It's a topic the family avoids, but since you asked, when they dragged my great-great-great-aunt to the guillotine, they left the ring on her finger. Her young nephew—my great-great-grandfather—found a way to retrieve it."

Some of the younger ladies looked decidedly pale. One retched and slapped a hand over her mouth. With a frantic glance around her, she jumped up to her feet and hurried off in the direction of the convenience. The flicker of satisfaction across Marshal Hunter's face was over so quickly, Rowena doubted anyone else had noticed it.

In a hurry to make it to the jeweler before the store closed, Dale chose to decline the meringue dessert. It saved no time, though, for Rowena nibbled through her portion, taking forever over each bite. When she'd finally scraped her plate clean, Dale bundled her into her shawls and steered her out of the building.

Breathless, she sauntered after him, trying to keep up with his long strides. "That thing you said…about a ring…and a countess who lost her head on the guillotine…you were just jesting…surely?"

He gave her a smirk and a wink. "The fewer questions you ask, the fewer lies you'll be told."

In the store, while they waited for the small, balding jeweler to bring out the trays of wedding rings, Dale noticed the longing looks Rowena cast over the display of earrings. He leaned down to her and spoke quietly. "Would you like to choose something? A wedding gift?"

She shook her head, a wistful smile playing around her mouth. "I have jewelry from my mother and grandmother. For all I know, the pieces could still be in Twin Springs, safe at the bottom of my traveling trunk where I left them when I returned from Boston."

"I hope you're not telling me that you have some other man's ring tucked away somewhere?"

Instead of laughing, Rowena flustered. So, there might have been a man she'd loved once, had wished to marry. Perhaps there had even been a lover. Dale tried to push aside the thought. It had no bearing on their bargain.

When Rowena had made her choice, the jeweler, speaking in his thick Eastern European accent, asked if they would also like a man's ring. Dale contemplated his bride, brows lifted in question. "Would you like me to wear one?"

Awkward, as if struggling between pride and admitting to what she wanted, Rowena replied, "Yes. I would like you to wear a wedding ring."

"Remember," Dale told her. "If you ever want me to do something, you only need to ask." And without further comment, he examined the display of rings and picked out a plain, narrow band that matched the one she'd selected.

On their way back to the hotel, Dale brought his wife to a halt outside the milliner's shop. "Would you like to wait here while I go to the telegraph office next door and check for replies?"

"Oh, yes." She waved him away, already engrossed in the pastel-colored capes and frilly bonnets that heralded the arrival of spring.

Dale went into the telegraph office, filled in a form and double-checked the message addressed to his mother in New York.

*Got married. You'd approve. Send Clairmont
ring. Wells Fargo office Cheyenne.*

Regret churned within him; regret and guilt. It was
his mother who had brokered his pardon. A close friend
to the late wife of President Arthur, in office at the time,
she had used her influence in Washington. Dale wished
he could have done more to reward his mother for her
efforts on his behalf, but the past stood between them.

He told himself it was the scars, the nightmares,
the legacy of his lawless life, but during the darkest
hours of the night he admitted to himself it was more.
He could not face his mother, for unresolved guilt and
blame lay between them. Guilt and blame, because he
had let Laurel die.

Restless now, unable to deal with the surge of emotions, Dale paid the fee to have the message sent and
took his leave from the uniformed telegraph operator.
At least now he had done one thing right in his mother's
eyes—acquired a wife.

He pushed the door open, his thoughts now on Rowena. Tonight, they would consummate the marriage. It
would bind them together for the rest of their lives, but
his bride had no idea of the true nature of the man she
was marrying—a killer, a former outlaw, a man with
so much darkness inside him it could blot out even the
brightest summer sun.

Surely, he ought to tell her.

Reveal his violent, criminal past.

Let her make an informed decision.

Outside, a young man was standing next to Rowena,
talking in the loud voice of a troublemaker with too
many shots of whiskey inside him. The electric street-

lights had come on, and a sphere of yellow light fell over
the couple. Short, with curly brown hair, the young man
was dressed like a cattle baron, in hand-tooled Montana
boots and an expensive sheepskin coat. Fawning over
Rowena, he leaned forward with such eagerness that a
small shove on his backside would have sent him toppling onto the cobblestones.

As Dale strode over to the couple, the cowboy
whirled about, clenched his hands into fists and took
on a combative pose. "Get lost, mister. I saw her first."

"You may have seen her first in the last five minutes, but a few days ago I stood beside her in front of a
judge and we both said 'I do'."

"What…what…?" Struggling to unravel the comment, the cowboy swayed on his feet.

Rowena laid a hand on the young man's arm. "What
my husband means is that he is grateful because you
kept me company while he was in the telegraph office."

Spellbound, the cowboy stared at the slender, un-
gloved hand resting on his sleeve. His eyes widened, the
triumph of discovery evident on his face. After glancing up at Rowena's worried expression, the young man
turned his attention to Dale. A cunning smile spread
over his features, revealing a row of even white teeth.
"Don't see no wedding ring on her finger."

Dale gestured toward the jeweler's premises down
the street. "That's because it is still in the shop, being
engraved. Engraved with my name on it."

Frowning with concentration, the young man tried to
come up with a reply, but his addled brain failed him.
Appearing to give up the effort of thinking, he flapped
his hand in the air, as if to usher Dale away, and turned

back to Rowena. "Sweetheart, I could show you a good time. A real good time."

Rowena stiffened her spine, took a step back. "You have already done plenty, protecting me while I was waiting for my husband to return. I am grateful, and I would like to bid you a proper farewell, but I'm afraid I didn't catch your name, mister...?"

Uncertain, the cowboy stared at her. Then, with a shrug and a sheepish grin, he relaxed and gave up his claim. "Yates. It's Pearly Yates, ma'am. Not for me teeth, but I had me a pearl-handled pistol before I lost it in a poker game."

Rowena beamed at the cowboy. "Better luck next time, Mr. Yates. I'd love to talk with you a moment longer, but my toes are frozen. My husband and I need to return to our lodgings. Goodbye, Mr. Yates." Smoothly, she edged past the cowboy. Seizing Dale by the elbow, she steered him down the street.

"That was a neat maneuver," Dale remarked as he let himself be dragged away.

"You said it yourself once. It takes more courage to avoid a fight than to lose one."

"I wouldn't have lost," Dale muttered.

"I know, I know." Rowena slanted him an impish glance. "But I would have gained no pleasure from seeing Mr. Yates lose some of those pearly white teeth."

Despite her lighthearted reaction, Dale felt another stirring of guilt. Rowena was a gentle soul, a peacemaker. She'd run away from her father's ranch to avoid being caught up in a battle, and two years in a Quaker town must have added to her dislike of violence. He had just witnessed how eager she was to avoid a confrontation. He owed it to her to be open and honest about his past.

The front steps of High Meadows loomed in front of them. Dale stopped walking, tugged Rowena to a halt. He waited to speak until she stood facing him. "Listen," he said. "I'm sorry about the scene with that puppy dog of a cattle baron. Without your intervention, I *would* have bashed his teeth in, make no mistake about that. I'm—"

Shaking her head to silence him, Rowena reached up and traced one fingertip along the scar on his cheek. Her touch was so gentle, so featherlight, it made Dale hold his breath. "Don't apologize," she told him. "It doesn't matter. Remember what we agreed? Tonight everything is perfect, and that means the incident is already forgotten."

Tonight everything is perfect.

Dale could not stop the faint trembling that seized his body. Every part of him screamed with need—need for her softness, need for her comfort, need for her warmth. Need for forgetfulness in her arms. Need for respite from the nightmares. He already knew it would be perfect between them tonight. He would make it so. What he didn't want to think about was what it would be like when his wife learned the truth about him.

Chapter Seven

Apart from the adjoining bathing room, their accommodation was a suite in name only. A single, large room, it was furnished with heavy antique pieces, including a polished rosewood table and chairs that would allow the occupants to dine in privacy, should they wish to order room service instead of going downstairs to the restaurant.

While they'd been absent, someone had been inside to light the lamps, and the coal stove in the far corner radiated heat. Outside, darkness was encroaching. The pair of tall windows faced the rear garden, where the reflected glow from the electric streetlights illuminated a row of neatly clipped ornamental trees.

"I don't want any dinner," Dale said. "Do you?"

Rowena did not reply. In silence, she took off the layers of shawls and hung them on the bentwood stand by the door. Still not talking, she crossed the room to the stove and held her hands out to the heat.

"Be careful," Dale said. "The metal gets hot. It's easy to burn your skin when your hands are numb from the cold."

Finally, she replied to his question. "If we don't have dinner, what shall we do while we wait…?"

Wait for the night. Wait for it to be the time to go to bed. She didn't have to say it. Didn't have to put her tension into words. The rigid set of her shoulders within the green gown, the quiver in her quiet voice, the way she had averted her face: they all spoke of nerves…of a woman's wedding night nerves.

"We don't have to wait for the night darkness to go to bed," Dale replied. Although his tension must be as great as hers, he managed to keep his voice light. "In fact, I would prefer not to wait."

Rowena glanced at him over her shoulder. A pink flush covered her cheeks. Her eyes traveled over his body in a way that made his gut tighten. On the train, she'd made the initiative, had climbed into bed with him, had offered herself to him. Up to now, she had shown no sign of being a reluctant bride, but that might change once they had removed their clothing.

"I also prefer not to wait," Rowena told him. She turned to face the stove again and spoke with her back to him. "Shall I change first? We can take turns in the bathing room."

"Look at me, Rowena."

He saw her flinch. He didn't know if it was because she resented the way he had issued a command, or if his sudden use of her given name had startled her. Slowly, she eased around on her feet. Her attention hovered on the intricate patterns of the Oriental rug that covered the floor, and then it slowly climbed upward, until their gazes met.

Holding her eyes, Dale spoke quietly. "Couples, at least those in polite society, can choose to live their lives without ever seeing each other naked. Even if they share a bed, they have dressing rooms in which they can hide to change into their nightgowns. To allow for a physical union, they only uncover their bodies to the extent it is necessary."

He paused, waited for Rowena to react. When she made no reply, Dale went on, his voice gaining in strength as the force of his conviction broke through. "I will not be one of those couples. I refuse to live my life in such pale imitation of companionship. We may have struck a bargain, made a practical arrangement to marry, but that should not stop us from trying to please each other in bed."

Rowena was scandalized. He could see it in her expression. A lady did not discuss such matters, and certainly not with a man. Most likely, she had expected to consummate the marriage because it was required of her, and then retreat to the kind of cool, formal coexistence he had just described. But to her credit, she rallied.

"I'll...I'll do my best to please you...but you'll have to teach me how..."

So, there had been no lover. Dale tried to ignore the flicker of satisfaction.

"We'll work it out together," he told her. "And remember what I said before—if you want something from me, the best way to get it is to ask. It is hard for a man to figure out a woman's mind if she guards her thoughts and desires."

"Can I call you by your given name?"

"You don't need to ask my permission for that. You gained the right the moment you stood beside me before a judge and said 'I do'." One corner of his mouth tipped into a smirk. "And, if you ask me, it's high time you did stop calling me Marshal Hunter."

She offered him a shadow of a smile in return. "Dale…"

"Yes, Rowena."

"What do you want me to do? Help me. Guide me."

"I want you to get undressed, the way you would do if you were alone. Don't mind me. I'll be busy undressing, too, instead of spying on you. But we'll be in the same room together, with the lights on. If I decide to take a peek, it's only natural. And I might feel downright offended if you resisted the temptation to take a peek at me."

Rowena lifted a hand to her chest. At first, Dale thought she was bold enough to get started at once, was reaching for the buttons at the bodice of her gown, but then he realized she'd pressed the flat of her palm to her breastbone and was staring at him, a frown of disbelief on her face. "With…with the lights on…?"

"With the lights on, Rowena." Dale strode to the window, pulled the drapes closed and proceeded to do the same with the other window along the wall. "With the lights very much on," he added as he toured the room and turned up the wicks on each of the lamps, both in the wall sconces and on the pair of nightstands.

When Rowena emitted a tiny, protesting sound, Dale lifted his brows at her. "Do you normally undress in the dark?"

"No…but…"

He held up a hand, palm out, to let her know that her protestations were a waste of time. "No buts, Rowena. Just get on with it, and I'll do the same." He sank to sit on the edge of the bed, pulled off his left boot, let it thud to the floor and then repeated the action with the right.

He knew he was asking a lot, expecting a gently bred woman to disrobe in the presence of a man, but he wanted to make sure Rowena got a good look at his body before they went to bed. If she touched him without being prepared, without knowing about his injuries, she might pull her hand away in disgust when she met the puckered ridges of his scars. And he could not bear the thought of that happening.

Impatient now to find out how she would react to his scarred body, Dale got up, removed his clothing and tossed the garments on the back of a padded armchair. Rowena was undressing, too, but slowly, casting nervous glances in his direction. When he had finished, she was still in her undergarments. Dale stood in a well-lit spot near a lamp and let his arms hang by his sides.

Rowena's movements stilled. Then stopped altogether. She looked at him over her shoulder and then turned around to face him. Her eyes flickered all over him, lingering on his chest where she had already seen the scars from the knife fight with Krieger, the soldier who had fired the bullet that killed Laurel.

After a few seconds of quiet inspection, her gaze drifted downward, paused at his erection for an instant, before settling on the ugly maze of jagged lines and ridges that covered his lower legs. For a long moment, she merely stared. Her eyes grew bright with tears. She kept shaking her head, as if to deny the suffering that must have been the cause of such terrible injuries.

"What happened to you?" she asked in a whisper.

"I told you once that a coyote tried to have me for his

supper." Dale touched the scar on his cheek. "My face wasn't the only part of me that he found tasty."

Rowena took a step toward him, but Dale shook his head in a stalling gesture. "Your clothes," he prompted her. "You need to finish undressing."

For an instant, she froze. Then she moved, slow and awkward. Shoulders hunched in an effort to protect her modesty, she slipped off her undergarments and let them drop to the floor. Attempting to distract her, to ease her way through the moral scruples he knew were drummed into well-bred females, Dale talked in a light, even voice.

"I was wounded in a gunfight against a gang of outlaws, and they left me for dead. A hungry coyote found me. He took a bite out of my face, but I regained consciousness and fought back. Every time the coyote came near, I took a swing at him. But I couldn't reach all the way down to my lower legs. He kept nipping at my legs and feet, biting through the leather of my boots. Then a company of soldiers arrived and rescued me."

Dale almost winced at the banality of the final part of his statement. *"Then a company of soldiers arrived and rescued me."* That single sentence summed up an escape from a near certain death, followed by months of painful rehabilitation that had almost exhausted his physical and mental strength.

Rowena appeared not to notice his momentary gloom. She was fully naked now. In the glow of the lamps burning around the room, her hair shone rich brown and her skin looked white and smooth, like alabaster. Soundless on her bare feet, she closed the distance between them with a few easy steps, her hesitation forgotten. Gingerly, her head bent, she lifted one hand and stroked the damaged skin on his chest.

"Does this hurt?" she asked.

"No," he replied. "And I don't want your pity."

He buried his fingers into her glossy upsweep. The hairpins slipped free from their moorings, and he kept mussing her hair while she ministered those comforting caresses to his scars. Soon he had her upsweep unraveled, the long tresses cascading like glossy mahogany against the paleness of her skin.

He fought to control the rush of desire but lost. "I don't want your pity," he said again, this time on a hoarse growl. Curling his hands around her upper arms, he hauled her naked body against his.

"Then what do you—"

He silenced her with a kiss. At first, she froze. Then, like a long, slender vine, she wrapped herself around him. One slim leg rose to hook over his hip, as if offering access, inviting him to slide inside her. Her arms coiled around his neck, anchoring him close. Her lips parted beneath his, shy and uncertain, but open and without guile.

For a long time, Dale kissed her. He could no longer deny that he'd been waiting for this moment ever since he first saw her. He'd told himself that he'd felt compelled to save her because he hadn't been able to save Laurel. He had told himself that he'd married her because of the land. But the truth was that he had wanted her from the beginning. Wanted her like this, her naked body against his, ready to accept him despite the nightmare legacy of his scars.

Dale broke the kiss and cradled Rowena's face between his hands, his thumbs stroking her skin. So soft. So beautiful. So perfect. Without flaws, unlike him.

Bolder now, Rowena made no effort to avert her face but she looked straight into his eyes. "What do you want?" she asked, the quiver in her voice betraying her nerves. "I'll do anything you want."

He shook his head, a small, rueful half smile playing around his mouth. "That's exactly what I don't want from you. You may have been given the idea that in bed it is a woman's duty to surrender and a man's right to make demands, but it shouldn't be like that. It ought to be mutual giving and taking. That is what I want from you. I want you to be my equal in the giving and taking. I want your passion, not your pity."

Although, he added in his mind, *I'll accept your pity, if it is all I can have.*

Rowena lifted her chin in a gesture of pride. "Of course I want to be your equal. Not just in bed, but in every aspect of life." Her expression grew wistful. "My mother...when she married my father, people said she married beneath herself, but according to my father she never had a moment's regret. She loved the pioneer life. My father says she worked beside him. They tamed the land together. That's the word he used. They *tamed* the land. I can't remember much about my mother, but I want to be brave and strong, the way she was. I want to stand beside you while we take over the land and build on what my parents achieved."

"Perhaps we *are* equal in some aspects," Dale told his wife. "But not all. Like physical strength." Giving her no other warning, he ducked down and scooped her into his arms. Her laughter rippled over him, soothing his anxieties, like smooth whiskey. He carried her over to the bed, a heavy affair of carved oak with a purple velvet canopy above.

Without finesse, he dropped her on top of the purple-and-gold-embroidered cover. She gave a little startled cry. It had been his intention to lighten the situation with humor, but he might have hurt her with his carelessness. Terrified by the thought, he sank to his knees by the bedside. "Is something wrong?"

"Yes!" She wriggled against the embroidered brocade cover beneath her. "The gold thread is prickly. It's like sitting on prairie grass." Looking up at him, she gave him one of those impish smiles that did something strange to his heart. "I think we are meant to be underneath the bedspread. Not on top of it."

"I can fix that." He gripped the brocade cover and pulled at the fabric, tugging it away. The impact sent Rowena rolling across the bed. With a tiny shriek, something between amusement and alarm, she controlled her tumble and burrowed beneath the covers.

Dale climbed in beside her. Rowena was lying on her back, the crisp linen sheet pulled up to her chin. He could feel her eyes on him, watching him, aware of his every move. He settled on his side, braced up on one elbow, and let his right hand rest on her belly. Fingers splayed, the gesture made no demand but the pressure of his palm formed a steady presence that she would find impossible to ignore.

"Do you know what will happen now?" he asked.

She nodded. Normally so expressive, her face had lost its animation. Only the eyes seemed alive, her gaze flickering over him.

"Are you sure you know?" he pressed her.

She nodded again. "I worked as a waitress for two

years. It was impossible not to overhear. Some men like to brag about their prowess, even when there is a lady present." The corners of her mouth tipped into a smirk. "*Especially* when there is a lady present."

"Good," he said. He didn't mean it, not the way it had sounded. It might ease the situation if she had an idea what to expect, but he didn't wish anything that happened between the two of them to be tainted by crude barroom talk, and he felt compelled to add, "I mean, it is better if you don't have to be afraid of something unknown."

"Is it going to hurt?"

How the heck would I know?

"Maybe. A little. Not too much."

It would probably hurt like a poke in the gut with a bayonet, but he wasn't going to tell her that. Slowly, Dale moved his hand, letting it slide upward until he could cup her breast.

Now it was *his* turn to watch *her* every move. He brushed the pad of his thumb over the peaked nipple, watched her lips part on a sigh of pleasure. Their poker lessons came in handy, for they had taught him to read her reactions. Taking his time, he stroked his fingers along the length of her arm, the indentation of her waist, the curve of her hips, seeking out places that rewarded him with soft moans and artless tremors.

His body quivered with the urge to rush, driven by the single-minded masculine instinct to seek satisfaction. Ruthlessly, he clamped down on the need. This was for her. This was to fulfill the promise he had made to himself on the train, that he would give Rowena a taste of romance, a honeymoon, however brief, instead of just a greedy coupling.

When he judged her ready, he settled into position above her. There was anxiety in her eyes, but he could see trust there, too. *Shouldn't have lied to her about how much it might hurt.* The thought rushed through his mind as he eased inside her.

He could feel her pain. It was there, in the startled gasp she gave. In the way her body went rigid beneath him. In how she dug her fingers into his shoulders, as if to stop his motion. "Hush," he told her. "The bad part is over. It will get better now."

He hadn't kissed her since they got beneath the covers, but now he lowered his mouth to hers and gave her gentle kisses, meant to soothe and reassure. He waited until that rigid tension in her body had subsided, and then he began a slow rhythm of thrust and recoil, murmuring soft words of encouragement and praise. Soon she learned to follow his movements, and he took it as an invitation to increase his pace.

In the past, even when he'd paid for a woman, he had taken pride in leaving her satisfied. Now he put no effort into making it last. She might be too sore. He had no experience of virgins. When the pressure built up inside him, he let it come.

Three years of celibacy was a long time, but he had no recollection of it ever being like that, a violent explosion of pleasure that swept his sanity away. Just as he bucked and shuddered in the throes of release, Rowena arched beneath him. He could feel those small contractions, could hear her throaty cries, could feel her straining beneath him, her head shifting restlessly on the pillow.

Slowly, clinging to the sensation of their bodies pulsing together, Dale let the pleasure ebb until the last of the tremors had faded away. Fully spent, he slumped down on the bed beside Rowena. He wrapped his arms around her and cradled her to his chest. All that gentle stroking at the start had been for her, to make it easier for her, but he had been the one to reap the benefit. For it was her reaction—so raw and real it had left him in no doubt that she'd reached completion—that had made the night perfect. Just as he'd wanted it to be.

Dale remained awake, too afraid to risk a nightmare. Rowena was sound asleep, curled up against him, warm and cozy beneath the blankets. Occasionally, she snuggled closer to him. Dale responded by tightening his arms around her.

As the night hours wore on, his mind grew troubled. He'd boxed himself into a corner. When he'd married Rowena, he had focused on the legal aspects of ownership, not on the battle to take back the ranch. One way or another, he had taken it for granted that he could keep his wife out of harm's way, perhaps by leaving her to wait in some nearby town while he cleared out any squatters who might have occupied the land.

Rowena's voice echoed in his mind.

"I want to stand beside you while we take over the land and build on what my parents achieved."

She might be kind and compassionate, but her refusal to prove her innocence when accused of murder had revealed an obstinate streak. There was no way she would agree to remain behind, and the possibility that he might fail to protect her, just as he had failed to protect Laurel, filled Dale with dread.

Restless now, he untangled himself from his sleeping wife and got up, relishing the cool night air against his naked skin. Two of the oil lamps in the wall sconces had guttered out, and he went around the room, turning down the wicks in the rest, until only a muted glow eased the darkness.

After pulling his clothes on, Dale took out his fob watch to check the time. Just after midnight. With quiet footsteps, he left the room. Downstairs, there was bound to be a gentlemen's smoking lounge where he could get a drink.

He found such a room, but to his dismay the place was not empty. A man in a blue uniform with an officer's insignia on his shoulders, sat sprawled in one of the overstuffed leather armchairs by the far wall, a curl of smoke rising from the tip of his cigar.

"Evening," Dale said with a curt nod and strode over to the ornately carved wooden cabinet where bottles and glasses stood lined up on silver trays.

"Good evening," the officer replied. He glanced at the grandfather clock by the entrance that marked the passing of each second with a loud *tick-tock*. "Or good morning, as it may be."

Dale did not reply. He studied the selection of whiskey, chose a bottle of Old Crow, took out one of the crystal tumblers and poured himself a hefty measure. Good manners forced him to turn around and address his companion. "Care for a refill?"

"Just the ticket, my man." Dale could hear the crisp sounds of a British accent. "Mine's a Courvoisier," the officer added, and held out his empty glass.

Dale located the correct bottle, picked it up and carried it across the room, weaving past the card tables. When he reached the man in the corner, he poured without making eye contact. He'd never quite been able to reconcile his hatred of the Union soldiers who'd killed Laurel with his gratitude toward the troops wearing the same uniform who had rescued him after he broke away from the Red Bluff Gang, the band of outlaws he used to ride with.

"Good heavens. It's Hunter. Dale Hunter."

Startled, Dale righted the bottle too fast, making the amber liquid slosh inside. He let his attention sharpen on the man sprawled in the armchair. Tall and wiry, with a hooked nose and a thin-lipped mouth, there was an air of a dedicated career soldier about him. A hard, hungry look, softened only by the warmth in the clear gray eyes.

With a shudder, the memory of all those months in a hospital, the pain, the surgical operations, flooded over Dale. His mouth went dry and he clutched the bottle in his hand so hard the imprint of the patterned glass pressed against his palm. He'd left his shot of whiskey untouched on top of the cabinet, an oversight he regretted now.

"Captain Parks?" he said in a low voice.

The officer lifted his free hand, tapped the insignia with a pair of golden oak leaves on his shoulder with his forefinger. "Actually, it's Major Parks now."

Dale nodded, his mind in turmoil. Major Parks—a captain at the time—had been the officer who had debriefed him after he'd been rescued. It had been up to Captain Parks to determine if Dale's contribution to the disbanding of the Red Bluff Gang merited a pardon.

"Go on, son." Major Parks leaned over the ashtray on an inlaid circular table beside him and stubbed out his cigar. "Fetch your glass. You look as if you need a drink even worse than I do."

With a deep inhale, Dale dismissed the shadows of his past. "I'm pleased to see you, sir, of course I am. It's just that the memories…"

"I know, son. Never known a man to recover from such severe wounds. You have more lives than a cat."

Dale set down the bottle of cognac and went to fetch his glass of whiskey. On second thought, he brought over that bottle, too, and sank into a matching armchair on the other side of the small table.

The older man held up his glass in a toast. "To reunions."

"To reunions," Dale replied and knocked back his drink.

Major Parks made an airy gesture, taking in their opulent surroundings. "Surprised the Marshals Service pays for a hotel like this."

"How do you know I joined the Marshals Service?" Dale asked.

The major whirled his glass, his attention on the amber liquid inside. "Your mother might have mentioned it."

Dale's ears perked up. He'd always assumed it was his mother's friendship with Nell Arthur, the late wife of President Chester Arthur, that had been instrumental in brokering his pardon. But perhaps his mother had other connections. In her late fifties, she was still an attractive woman. With a speculative eye, Dale studied Major Parks, a lifelong bachelor, while at the same time keeping up the conversation.

"In fact, I'm not here on business. I just got married, and I'm on my way to inspect a ranch my wife inherited here in Wyoming."

"Married?" Now it was the older man's turn to spring to attention. "Does your mother know?"

Definitely something there, Dale decided. "I wired her with the news."

Major Parks kept nodding. Dale could see he wanted to say something, but discretion made him hold his tongue. Something about the man's calm, companionable presence made Dale feel at ease. Almost against his will, he found himself unburdening his mind.

"In fact, I'm facing a bit of a dilemma. My wife hasn't been back since her father got gunned down in a range war over two years ago. I have no idea what we'll find. I'd hate to walk into a pack of trouble with a woman by my side, but I know she'll insist on coming along."

"Headstrong, eh?"

"Gentle, but obstinate like a mule."

"Reminds me of someone else. Tempered steel wrapped up in silk and lace."

Dale smiled. It was a good description of his mother. And it fitted Rowena, too. "What do you think I should do?" he asked. "Order her to stay away and face her anger? Or let her come and expose her to danger?"

"Where is this ranch of hers?"

"Northwest from here, on a tributary of Sweetwater Creek, some way beyond Muddy Gap. I understand the best way to travel is Union Pacific west to Rawlins and then northwest on horseback. It will be a two-day ride. Around a hundred miles."

Major Parks gave his brandy another twirl. He held the glass to the light, then finished the drink and laid the glass down on the table with a clunk. Twisting sideways in his seat, he faced Dale, mouth pursed. Appearing to reach a decision, he spoke without emotion, although the expression on his face betrayed some kind of an inner struggle.

"Young man, I might be able to solve your problem."

Dale said nothing, merely lifted his brows in question.

An eager look entered the older man's gray eyes. "Could you convince your wife to be ready at dawn, when the first westbound train comes through?"

"If it solves my problem."

"Splendid. It just happens that although I am in Cheyenne with matters concerning the statehood for Wyoming, I have also been tasked with leading a company of green recruits to Fort Washakie. We'll be going through Muddy Gap. Only a small detour is required to pass by your wife's ranch."

"Are you suggesting what I think you're suggesting?"

"I'm offering you a military escort, all the way to your doorstep." The major's manner grew guarded. "And, if in future we might meet under different… more familiar circumstances, I hope you'll remember the favor and let it count to my benefit."

Chapter Eight

Rowena did not mind the hurry, for at least Dale had been able to rouse the jeweler and collect their wedding rings before they left Cheyenne. Neither did she mind the rough traveling, even though her muscles ached from a day in the saddle and her skin itched from sleeping fully clothed on the ground. Fortunately, spring had finally arrived, sending the temperatures soaring, although the melting snow had turned the trails across the prairie into rivers of mud.

But with each passing mile her edginess grew. What would happen when they reached Twin Springs? Would Dale find the place lacking and make his displeasure known? Would it turn out that she'd had no reason to flee, and she'd be branded a coward? She swept a worried glance over the two dozen uniformed recruits surrounding her. She valued the safety of an army escort, of course she did, but if she faced a humiliation of some sort, the presence of the soldiers meant it would be a public one.

When they reached the end of the valley, a sturdy rail fence marked the boundary of her father's land. A fence that had not been there before. And on the other side of the fence, next to a closed gate, stood a small, square log cabin. And through the narrow slit in the solid timber door of the cabin, a rifle barrel poked out.

The soldiers, seated on their horses, fanned out along the fence line. Major Parks called out an order for the rifles to remain in their saddle scabbards. Some of the recruits revealed their inexperience through nervous gestures, hands settling on their sidearms. Rowena could hear the faint popping of holsters being unsnapped.

"Who are you and what do you want?" a muffled voice shouted from inside the cabin.

"Name's Hunter," Dale shouted back. "But that's not important. The important part is that I have a wife with me, and her name used to be McKenzie."

"What's her given name?"

Gathering her courage, Rowena urged the big chestnut gelding toward the gate, where anyone hiding inside the cabin could get a clear view of her. With a quick flick of her wrist, she rearranged her skirts to make sure they covered her legs, and then she tightened the reins to hold her skittish mount steady. The United States Army did not provide sidesaddles, and neither did they provide horses accustomed to female riders. The powerful quarter horse beneath her took a frightened sidestep every time a gust of wind whipped her petticoats around the animal's flanks.

When the horse had settled down, Rowena pulled aside the shawl that covered her head. "My given name is Rowena. My father's name was Duncan McKenzie, and my mother's name was Isla McKenzie. On her gravestone up on the hill behind the house it says 'Beloved mother and wife, a woman of courage'."

"And what do you want, Rowena McKenzie?"

"I want to come home, claim what is lawfully mine."

The rifle barrel pulled out of sight. The door creaked open and a young man wearing a double rig of pistols and a flashy, silver-studded jacket in black rawhide edged out. Rifle clamped in one hand, he swept an arrogant look over the group of soldiers while a sorrel horse followed him out of the cabin and halted beside him, as obedient as a well-trained dog.

The young man vaulted into the saddle, adjusted the brim of his hat against the evening sun and looked down at Rowena. "Ride slowly. I'll let Mr. Reese know you're on your way." With a jerk of his chin, he indicated the line of recruits. "Tell those soldier boys to keep their hands away from their guns."

The house loomed in the distance, a two-story timber structure nestling at the base of the foothills that heralded the change of terrain. Behind the house, rocky slopes created a patchwork of gray and green and brown. Rowena felt her heartbeat quicken, not just with foreboding, but with the bittersweet nostalgia of homecoming.

Earlier, while the soldiers filed through the gate, Major Parks had sought her out and bombarded her with questions. Seated on his horse beside her, Dale had listened in on the conversation but had made no comment as she described how two and a half years earlier an army supply wagon had dropped her off and unloaded her trunks in the courtyard.

"The house felt stuffy, the stoves blazing, the air too hot. Before going upstairs to inspect the bedrooms, I opened a window in the parlor. I heard sounds from outside. Like distant singing. When I went out, I saw men gathered on the hill behind the house."

She told them how she'd discovered her father had been shot, and how she had refused to listen to Reese's explanations. "I watched the burial, and then I shut myself away in my father's study. After nearly a decade away, I'd been dreaming of coming home, of a reunion with my father. And now he'd been killed, murdered for the land, just like my mother had been killed by the Shoshone. My mind snapped. I can't remember much, but when the night fell, I simply walked out into the frozen darkness, and I have never tried to get in touch since."

But now she was back, and this time the ranch was the opposite of quiet. Men were rushing about in the stable yard, leading out their horses and saddling them. Some darted into the bunkhouse, carried out bedrolls and strapped them behind the saddles.

By the time the double column of soldiers drew up outside the house and the bugler announced a stop, Rowena had counted eight men, and she had picked out Reese and his part-Indian son. Even though Reese had light brown hair and pale skin, the kind that did not tan easily, the likeness was evident. It was there in the way they sat on their horses, in their lithe movements, in the way they seemed to notice everything around them without even looking. It was in the quiet, confident manner in which they issued orders and had eight men saddled, mounted and ready to ride out before Major Parks had even been given the opportunity to demand that they leave.

Rowena had been placed at the back of the column for safety, but something, perhaps a need to prove her courage, made her kick her heels into the flanks of her mount and urge the tired horse forward.

Or, she told herself with a flash of wry humor, *perhaps I simply want to be beside Dale because I feel it is the safest place to be.*

Reese followed her approach with his eyes. When she came to a halt, her chestnut gelding almost nose to nose with his shiny black mustang, Reese leaned forward in the saddle and touched the brim of his hat. "Miss McKenzie. Welcome home. I hope you'll find everything to your satisfaction."

Coward. Coward. The shame of it thudded in her heartbeat. She had been a coward, needlessly fleeing from her home, for now she had been welcomed back with a formal courtesy, not a hint of danger in sight. She managed a stiff nod. "Mr. Reese."

He jerked his chin toward a young man seated on a gray Appaloosa beside him. "So, my son wasn't good enough for you. You must have married an important man, to have the power to bring the army along. You might be kind enough to ask the soldiers to let us go in peace."

Two years of doubt, of wondering if she'd been wrong, made her burst out. "You were living in my father's house, and my father was dead. What was I to think?"

"You might have listened. I made a bargain with your father. After Luke's mother died, I married again. Married a lady, and her family disowned her because of me. When she got sick, I took on the job with your father. Part of our bargain was that I could live in the house, offer my wife some of the comforts she'd lost because of me."

Rowena recalled the heat, the fires blazing. The stuffiness of a sickroom.

Reese spoke quietly. "My wife died a week after we buried your pa. I could have left, but I had promised your father that I'd stay on and hold the ranch for you. And I've kept my word. But now that you have a husband, the ranch is his worry and I'm free to leave."

Up to that moment, both Dale and Major Parks had been listening in silence. Now, with a creak of leather, Dale shifted in the saddle. "The name's Hunter. And, provided my wife agrees, you're welcome to stay on as the ranch manager."

Reese contemplated Dale. "So, she married into gentry. I can see that. I would have liked her to marry Luke, but she appeared to be more inclined to spit in his eye."

Throughout the conversation, Rowena had been aware of Luke Reese's attention on her. Perfectly blank, without expression, hiding all his thoughts, he kept staring at her. Something—perhaps the memory of her own rejection by Freddy—made her speak up.

"Surely you understand that I couldn't consider tying myself to a man who might have been part of a conspiracy to kill my father." She hesitated and went on, a plea in her tone. "Even if I had listened to you, even if I had believed you, the doubt would never have gone away. I couldn't have married your son because every time I looked at him, I would have wondered if he had fired the bullet that killed my father."

"Don't torture yourself with my hurt feelings."

The words came in a deep, gravelly voice, without a trace of an accent. Startled, Rowena whipped her head around to look at Luke Reese. In his late twenties, he was lean, with high cheekbones and a full, wide mouth.

The tanned skin and black hair marked him as partly Indian, but even without the dark coloring his ability to sit absolutely still on the horse and yet appear graceful would have hinted at his Native blood.

Their gazes collided and held. Unable to look away, Rowena felt herself blush. Deep down, in those inscrutable eyes, she could read derision.

Why, he knows, flashed through her mind. *He knows how I feel about Indians. That I hate the Shoshone for killing my mother and would never have married him, whatever the circumstances.*

"My men will ride out with me." Reese shifted his focus back to Rowena and went on with that curious note of wry humor in his tone. "There's no cattle left, but before you accuse me of robbing you, check the accounts. I sold the herd back in eighty-four, soon after your father died. I'm not a rancher, and I didn't want a bunch of cows to nurse. As luck would have it, I did well for you. Since then, beef prices have tumbled. I've drawn wages, and so have my men. Some of the grazing is rented out to Faraday. You'll find every cent accounted for, and we'll leave a few spare horses in the stable."

Reese directed his attention to Major Parks, glancing at the oak leaf insignia on the older man's shoulders. "Well, Major, what it is to be? Do we ride out peacefully, or do you wish to give your troops an opportunity for target practice?"

The major pulled a face. "You must know as well as I do that this bunch is so green they'll scarcely know which end of the gun the bullets fly out from. Go in peace. And should any of your men wish to enlist, tag along and we'll get you signed up at the fort."

A burst of laughter rippled around the band of gunfighters. Even Luke Reese's lips slanted into an amused half smile. His father joined in, then fell serious again. "Miss McKenzie, there is one more part to my bargain with your father. My wife's buried on your land, and I want to be buried next to her." He patted one hand at his chest. "I carry a letter in my pocket, promising a hundred dollars to the man who brings my body back to Twin Springs. The money's in the strongbox, clearly labeled and separate from the ranch funds."

"Don't forget Katherine's things," Luke Reese said.

"Right. There's a trunk with my late wife's belongings up in the spare bedroom. She set great store by the few mementoes she had from her affluent life. I'd be grateful if you held on to them. If Luke manages to find a woman who'll have him, he'll send for the trunk."

It felt odd to Rowena, having eight heavily armed men on one side and two dozen uniformed soldiers on the other, all keeping quiet, out of the way, letting her—a woman and hence a person of no consequence—conduct her difficult conversation uninterrupted.

Thank you, Rowena wanted to say to Reese. *I appreciate everything you have done. I'm sorry I didn't listen. I made a mistake.*

But somehow, her error of judgment seemed so monumental, her behavior at the time of her father's death so foolish, words failed her. She needed time to rearrange her entire thinking.

For once, she was grateful for her expensive education, for now those formal good manners came to her aid. "Please be assured, Mr. Reese, that when the time comes, we will act according to your wishes. We will bury you beside your wife, and in the meantime I shall make sure there are flowers on her grave. And I will look after her belongings until your son sends for them."

Reese nodded. He signaled to the men. The horses shifted. Leather creaked. Bits jangled. Hooves scraped against the ground. *They are about to leave,* Rowena thought, and her chest clenched at the prospect of a parting with so much left unsaid.

And finally, the words flowed, as easy and free as the springs that gave the ranch its name. "Thank you. Thank you all, for everything you have done, for the way you have taken care of my home. If any of you ever needs a resting place—perhaps a final one—you are welcome here." She laid her palm across her heart and said, "Go with God." A sincere farewell that came out choked with emotion, and then she watched the eight men who had guarded her father's legacy ride out.

The soldiers left immediately afterward, the call of the bugle leading them away in a neat formation, a flag flapping at the head of the column. Although she'd miss the big chestnut gelding, in truth, Rowena was glad to see the troops go. Each time they had halted on the trail, the soldiers had hurried to picket their mounts and join the stampede to help her down from the saddle. Like lemmings, they had crowded around her. Despite her kind nature, the constant attention had begun to grate on her nerves.

When the rhythmic thud of the heavy quarter horses no longer shook the ground beneath her feet, she had lost the excuse to avoid looking at Dale. The sun was low on the horizon, and she had to shade her eyes with her hand to make out his expression.

"You think I'm a coward, don't you? The way I ran away."

"Fear can make a person act without reason," he pointed out.

"I can't see you ever being afraid of anything."

"Can't you?" Dale replied softly. "Can't you?"

The memory of the nightmare she'd witnessed on the train, the terrible sounds he had made, echoed in Rowena's mind. Feeling ill at ease, she shrugged the question away and turned toward the house. She lifted her arm and made an expansive gesture. "So, what do you think of Twin Springs?"

"The house seems solid enough."

Rowena tried to assess her home with the eyes of a stranger. Two stories high, constructed of sturdy logs mellowed golden, the house seemed as much a part of the landscape as the grass-covered prairie and the rugged hills. Above the entrance, a canopy provided shelter, and the glass in the windows reflected the setting sun.

"And the land?" she pressed him. "What do you think about the land?"

"Haven't seen enough to form an opinion."

She gave up quizzing him in the hope of some positive comment. "Let's go inside."

The front door gave way to a small vestibule, designed to keep the heat in during wintertime. Beyond was a big parlor, furnished with homely pieces her father had crafted himself. The rest of the ground floor comprised a simple kitchen and a study lined with bookcases.

"Papa didn't employ a housekeeper after Mama died. He did the cooking, and I did the cleaning, until I went to school at fourteen." Rowena swept one fingertip along the top of an oak cabinet in the parlor and studied the line in the dust. "And it seems that after I left nobody took over the task."

However, contrary to her remark, the desk in the study shone spotless, the inkwell full, the ledgers arranged in neat stacks. "Do you wish to examine the accounts?" she asked. "Find out if we are paupers?"

"It can wait."

Rowena led the way into the kitchen and peeked into the meat safe and the pantry. "A side of beef," she announced her findings. "Tins of milk. Canned vegetables. Sacks of flour. At least we won't have to starve right away."

Dale crossed the room to the ancient iron range by the window. Rowena watched as he dipped his finger into the big cauldron of water on the stovetop to test the temperature before bending to open the hatch below. While he stirred the glowing embers, Dale spoke in a casual tone. "I don't think you're a coward."

Surprised, Rowena abandoned any pretense of inspecting the supplies and stared at him.

"You were faced with an impossible situation," Dale went on. He fetched firewood from the rack in the corner and filled the stove. "If you'd stayed, you might have been coerced into marrying a man you suspected of murdering your father. Running away was as good an option as any. Your only failing was not to make better preparations for your flight."

When Rowena made no reply, Dale closed the hatch with a clunk and straightened. Facing her, he leaned back against the kitchen counter and crossed his arms over his chest. He hadn't removed his hat, and he slanted a curious glance at her from beneath the brim. "I expect it wasn't your first proposal of marriage. How did you deal with the others?"

"I…" She wanted him to understand, so much that she burst into a confidence when it might have made more sense to hold her tongue. "In fact, I was engaged to be married, in Boston…the brother of one of my school friends. He…he thought I was an heiress to a big ranch… I never misled him, he simply made a false assumption…and when he learned the truth about Twin Springs, he broke off the engagement in a very public manner… That's partly why I recoiled from the suggestion that I marry Luke Reese…one man had already wanted to marry me for the land, and now another…"

"And you ended up married for your land anyway."

"I didn't mean…" Fraught now, Rowena closed her eyes and gave a small huff of frustration. She opened her eyes again and swept an awkward look at Dale. "I think I'd like to go and see the cemetery now, before it gets too dark."

Dale pushed away from the kitchen counter. "I'll come with you."

The wind had gathered force, and Rowena's skirts whipped around her legs as they made their way up the hillside along the narrow, winding path behind the house. She pulled her shawls tighter around her shoulders against the cold. Her thoughts ran in nervous circles while she picked her steps between the rocks and clumps of coarse grass that might trip her up in the evening twilight.

After the success of her wedding night, she had hoped her marriage could become more than just a practical arrangement. That they could build on the physical closeness between them, form an emotional bond.

But in the last two days the constant presence of the soldiers had prevented any intimacy. The memory of that night was already becoming distant, like a dream, never to be repeated. The question of their sleeping arrangements in their new home pricked like a thorn in her flesh. Deep down, she felt that whatever happened between them tonight would act like a trail marker and determine the direction their life together would take.

She came to a halt by a pair of granite headstones and studied the inscription that she recalled by heart. *Beloved mother and wife, a woman of courage.*

"I've never seen my father's grave," she said quietly. "Not covered up, I mean." She took a step to the right. Because they were higher up, the last rays of the setting sun were still peeking over the western horizon and fell on the letters chiseled into the stone.

Rowena read the words out loud. "Duncan McKenzie. Beloved husband and father and a good friend. A man of honor." Her eyes misted. Not only had Mr. Reese made an effort to find a headstone that matched her mother's, but he had chosen words in keeping. A swell of gratitude rose inside her at the man she barely knew, a man she had treated with suspicion and mistrust. "I'd like to see his wife's grave."

Despite the vagueness of her comment, Dale appeared to understand, for he set off higher up the hillside. Rowena listened to the crunch of his footsteps, then heard his voice calling out for her. "Up here."

She hurried after him. The grave was almost at the crest of the hill, where a sweeping view opened up over the valley. The simple gray stone headstone only had a name, Katherine Reese, and the dates of her birth and death engraved on it. Around the grave, stones in the same pale gray granite formed a decorative border. Circular in shape, perhaps eight inches across, each stone had been chiseled into a pillar-like ornament with a ball on top, a bit like pawns on a chessboard, the surface polished smooth.

"He must have hacked out these stones by hand," Dale commented, awe in his tone. "It must have taken him forever." He counted the ornamental shapes, his forefinger hovering in the air, dipping as he silently added up the number. "There's thirty of them in all."

"He must have loved her very much," Rowena said quietly. She stole a glance at Dale standing beside her. The brim of his black, flat-crowned hat shadowed his face, but she could see the stubble on his lean features, the scar on his cheek, the shadows of past suffering in his eyes. She felt her chest tighten with some emotion she dared not name.

Dale led the way down the hill in silence, each of them wrapped up in their own thoughts. The wind was blowing in fierce gusts now, and the narrow path required them to walk in single file, which would have made conversation difficult anyway, even if he had known what he wanted to say to Rowena. She had lost just as much as he had, Dale realized, perhaps more, and he chose to allow her a moment of privacy to remember her parents.

"The water should be warm by now," he remarked once they entered the heat of the kitchen. "If you tell me where to find a tub, I'll prepare a bath for you."

"In here." Rowena went to the far side of the kitchen and opened a narrow door. Edging past her, Dale stepped into a small room with a cement floor and a single window high up on the wall. The space reminded him of Rowena's jail cell in Pinares.

Three weeks. Three weeks was all it had taken for those edgy emotions inside him to grow until it felt as if his skin was too tight, his blood on fire. In the last two days, he'd come close to ignoring the rules of propriety and taking her on the hard ground while he hoped the soldiers had the decency to look the other way.

During the journey, he'd felt Major Parks watching them. Dale had no doubt that a letter would soon find its way to his mother in New York, with details about him and his bride. Somehow, the thought pleased him. He wanted his mother to know about Rowena. Know that he was no longer alone, with only nightmares to keep him company.

He turned around to face his wife. She was hovering in the doorway, silhouetted against the last of the daylight through the kitchen window. It struck him again, the serene grace and dignity he'd noticed when he first saw her in Pinares. It was not just her beauty that had enchanted him, had drawn him to her. It was her gentleness, her compassion, her sense of humor. She made him forget the ugliness of his outlaw years, allowed him to believe in redemption. With her, he could remember the happy years of his childhood, before the war, before the killings, and imagine life could be like that again.

As he watched her standing there, shy and uncertain, he wanted to tell her that he hadn't married her for the land alone. That she meant more than the ranch. But her tale of a past betrayal kept him silent. There had been a wistful note in her voice when she revealed her broken engagement. For all he knew, Rowena was still in love with the man she'd hoped to marry, pining for him, and someone else's reassurances of her worth might mean nothing to her.

"I'll bring in the water, then," he told her, his casual manner giving no hint of his hopes and longings. "You might like to hunt up towels and clean clothing."

Rowena nodded and whirled and vanished. Dale went back into the kitchen, lit the lamps there, put candles in the wall brackets in the bathing room and lit them, too. He took off his coat and rolled up his shirtsleeves, then lifted down the tub hanging on the wall and gave it a good rinse before hauling over the cauldron of hot water from the stove and tipping the contents into the steel tub. He tested the temperature. Just right for a woman's delicate skin.

He closed his eyes, dreamed, imagined. But a jarring note shattered the picture of a contented future he tried to create in his mind. Even though their wedding night had been a success, Rowena had married him as a business arrangement. Would she one day feel trapped because she had tied herself to a man she did not love and make him suffer because of it?

And what about himself? He was allowing pretty dreams to fill his head, but did he even possess the capacity to love? Was he worthy of love?

He thought of his past, how for so long hate had been a greater force in his life. And deep down he knew that he had no hope of building something lasting until he had purged those memories from his mind. Shared them with Rowena. Let her know what kind of a man he had been, so that if she ever loved him, she would love all of him, not just the thin veneer of a gentleman officer of the law that she could see on the outside.

Chapter Nine

The sound of Rowena's footsteps across the kitchen floor warned Dale of her approach before he heard her voice and saw her standing in the doorway. "Success," she told him with a note of triumph. "Towels. Underclothes. A clean gown." She dumped the stack of items on the single rickety chair in the bathing room. "There are plenty of blankets, too, not too musty, and the sheets look clean. I've opened the windows upstairs to air the bedrooms."

Dale lifted up the empty cauldron. "I'll leave you to it."

After Rowena had closed the door behind him, he stood still in the kitchen, listening. The rustle of clothing. The slosh of water. He knew she was naked in the tub, illuminated only by the warm glow of candlelight, droplets glistening on her skin, her unbound hair tumbling down her shoulders.

He could go inside. *I'll help you wash. We'll share the bathwater while it's hot.* He could think of a dozen excuses, lighthearted phrases. But there was nothing lighthearted about the ache he felt inside, about the way his body trembled and his blood throbbed.

Unable to give in to the need, equally unable to resist it, Dale stormed out of the kitchen and went outside. The stables and the barn on the other side of the courtyard loomed like giant shadows in the falling darkness. He returned to the vestibule where he'd noticed a storm lantern hanging from a hook on the wall and beneath it matches in a leather pouch. He checked the lamp for oil, found the container full. He took out a match, scraped it against the strip of sandpaper attached to the leather pouch for the purpose and held the flame to the wick.

Using the lamp to illuminate his path, Dale went into the stables. The place smelled of fresh hay and horse liniment. He held the lantern high. A row of stalls on the left. Two loose boxes on the right. Behind him came an angry hissing sound. Alert, Dale whirled around on his feet. His right hand settled on the pistol at his hip. In the lantern light, the eyes of a cat glowed at him, like a pair of burning coals. Dale let out a long, slow sigh. His nerves had to be on edge if a barnyard cat had him reaching for his gun.

Feeling his way forward with cautious steps, Dale inspected the horses in the stalls. In the first, a big bay wagon horse greeted him with an eager whinny. By the looks of him, the horse was so old Rowena might be familiar with the creature. Next, two dun geldings, so alike Dale judged them to share a bloodline.

In the first loose box, a big black stallion bared his teeth and neighed in fury. "It's all right, boy," Dale told the animal. "I mean you no harm."

When he eased closer, the horse kicked the stable wall, then craned over and tried to take a bite out of Dale's shoulder. "Whoa," Dale said with a leap back. He held his hand out to the horse and spoke softly. "Easy... easy now."

Edging past the angry stallion, Dale peeked into the final box, which appeared to be empty. But it was not. A gray mare lay on her side, pregnant belly ballooning before her. Dale glanced back at the stallion and smiled. "So, you were only protecting your lady. But you'd best understand there's only one master around here, and that's me." He released the bolt on top of the gate and slipped into the mare's enclosure.

The stallion increased his protestations, but Dale ignored him. He hung the lantern on a nail hammered into a rafter and gave his attention to the mare. A week longer, or perhaps two, Dale reckoned, and they'd have a foal. He couldn't wait to tell Rowena.

"It's all right, pretty lady..." He ran his hand over the mare's belly, feeling the new life inside. "I won't hurt you. When the time comes, I'll do my best to help."

He'd only intended to make a brief inspection, but he remained at the stables, letting the mare get accustomed to him—his voice, his scent, the play of shadows on the rough timber walls and the rustle of straw beneath his feet as he moved about—so his presence would not add to the stress of birthing when the time came.

By the time Dale returned to the house, it was pitch-black outside. The wind had stilled and the night chill had fallen. Shivering in his shirtsleeves, Dale made his way across the yard, using the lantern to illuminate the ground before his feet.

The kitchen was quiet, the lamps burning low.

"Rowena?" he called out. When there was no reply, he inched open the door to the bathing room. Steamy heat enveloped him. The candles had been extinguished, but the tub was full, soapsuds floating on the surface. He lowered the lantern to the floor and dipped his fingers into the water. Still lukewarm.

At first, Dale assumed Rowena had lacked the strength to tip out the water, but then he noticed the pile of clean towels and clothing arranged on the rickety wooden chair. She'd left the water for him, Dale realized. It caused an odd stirring within him. In all his adult life, no one, apart from a paid servant, had ever looked after his comfort and welfare.

Wasting no time, he stripped naked, sank into the water and leaned back with a satisfied sigh. His earlier hesitation about forging a future with Rowena seemed foolish now. Tonight, and all the nights to follow, filled his imagination with visions that made his body respond. Impatient to join his wife, impatient to turn those mental images into reality, Dale scrubbed himself clean with soap and a piece of coarse linen cloth.

Water cascading down his body, he pushed up to his feet and hastily dried himself. Puzzled, he examined the clothing she'd left for him. A tent? A curtain? No, an old-fashioned man's nightgown in thick, unbleached cotton. With a grin, Dale tossed the garment back onto the chair. He'd rather sleep naked.

With only a towel wrapped around his waist, he picked up the storm lantern from the cement floor and set off, barely pausing to extinguish the lamps in the kitchen before continuing upstairs. He'd not seen the bedrooms yet, and he surveyed his surroundings, mentally reviewing the layout of the house.

Three doors, leading to three bedrooms. And all of them closed. None of them open in invitation. But in a cold climate one was wise to avoid drafts.

He opened the first door, held the lantern high. A small bedroom, filled with a jumble of furniture and trunks. He closed the door quietly, tried the room across the hallway. A large bedroom, uncluttered, furnished with a mirror-fronted armoire and two matching chests and an enormous bed—a bed with no one in it.

His heart was pounding now with impatience, with anticipation. He closed the door too quickly, and the sharp click disturbed the quiet of the night. Dale came to a halt. He chuckled, a wry note of amusement at his schoolboy eagerness, but the nervous quality of the sound betrayed his unease.

Edgy, he went to the final door at the end of the hallway. It opened to a serene, feminine room with gauzy drapes in the window and a matching set of simple, white-painted furniture. And, in the small bed, his wife slept, curled up beneath a patchwork quilt.

It was a girl's room. The room she must have occupied before leaving home. And like a homing pigeon, she'd returned to her own room, to her own bed. A bed that did not have enough space for two.

Standing in the doorway, Dale held the lantern high. He saw the rosy glow on her cheeks, the slight rise and fall of the patchwork quilt with her calm, even breathing. She must be exhausted after the journey, after all the topsy-turvy changes in her life. He ought to let her sleep. A gentleman did not rouse a lady from her rest to satisfy his physical needs.

As Dale let his eyes linger on Rowena's sleeping form, a wave of warmth swept over him. He felt breathless, his chest constricted. He ached to hold her, nothing more than to hold her, have her slender body curl up against him. He could pick her up and carry her to the big bed without waking her. Surely, he could do just that?

But the unease that had been growing inside him sharpened. He could feel the shadows of violence flickering in his mind. The presence of soldiers, the reunion with Major Parks, the expectation of a battle with squatters, they had all served to stir up the memories, and his finely tuned nerves warned him that a nightmare hovered on the edge of his consciousness.

He turned around on bare feet and returned to the big bed that had no one in it.

But all too soon, it became crowded. When the nightmare came, it spun Dale back in time, into a dusty red desert canyon where he stood hidden behind a boulder, waiting for his executioners to arrive. Roy Hagan and Celia had already made their escape, with Roy draped across the saddle, so badly wounded it would be a miracle if he survived. But Dale had insisted on staying behind, willing to sacrifice his life to give his friend a chance to get away to safety.

Riders thundered up. Guns roared. Dale could feel the bullets slam into his flesh. He could feel the heat, the dust, the brightness of the sun, a jumble of sensations, a cacophony of sounds, men shouting, horses neighing, bullets ricocheting from the rocks.

The battle noises faded away, and he lay sprawled in the dust. He could feel a bullet in each leg. In his left arm. In his side. And he'd broken his right arm when he tumbled down from the rocks. The pain enveloped him, like a dark curtain that dulled the rays of the midday sun that reached the canyon floor.

Dimly, Dale became aware of sounds. The scrape of

footsteps on gravel, easing toward him. Voices, muffled and cautious. He kept his eyes closed and remained still.

"You reckon he's dead?"

"I'll check."

Dale cracked his eyes open. The canyon walls rose around him, the sky a blue ribbon above. He tried to lift his gun, but a boot stamped over his forearm.

"Lookit—he's still trying to fight."

Dale felt a kick in his side and the silver-decorated pistol was wrenched from his hand. One of the outlaws found the other matching pistol Dale had dropped when the bullet struck his arm. The outlaw toyed with the revolvers, spinning them back and forth. When he got tired of showing off, he pointed the barrels at Dale's head and cocked the hammers.

Unwilling to let his killers have the satisfaction of watching the final spark of life fade away, Dale closed his eyes. But no sound of gunshot came, no slam of a bullet against his skull. Instead, pain exploded in his right leg. Then left leg. Biting back a scream of agony, Dale opened his eyes. The outlaws were circling him, delivering kicks.

"His legs are busted. Both of them."

"I'll shoot him. It will be an act of mercy. Like shooting a crippled horse."

"Patience, my friend." One of the outlaws poked at the gunshot wound in Dale's left arm with the tip of his knife. Dale stifled a moan. The man tugged at Dale's right arm so hard the broken bones crunched. "Both his arms are busted, too."

Even in the dream, the pain overwhelmed Dale. He longed for a drink of water, but he knew they wouldn't give him any, so he chose not to let them have the victory of hearing him beg.

"Step out of the way," one of the outlaws ordered his companions. "I'm gonna shoot him. I'm gonna shoot the sumbitch with his own fancy shootin' irons."

Another man slanted him a sly glance. "Why bother? An act of mercy, you said. Why not leave him to die a slow death? He can't move. We've taken his guns. He can't defend himself and he won't have the means to end his life. If we haul the other bodies away, he's the only thing left for the buzzards. Look—" the man gestured toward the sky "—they are waiting to start their feast."

Dale could see the battle of conflicting desires in their expressions. The prospect of greater cruelty, compared against the instant satisfaction of watching him die. Undecided, one of the outlaws turned around and spoke to another man partly hidden by the rocks.

"Halloran, what do you reckon?"

At this point in the dream, Dale always felt a flicker of hope. Halloran, a stocky, brown-haired man with a wife hidden away in some quiet town, was one of the few decent ones in the Red Bluff Gang. But the hope always died before it could take hold. What could Halloran do, except prolong his suffering?

"I reckon it's a fine idea." Halloran spoke with a carefully controlled air of indifference. "Let Hunter die slow, Indian style. The buzzards will go for his eyes first. The coyotes, too, will find him. It might be fun to come back tomorrow and see how much of him there's left."

Dale saw a glint of gold as Halloran pulled a coin from his pocket, tossed it in the air and caught it in his fist. "I bet ten dollars he lives until noontime tomorrow."

The other outlaws grinned. "You're on."

Dale gritted his teeth. They would leave him for the scavengers. He listened to the outlaws arguing who should fetch the horses picketed down the canyon. Halloran gave a piercing whistle, and a moment later Dale heard the clip of hooves.

Halloran spoke in that same casual tone. "I reckon I have the right to improve the odds a mite, since I've saved us a walk to get the horses."

He went to his sorrel, took down a canteen, walked over to Dale and uncapped the canteen. Sympathy flickered across the older man's features as he slipped one arm behind Dale's head to lift him up and tipped the canteen to his mouth. Dale drank. Even in the dream, he could feel the cool water sliding down his throat, reviving him. After lowering him down again, Halloran gave him a small, comforting squeeze on the shoulder and propped the canteen on the ground beside him.

Dale moved his lips. Halloran leaned closer.

"Hide," Dale whispered. "Soldiers will come."

Halloran gave the briefest of nods to indicate that he had understood, and then he straightened on his feet and returned to his horse.

"What about the girl and Roy Hagan?" one of the outlaws asked, grouchy and irritable. "Shouldn't we go after them?"

Dale spoke up, startling the men. "Hagan's dead. The girl took the body. Wanted to bury him proper, have a grave to cry over. Women are like that."

The outlaw gave a cackling laugh. "There won't be nothing left of you to bury after the buzzards and coyotes have finished with you, and there sure won't be no woman to cry over your grave."

After collecting the dead bodies, the outlaws got on their horses and set off down the trail toward their canyon hideout. When the sounds of their departure had faded away, Dale gave up fighting the pain. Twilight fell, and the buzzards circled lower in the sky, and loneliness closed around him, deeper than he had ever known.

Let me wake up. Let me be free of past suffering. I'm not alone anymore.

The hazy fragments of consciousness pierced Dale's sleep, but the nightmare did not release its grip. In the dream, darkness surrounded him. Pain seared his left cheek. He could smell a hot, rancid breath on his face, could feel something lurking in the shadows beside him. His body throbbed with agony, but he put all his energy into moving his left arm, the one not broken.

His muscles obeyed his will, and despite the pain of the gunshot wound high up near his shoulder, his arm rose from the ground. He fisted his hand and took a swipe into the darkness that surrounded him. "Git!"

The animal growled, scurried away. Dale lifted his hand to inspect his face. His left cheek hurt, as if someone had taken a knife to it. Gently, he touched his fingertips to the skin, found a ragged gash, like a flap torn open. Nausea welled up in his throat. He'd expected to die tonight, but not like this, not like a carcass, with scavengers fighting over him.

The beast crept closer again. Stars glittered in the sky, and somewhere out of sight the moon must be shining, for a faint light reached down into the canyon. Dale could see the outline of the coyote and a pair of yellow eyes glowing in the darkness. Snarling, the predator flattened its lean body against the ground, preparing to lunge.

If only he had a gun. Coyotes were solitary animals, not like wolves, inclined to hunting in packs, and he could only see one of them, easily dispatched with a bullet. Moving his left arm again, Dale searched the ground for a stone. His fingers met the strap of the canteen.

He curled his hand over the leather strap and tensed his muscles. When the coyote pounced, Dale flung the canteen at the beast. Water arched in the air, like a silver rainbow. Too late did he remember that to make drinking easier for an injured man Halloran had left the canteen uncapped.

The blow connected, and the coyote leaped back with a yelp. Gritting his teeth against the agony of motion, Dale slumped back to the ground. He drew short, swift breaths, staring into the darkness, searching for that pair of yellow, glowing eyes.

A few minutes later, the coyote launched another attack, and Dale deflected it with a blow from the canteen. The fight acquired a pattern of retreat and advance, like a military campaign. As the night hours wore away, Dale pitted his stamina and patience against that of the coyote, the precious water spilling out of the canteen with each swing, going to waste.

Half-delirious, Dale let his mind wander. Had he been wrong to accept the deal his mother had brokered with President Arthur, to cooperate with the law in exchange for a pardon? No, he told himself. He had become an outlaw against his will, forced into hiding after he'd avenged the murder of his sister. He had never killed a man who didn't deserve killing. Other men in the Red Bluff Gang in similar circumstances, such as

Roy Hagan and Burt Halloran, would also be recommended for a pardon.

By the time the first hint of gray eased the darkness in the sky, Dale could feel a fever setting in. He shivered, alternately hot and cold. His body felt too exhausted to register pain. All his concentration went to watching the coyote and swinging the canteen.

I'm already a dead man, he had told Roy Hagan's woman, Celia, when he'd sent her along the trail to safety, with Roy barely clinging to life. Only he hadn't expected that dying would involve so much pain.

His arm grew heavier and heavier. The coyote, emboldened by the weakness of its opponent, snapped and snarled, biting at Dale's feet and legs where the canteen didn't reach. Soon the leather of his boots gave way and the sharp teeth of the animal tore at his flesh.

It was only a matter of time now.

Come midday, Halloran would lose his bet.

Sometimes, the nightmare went on and on, the coyote biting chunks out of him, until he turned into a skeleton. Sometimes, Dale woke up in the middle of the battle, shaking, covered in icy sweat, his breath rasping in his lungs. At other times, he held the coyote at bay until dawn crept over the canyon and the steady drumming of hoofbeats in the distance announced the arrival of the soldiers who would rescue him.

In tonight's nightmare, dawn came, and he could feel the ground vibrating beneath him with the approach of cavalry troops marching in an orderly procession. But no column of riders in blue uniform emerged from the opposite end of the canyon. It was a girl in a green gown, sitting on a big chestnut quarter horse, her hair flowing like a mahogany-colored cloak down her shoulders.

* * *

Rowena came awake in stages. Lifting her head from the pillow, she studied her surroundings. In the faint glow of moonlight through the window she could see a white-painted chest…a striped rug…an oval mirror on a stand.

Familiarity enveloped her, comforting and safe.

But then a muffled cry cut through the quiet of the night, and the sense of safety shattered, with the present sweeping aside the childhood memories. Quickly, she got out of bed and tiptoed into the corridor wearing only a thin cotton nightgown.

Why hadn't Dale awoken her when he came upstairs? She'd only planned to lie down in her old bedroom for a moment, for it hadn't seemed right to settle in her father's big bed alone. She'd wanted to let Dale claim the role of the master of the house, make that large bedroom his and then invite her to share it with him.

For a long moment, Rowena stood outside the closed door, irresolute. Did her husband wish to keep his restless dreams private? Was she intruding?

"Next time you hear me moan in my sleep just turn away, or throw something at me to make me wake up."

Surely, those words gave her permission to enter.

Gingerly, she turned the brass knob and eased the door open. On this side of the house, the moonlight did not reach into the room, and the dark rosewood furniture deepened the shadows.

She crept closer to the bed. Dale lay on his back, the bedclothes in disarray. His face seemed deathly pale, his expression grim. The coal-black hair formed a stark contrast against the white linen sheets, making the whole scene appear monochrome, drained of color.

Rowena leaned over him, uncertain how to best awaken him. Without warning, Dale swung his arm in a wide circle, nearly hitting her. The bedclothes slipped aside, exposing him to the waist. Even in the dim light, Rowena could make out the scars that crisscrossed his chest—scars she had already seen on their wedding night, but now a baffled thought flashed through her mind.

He said the coyote went for his legs...

She brushed aside the inconsistency of it, for Dale gave another one of those tortured cries. His arm rose again. This time Rowena was prepared and kept out of the range of that swinging fist.

When Dale had slumped back to the mattress again, she sank to her knees beside the bed. She could hear his labored breathing, could see his body trembling with the tension and fatigue of the nightmare. She curled her fingers around his shoulder. Beneath her touch his skin felt feverish and damp with perspiration.

"Dale… Dale…" She shook his shoulder and spoke in an urgent whisper, a compromise between attempting to pull him out of the nightmare and trying not to startle him. "Wake up…wake up… Dale, wake up."

He shuddered. His eyelids lifted. For a few endless seconds, he stared at her, unblinking. A look of confusion flickered across his face, as if he couldn't tell if she was real, couldn't tell where the nightmare finished and the reality began.

"You had a bad dream," she told him softly. "I think it was the one with a coyote. You were swinging your arm."

"Sorry…to trouble you."

"It's all right," Rowena replied. Without thinking,

she lifted her hand and smoothed the tangle of straight, jet-black hair away from his brow. "It's all right," she told him, and the words gained a wider meaning. She spoke with a confidence she had never felt before, her wish to heal and comfort ignoring the bonds of reason, rising above the realm of possibilities.

"I'm here now." She bent closer to him, her fingers sliding through his hair. "The coyote has gone away, and I won't let him come back. I won't let him get at you again."

Dale made a harsh sound, something between an exhale and a groan. He reached out for her and pulled her toward him, his hands curled around her upper arms, tugging so hard she heard a seam rip in her nightgown.

Ignoring the mishap, Rowena climbed in beside him. When she lay facing him, Dale wrapped his arms around her and held her tight. He crushed her to his chest with such fierceness that for an instant she felt trapped, but she overcame the flare of panic. She'd offered to shield him against the nightmare, to be the force that anchored him to reality, and she must keep her promise. Instead of struggling to be free, she slipped her slender arms around him and clung to him, their bodies so closely fused that despite the barrier of her nightgown she could feel the pounding of his heart, the urgent rise and fall of his chest, the uneven texture of his scarred skin.

His arms around her eased their hold a fraction. His hands fisted behind her back and shifted in a quick series of motions, separating and joining. She heard tearing sounds, and then there was no more nightgown, only ragged strips of fabric that fell away to tangle with the bedclothes.

Dale spoke in a hoarse growl. "I need… I have to…"

With no further warning, he edged backward along the mattress, so he could pull her into the center of the bed. It felt a bit like dancing, the flat of his palm pressed across the small of her back, urging her toward him. When he had her where he wanted, he slid one knee between hers to nudge her legs apart and rolled on top of her.

He paused to look into her eyes. "Do you mind?"

"No," she replied. In truth, she didn't know if she should acquiesce or not. Her single experience of a physical union on their wedding night might not have prepared her for what would take place next. But it was too late for misgivings, for he entered her in one swift, powerful thrust. There was no pain, only that startling sensation of having something inside her that she remembered from before.

Braced up on his arms, Dale began moving over her in deep, rhythmic strokes that had her sliding against the mattress. His expression was fierce, his brows furrowed in concentration, his mouth flattened into a determined line.

She should have been frightened of his grim mood and the ferocity of his need—a need that he did not even try to rein in and control—but it was not fear that made her heart pound and her body quicken. Acting by instinct, she wrapped her legs around his waist, tilting her hips toward him, inviting him deeper inside her.

At first, when Dale felt her anchoring him into place like that, he ceased his motion. For an instant, he remained absolutely still. Then he lowered his head and pressed a rough, hungry kiss on her lips. It was over in seconds. Then he straightened his arms again and resumed his motion, even more forceful than before.

As they rocked together in their coupling, his eyes held hers, intense in the darkness of the room. Rowena had a sudden sense of falling, of weightlessness. Emotions that seemed too frightening to accept, yet too powerful to fight, soared inside her. In an effort to block out those emotions, she closed her eyes.

"Open your eyes, Rowena."

"I can't," she said. "I can't."

"Yes," he told her. "You can. And you will."

He thought she was talking about a physical release. She gave her head a tiny shake, her hair tumbling against the pillow. "I won't…"

"Look at me, Rowena."

She couldn't resist the demand in his voice. She opened her eyes. Poised above her, Dale nodded his approval, and then he bent his arms and gave her another one of those quick, fierce kisses.

"Don't close your eyes," he said, and drove himself to completion.

It was thunder and lightning, and it was glorious, even if she didn't achieve any of those rolling waves of pleasure he'd given her on their wedding night. When Dale finally arched above her, his body taut, his face stark, Rowena clung to him and shared the sensations of his release.

When it was over, Dale slumped against her, his weight pinning her to the mattress, his face pressed to the crook of her neck. Rowena could feel the warmth of his breath, could feel the faint tremors that continued to ripple through his body, and she took pride in having brought him comfort, in having chased away the nightmare.

"Sorry," he muttered, his lips grazing her ear.

"There is no reason to apologize."

He ignored her reassurances. "I'll make it up to you. I promise."

Slowly, his breathing calmed and the last of his tremors faded away. With a sigh, he shifted his weight off her and let his body relax against hers. When he didn't speak again, Rowena thought he had fallen asleep, but Dale proved her wrong by lifting his head and brushing a gentle kiss on the crest of her cheek.

For what seemed like hours, they lay like that, side by side, his palm resting on her chest and his leg thrown across hers, his face buried in her hair. Every now and then he stirred, for another soft kiss, always in a different location…her shoulder…the shell of her ear…the edge of her collarbone…the corner of her mouth…the wispy curls at her temple.

Afraid of her own emotions, Rowena accepted those small caresses but offered none in return. If she didn't watch out, she would fall in love with him. Every day, every night, he would gain a little more of her, leaving her a little less, making her happiness a little more dependent on him. And whatever other challenges her marriage might bring, she could not bear the thought of loving and not being loved in return.

Chapter Ten

Something tickled her belly. Rowena swatted at it, but the tickle returned. She let sleep slide away and opened her eyes, squinting against the brightness of the light. Sunshine streamed into the room. Why, it must be nine o'clock, perhaps even ten.

"Good morning." Dale was kneeling on the bed, looking down at her. Sunlight fell on his naked skin, creating a play of shadows over the muscled ridges. The golden glow highlighted the scars on his chest, softening the jagged lines.

Fascinated, Rowena stared. She would never have guessed that a legacy of injuries could enhance a man's looks instead of detracting from them. Lean in build, elegant in carriage, Dale might have looked like a dandy, too beautiful for a man. The scars added a rough edge of masculinity.

"Good morning," she replied. She tugged at the rumpled sheet, attempting to pull it up over her breasts.

Dale yanked the sheet aside, baring her again. He lowered his head and dropped a kiss on her belly. Rowena recognized the tickling sensation that had awoken her.

"Stop," she protested. "I need to get up."

He slanted a glance at her. "You have to visit the convenience?"

"No, but—"

"Then lie back."

"But…" Edgy with nerves, a blush spreading from her bare breasts all the way up to her hairline, Rowena muttered, "It must be close to midday." An exaggeration, perhaps, but it made the point of the lateness of the hour.

Dale flapped his hand in a command for her to settle down again. "Lie back. Last night, I looked after my own pleasure, and I promised to make it up to you. Just relax, and concentrate on the sensations."

"But we can't—"

"Lie back, I said."

Unless she wanted to turn it into a fight, she had no choice but to obey. Rowena flopped back against the mattress. Every muscle tense with anticipation, she stared up at the ceiling, her eyes following the dust motes that danced in the sunlight. On her belly, she could feel a brush of lips. The featherlight sensation drew an instant response from her body.

Scandalized at her own wantonness, she spoke between panting breaths. "You can't… We can't… Not in daylight."

"Well, *ma cherie*," Dale replied smugly. "It might come as a surprise to you, but it is possible to do exactly the same things in broad sunlight as one can do in midnight darkness."

"But—"

"Hush. Just lie still and enjoy it. I promise you it will be good."

With a whimper of embarrassment, Rowena settled down on the mattress. The easiest way to deal with the situation was to let him do what he wished. All her senses seemed to heighten as Dale began to caress her body. Moving with the easy grace that was so much a part of him, he dipped and darted, touching her here and there, brushing his lips over her skin, finding sensitive places.

Unable to keep still the way he'd ordered, Rowena writhed on the bed, the response of her body impossible to contain. Hampered by the prudish attitudes drummed into her at school, she flung one arm across her face to shield her privacy.

"Don't do that," Dale told her. "Don't hide from me."

"Can't you let me retain any measure of dignity?"

"Dignity?"

At the sharp tone of his voice, Rowena shifted her arm, just enough to get a peek at him. He was on all fours over her. He'd been kissing the indentation of her waist, working his way upward along her body, getting perilously close to her breasts. In broad daylight.

"Dignity?" he said again. "I'm paying homage to you, to your beauty and your courage. I'm showing my gratitude for helping me banish my nightmares. How could that hurt your dignity?" He made an angry sound. "My God, what do they teach girls in those expensive schools? That a lady must live her life untouched, cobwebs between her legs? If she must surrender in order to have children, it must be with reluctance and distaste."

That's just about it, Rowena thought.

Aloud, she said, "I chased the coyote away." A childish remark, but putting it like that gave her a sense of pride, a sense of achievement. It eased the sting of the label of a coward she'd attached to herself.

"So you did," Dale replied, his tone gentling into amusement. "And now, will you just relax and let me get on with it?"

I'm a woman of courage, Rowena told herself.

And she needed courage, for, in broad daylight, with the sun streaming in through the window and making patterns on her skin, Dale kissed her breasts. While he did it, one of his hands slid between her legs. There, with his long, elegant fingers, the fingers of a gunfighter, he teased and rubbed and caressed until she came apart, her dignity in tatters.

Instead of ceasing his ministrations, Dale started again. He rolled her over to lie on her stomach and began seeking out new places on her body to awaken… the ridge of her spine…the side of her breast…the plump curve of her buttocks. Nothing was overlooked, no part of her left without attention. This time, when the pleasure of completion swept over her like a riptide, she screamed, actually screamed, her frantic cries of passion fading away in the dusty corners of the room.

Again, Dale repositioned her, now to face the ceiling. Languid, as if her bones had turned to water, her limbs so heavy she doubted she could remain upright if she tried to stand, Rowena did not resist. She didn't even have the strength to cover her face, which meant that she had an unobstructed view of the glow of masculine pride in Dale's green eyes.

"One more time," he said. "A *hat trick*, I believe the English call it, a sporting feat achieved three times in a row."

"No." She tried to shake her head but found it required too much effort. "I can't... I have no strength left..."

"Let me prove how wrong you are." Her husband crouched over her, like a sleek predator stalking its prey. As he inched downward along her body, the muscles in his arms and shoulders bunched and flexed. His naked skin gleamed in the sunlight.

Rowena closed her eyes.

Dear Lord, he is going to do it now, that thing I suspected might be possible but couldn't believe anyone would be bold enough to attempt.

She held her breath, every inch of her body on fire. Anticipation quivered within her. She knew that Dale would not have to wait long to accomplish his *hat trick*.

Boom, boom, boom. The sound reverberated around the house.

Rowena opened her eyes. Dale had lifted his head and was listening to the insistent, banging sounds that emanated from the front door. With a muttered curse, he jumped out of bed and began pulling on his clothes. "There's someone at the door."

Thank you, Rowena said in her mind to that unknown person, while at the same time wishing a gruesome fate upon them for the interruption.

Dale was hopping on one foot, shoving his legs into trousers, struggling to do up the buttons over his erection. He glanced at her and winked. "You'd best get up, too, Mrs. Hunter. Put some clothes on instead of lazing in bed all day. After all, it's nearly noon."

For an instant she stared at him, stunned at the criticism. Then her brain caught up with the lighthearted banter. It had not occurred to her before, but Dale had the capacity to adapt to changing situations in a heartbeat. A man must develop the skill when living on the edge, facing constant danger. He was a federal marshal, after all, a man who had spent his life fighting outlaws, keeping the country safe for peaceful, law-abiding citizens.

After Dale had vanished out of sight, Rowena flopped back onto the bed. Sensations, fragments of conversation, images chased each other around her head. Like a scandalous stage play, the events of that morning and the night before flickered through her mind.

But it seemed that a woman might possess some of that skill of adaptation, too, for curiosity about their visitor beat back those heated recollections. Rowena bounced out of bed. Wincing at the slight soreness in her private places, she hurried over to the mirror-fronted rosewood armoire. Voices drifted up the stairs, too muffled for her to make out the words. She surveyed the contents of the armoire, chose a navy blue wool shirt that had belonged to her father and slipped it over her head. The garment came down to her knees, not very ladylike attire but it would serve to keep her warm.

At the top of the stairs, Rowena came to a halt and crouched down to peek between the timber spokes of the balustrade. Dale was standing in the foyer, his back toward her. Facing him was a gaunt man of medium height. On the floor by the man's feet, Rowena could see a stone jug and a pair of burlap bags. She studied the visitor. There was something familiar about him…thinning gray hair…sunken cheeks…sharp blade of a nose.

When the recognition came, she had to slap a hand over her mouth to hold back a startled cry. Why, it was Mr. Faraday. Or a shadow of his former self. Surely, it was no more than eight or nine years since she had last seen the feuding neighbors. How would anyone age so fast?

"It's part of the lease conditions," Faraday was saying. "Twice a week. Milk, cheese, butter, eggs. Pork or beef, when we've slaughtered. Usually, I send a ranch hand over to bring the supplies, but today I wanted to come myself, in case Reese didn't explain things. The lease is up in August. Just wanted to flag it up, so you can draw up the paperwork to extend for another year."

"I'll have to think about it," Dale replied.

Rowena frowned. Dale was speaking in a thick Southern accent. She'd never heard him sound like that before. And his manner seemed odd, as if he was acting the role of a Southern aristocrat, out of his depth in these rough surroundings.

"Might bring in a herd of my own, stock the range," Dale went on.

"Man, you can't do that. I need…" Faraday paused, appeared to pull himself together. "You're a newcomer to the area and not a rancher. I'll tell you for nothing, it's hard times. The drought has been going on for three years…" He scrubbed his face with his palms, then lowered his hands again. "I need that grazing."

"It's my wife's land. The decision is hers."

"It became your land when you married her."

"Nevertheless, the decision is hers. I'll pass on your request to her."

"You'd let a woman dictate to you?" Strutting his sunken chest, Faraday blustered, cocky superiority in his tone. "A woman doesn't know her elbow from her backside. Heck, a woman doesn't know her own mind until a man makes it up for her."

Dale's manner cooled. "In my opinion, a woman's

brain is no less capable than a man's. Good day, Mr. Faraday. I'm needed in the kitchen. My wife hasn't had her breakfast yet."

Faraday's bloodshot eyes nearly bulged out of his head. He stared at Dale, as if looking at a circus side-show. Then he shrugged, gave a curt nod and left, leaving the jug and the pair of burlap bags on the floor.

"Stop lurking on the stairs, Rowena," Dale called out. "Come down."

She descended to the foyer in her bare feet and swooped down on the burlap bags like a buzzard on a carcass. "He wasn't lying...butter...cheese...a whole chicken, all plucked and dressed..." She looked up at Dale. "We can have a feast tonight."

He gestured at her bare feet. "Put some socks on before you catch a cold. And let me have those bags. You said your father cooked and you cleaned. I propose to continue the arrangement. Unless you'd rather I clean and you cook."

"You wouldn't like the outcome," Rowena warned him bleakly. "Alice Meek tried me in the kitchen, but she said she'd lose all her customers within a week."

"I know," Dale replied with a rueful smile. "You don't think I offered to cook out of the goodness of my heart?"

Dale cracked the eggs with one hand, showing off the skills gained by doing his own cooking, while making sure he could reach for his gun at all times. He let his eyes drift over Rowena. Swamped by the large man's shirt, thick wool socks on her feet, she looked happy and relaxed. Even better, she appeared to have lost some of that inconvenient prudishness. His marriage was getting off to a good start.

"Eat," he said, and slid a sizzling plate in front of her.

Ravenous, they devoured their breakfast, sitting side by side at the battered table, with the sun streaming into the kitchen. They talked easily, about the ranch, about the horses. The wagon horse was nearly twenty years old, called Samson, Dale discovered. When Rowena learned about the mare in foal, she dropped her fork with a clatter to the plate, jumped up and dashed toward the front door in her sock feet.

Dale hauled her back. "Later."

"But I must say hello to Samson, and see the others..."

He lured her into staying by pointing out that the other horses needed names, too. Instantly, Rowena immersed herself in the task. Dale described each animal. Color, size, what he had noted of their disposition. By the time they had finished eating, the pair of dun geldings had become Boston and Louis, the latter being short for Louisiana, the names in honor of the places important in their respective pasts. The mare was Ruby, and the stallion Flint.

When another knock sounded at the front door, Dale pushed his empty plate aside. "I believe doing the dishes counts as cleaning. You can get started while I deal with Spencer."

"How do you know it's him?"

"He wouldn't let Faraday get an edge over him."

Spencer was the opposite of Faraday. Tall and slim, with silver hair and an erect posture, he wore a brown suit of good quality. When they introduced themselves, Dale put on the abrasive manner of a brash New York Yankee.

"I'd like to buy your land," Spencer told him bluntly. "I'll pay any price, within reason."

"I have no intention of selling."

"Will you extend Faraday's lease?"

"That is no business of yours."

"I'm making it my business. When cattle prices went up to seven cents a pound, he got greedy. He overstocked his range and brought in another herd to graze on the reservation land. Last year, there was trouble with the Indians, and President Cleveland ordered all cattlemen to remove their stock from the reservation. Beef prices had fallen to three cents a pound, and Faraday didn't want to sell at a loss. With the drought, his grass is too poor to support a big herd. If you refuse to extend the lease, he'll be finished."

"And if I agree to extend the lease?"

"It will give him a reprieve. But if the drought continues, he'll go bankrupt. I assume you know about the animosity between us. For more than ten years, my sole goal in life has been to destroy Faraday. But now I have to do nothing. His greed has taken care of it. All I have to do is wait, and I'll see him ruined."

"In that case, what I decide to do with the lease should be of no concern to you."

Spencer took down his hat and turned it around in his hands. "Tell your wife I'm sorry about her father. I wish I hadn't hired those men. They are gone now, every man who was happier holding a pistol than a lariat. Faraday's hired guns have left, too. He could no longer afford to pay them."

Dale acknowledged the words with a nod. Spencer took his farewell, his erect carriage slumping. When he returned to his horse waiting outside, everything about him spelled out the despair of a broken man—a man who had lost everything and lived only for revenge, but now that he was about to taste that revenge, he'd discovered it was a bitter fruit.

As soon as the front door had closed after Spencer, Rowena gave up hiding in the kitchen and hurried into the foyer. "Mr. Faraday is from the North, and you spoke to him with a Southern accent. Mr. Spencer is a Southerner, but when you spoke to him you put on a Yankee accent. Why did you do that?"

"I wasn't going to let either of them think that I'll be an ally just because we share the same background."

Frowning, Rowena took a moment to figure out the comment. When the implication became clear, she broke into a grin. "You wicked, wicked man."

Dale ushered her toward the study. "Let's go and check out our financial situation."

Inside the big oak cabinet, they found a strongbox. The key had been left in the lock. Dale turned it and lifted the lid. Gold eagles, arranged in neat piles, glittered inside.

"Good heavens," Rowena breathed. She was hovering on her toes behind him, peeking over his shoulder. "Are we rich?"

"We're certainly not poor. And that means we can afford some groceries, and a warm coat for you, and anything else you might need. Is there a town nearby with stores?"

"Clayton, about ten miles to the west. It's a proper town, with a church and a school, and a post office, and several stores and saloons. A man from Baltimore tried to start a bank but no one would trust him so he closed down again."

"If that was almost a decade ago, things could be different now. Some towns flourish, some die out. We can ride over tomorrow and take a look. But first things first. Why don't you count the money while I take a look at the ledgers?"

He picked up the strongbox, carried it over to the desk and placed it on the far side, opposite to the big leather chair he intended to occupy himself. Then he fetched one of the balloon-back chairs lined up against the wall, positioned it by the strongbox and gave Rowena a courtly bow, inviting her to sit down.

With a smile at his playful gesture, Rowena dropped into the seat. Appearing to forget all about him, she stared into the strongbox. Reverently, she lifted one hand and touched the money. As Dale watched her, tenderness welled up within him. He'd been born affluent. In his outlaw years, only survival had mattered. After his pardon, guilt had stopped him from accepting the family wealth. But now, possibilities flashed like bright images in his mind. He could give Rowena anything she wanted. But in order to do so, he would have to reveal his past.

Dismissing those tempting images, Dale opened the first ledger in the stack and studied the neat entries. "Reese said he was no cattleman, but he has kept good records."

The only reply he received was a muttered *"Forty... fifty...sixty..."* and the clink of coins. He gave up the attempt at conversation and continued studying the ledgers. He found a neat list, noting beef prices every spring and fall. It was true, what Faraday had said—that prices had crashed to less than half of what they had been at their peak, only four years prior. He found newspaper cuttings about the decision by President Cleveland to disallow the grazing of cattle on reservation land, and a copy of the lease agreement with Faraday.

Rowena looked up from her stacks of gold. "We have four thousand three hundred and seventy dollars."

Dale closed the ledger. "It might sound like a lot of money, but this place will require upkeep. We can't simply live on the money until it's all gone. And we need to do something to occupy our time." He considered. "We could buy a herd and run cattle."

"Papa always said that Twin Springs is better suited for sheep, but he had no wish to take on the cattlemen who hate sheep farmers. He kept quoting something by a man called Silas Reed, who did a survey of the Wyoming Territory back in the 1870s." Rowena tilted her head, searching her memory.

"There seems to be no doubt that the vast quality of mutton can be grown here, pound for pound, as cheap as beef, and, if so, then sheep raising must be profitable if cattle raising is."

Dale shook his head. "That's no recommendation, considering the beef industry is in a slump." Slowly, his mouth tugged into a grin. "But I can't think of a better way to rile our neighbors. Filling those hillsides with a flock of sheep would be like waving a red flag at a pair of stampeding bulls."

The next morning, Rowena did the breakfast dishes while Dale went out to harness Samson to the wagon. The previous afternoon, she'd been to the stables, had received an eager welcome from the big wagon horse who remembered her. She'd made friends with the other horses, too, the pair of steady, workmanlike duns, the gentle mare, and even the big black stallion who seemed to sense that she posed no threat.

Before they set off for Clayton, Rowena changed into one of her Boston gowns. Nothing ostentatious that might make people think she was showing off, but elegant enough to prove that the money spent on her education had not gone to waste.

Brimming with optimism, she sat beside Dale on the wagon bench. Last night, he had made love to her again, and despite her lack of experience she knew they were well matched. The guarded warnings by some of her teachers that marital duties were a cross a woman had to bear had proved to be nothing but wicked lies. Or perhaps those teachers didn't know any better, poor souls, most of them spinsters, Rowena thought with a twinge of pity.

The sun warmed the air, the spring grass painted the hills green. Swallows dipped and dived overhead. The world smelled fresh, clean-scrubbed. She took deep breaths, anticipation buzzing inside her. She'd loved Clayton, the small school, the stores where people would greet her by her name and ask after her father. She'd been fourteen when she left for Boston, and it had been a wrench to leave everything familiar behind.

Her maternal grandparents had been of modest means, but they had wanted the best for their only grandchild. They had used their savings to send her to an expensive academy for young ladies. They had died when Rowena was seventeen, but there had been enough money left to fund the last three years of her education.

When the plan had first been put to her, she'd refused

to go, but Papa had played his one trump card. "Your mother would have wanted you to grow up a lady."

"Your mother would have wanted..."

That statement had preceded every difficult choice she'd faced in her childhood years. And, as always, it had persuaded her to yield. For she knew her father had been right—Mama would have wanted her to have a proper education.

But now she was back. The town rolled into view, a single thoroughfare with two-story buildings on either side, and a few side streets with homes behind white picket fences.

"Is it the way you remember?"

Her eyes were too busy searching, her mind too busy remembering. The Tin Drum Saloon with its wide balcony…Hannerman's Baked Goods…the dress shop, now painted yellow instead of pink…the general store run by Mr. Jenkins and his wife.

"Yes," she said, craning ahead, one hand atop her bonnet to keep it anchored while Samson picked up speed. "It looks the same…almost."

Dale pulled to a halt outside the general store and set the brake. Too impatient to wait for him to assist her, Rowena climbed down and hurried ahead, her heels clattering on the timber planks as she jumped up the single step to the boardwalk.

She pushed the door, and with the jangle of the bell she was through. Yes! Things were the same. With a warm flush of delight, she smiled at the heavy, bespectacled man behind the counter. "Mr. Jenkins. It is lovely to see you again."

He squinted at her. Rowena's smile widened. Everything was indeed the same, even the reluctance of

Mr. Jenkins to invest in a new pair of spectacles when he needed them.

"Don't you recognize me?" She tilted her head, pointed at the candy jars that lined the counter. "You gave me peppermint drops and licorice sticks and agreed to put it down on my father's account as laundry soap."

"Miss Rowena? Is it you?"

"Yes, it's me, Mr. Jenkins. And I'm married now." She heard Dale's distinctive footsteps on the boardwalk outside, waited for the door to open and gestured behind her. "This is my husband, Mr. Hunter."

Dale came forward and shook hands with Mr. Jenkins. With a tiny sting of unease, Rowena observed the pair of them. Dale's performance with Mr. Faraday and Mr. Spencer had reminded her how little he revealed of himself. Would he resent the inquisitive questions Mr. Jenkins was bound to ask?

True to form, the storekeeper pushed his glasses higher up along his nose and studied Dale through the thick lenses. "You plan to run cattle on Twin Springs, Mr. Hunter?"

"I'm considering running sheep. You think that would invite objection?"

Mr. Jenkins squirmed a little, unwilling to take sides. "Can't truly say. There's quite a few sheep farmers settled in the area, making a go of it. There's the Cosgriff brothers, and Evans and Homer, and young John Okie. In fact, I just saw Okie ride into town. Went to get a haircut, I believe. The word is, he is hoping to find himself a wife."

Unable to contain her impatience, Rowena cut in, interrupting a conversation between men, an act that would have sent Miss Malmaison, her etiquette teacher, into a swoon. "Mr. Jenkins, does Sharon still live here in Clayton? Or any other of my old school friends?"

The storekeeper beamed. "Yes, yes. Sharon married Davey, the youngest of the Madigan boys. They live with me and plan one day to take over the store. And Lainey Harrison is now Lainey Willoughby. Her husband works at the post office."

"Perhaps I could call on Sharon…?"

"Go. Go now. Anytime. She'd be pleased. And there's a ladies' sewing circle. Sharon can tell you about it, when they meet next, in case you have time to join."

She turned to Dale. "Could I…?"

Smiling, Dale flapped his hand at her, ushering her along. "Of course. And I'll take the opportunity to find this man, Okie, and talk to him about raising sheep. Why don't we plan to meet back here, say around two o'clock? If you are early, you can look through the shelves, pick out anything we need."

"Thank you," Rowena shouted, already on her way out. "Thank you, Mr. Jenkins."

It had never occurred to her grandparents that by sending her to a school that catered for the rich and well connected, they had condemned her to the fate of an outsider, with no true friends. Friends like Sharon Jenkins and Lainey Harrison had once been. And perhaps could be again.

Chapter Eleven

Dale wasn't used to talking to anyone about his plans. But today, ever since he had finished talking to the young sheep farmer he had tracked down outside the barbershop, the urge to share his findings with Rowena had been pressing inside him, like water against a dam.

On his return to the general store, he found his wife busy stocking up with canned goods and flour and soap and detergents. Impatient, he paid for the purchases, carried the boxes into the wagon and helped Rowena up. The sun was still high in the sky, allowing them plenty of time for the journey home, so he kept Samson to a walk, the slow pace making it easier to talk.

"This man, John Okie, he is young, much younger than me, younger even than you, and he's been raising sheep for four years now. He sells the wool, and he usually sells the lambs in the fall. He said he could let me have a small flock, to try my hand. He made mistakes in his first year, lost half his sheep. It's best to start small if you have no experience."

"How small is small?"

"Maybe thirty ewes and lambs, and a ram. I'd have

to fetch them with a wagon. A two-day trip. Would you like to come?"

"I'd like to stay behind…if you think it is safe."

Surprised by the comment, Dale contemplated his wife, noticed her pinched expression. He should be more understanding. He'd spent his life courting death. He ought to remember that Rowena would be more sensitive to danger. She'd be afraid to be alone, but equally afraid of being labeled a coward.

He spoke lightly, careful to reassure her without belittling her fears. "It is sensible to be concerned about Faraday and Spencer, but they won't trouble you. Faraday needs you willing to sign the lease, and Spencer no longer needs Twin Springs to crush his enemy. There is a lull in their feud."

Rowena's expression brightened. "In that case, I'd like to stay behind. Sharon has offered to help me give the house a spring clean. A welcome home present, she called it. She'll come on Monday and bring her baby with her. Lainey Harrison might come, too, and bring her little boys."

Baby. Little boys. The words caught in Dale's mind and stuck there, like a pair of terriers trying to tear apart all his misgivings and doubts. The future that only a short while ago had seemed too impossible even to imagine now began to feel all too real.

When they got home, he felt edgy and restless. They put away the provisions they had purchased and took turns to wash away the trail dust. Rowena toured the house, planning how to clean each room, and he cooked supper, a simple stew with beef and dried vegetables.

After they had eaten and cleared away the dishes, Dale went to stand in the kitchen doorway. He held out his hand to Rowena. "Will you come and keep the coyote away?"

"Yes." Without any sign of shyness or hesitation, she rushed over to him and slipped her hand in his. Dale led her upstairs. A sense of contentment settled over him. Surely, the hard part was over now, that period of doubt when the two of them rattled in the undefined space of their marriage and tried to find a firm foothold. Now the foundations for their future together had been laid. All they had to do was to build on those foundations and make sure the construction remained solid enough not to topple down at the first gust of an adverse wind.

"That's Molly. No, it's Iris. Or Poppy. Damn you, don't laugh at me."

Dale suppressed his smile and surveyed the flock of thirty ewes and lambs milling on the sunlit slope before them. He'd fetched the animals two weeks ago. With Rowena's help, he was nursing them as if they were babies. Every morning he moved the flock into a new spot and studied the reactions of the sheep, to learn what kind of grass they liked, if they preferred sunlight or shadow, easterly aspect or west.

"How can I not laugh when you attempt to name creatures so identical they're impossible to tell apart?" he pointed out.

"Not so," Rowena protested. "Molly is bigger than Iris. And Poppy has longer ears. They just refuse to stand next to each other long enough for me to compare them and decide which one is which."

During the day, Rowena wore denim trousers and wool sweaters from her girlhood, the fit so snug they showed off her figure in a way that made Dale's pulse spike. And every night, she slept in his arms. Often he would have been content just to hold her, feel her against him, inhale the scent of her fragrant soap and listen to the even sound of her breathing. But sometimes, when he planned to let her sleep, she took the initiative, gently trailing her fingertips along his chest until she got the reaction she wanted. It was those nights he liked the best.

"Faraday," Rowena said in a mutter.

Dale nodded his understanding but showed no other reaction. Rowena's hearing was keener than his, and she could tell an approaching rider from the faintest sound of thudding hooves. Ever since Dale had brought the sheep over in the wagon and let them loose on the range, Faraday had been skulking about with two big dogs running alongside his gray gelding. He was a shadow on the horizon, a flicker behind a tree, always nearby.

But this time, he rode straight up to them, leaving them at a disadvantage as they stood on foot, their horses tethered nearby. Dale heard Rowena's frightened gasp and stole a glance at her. She was not staring at Faraday but at him, and then she directed her attention at the pair of dogs that were running toward them, teeth bared. "I'm not scared of dogs in real life," Dale told her quietly. "Or even coyotes. Only in dreams."

He could sense her relief, wanted to add to the reassurances he had given her, but Faraday pulled to a halt in front of them and prevented any further confidences.

"Please keep your dogs away from our sheep," Rowena called out.

Faraday ignored her, but nodded a civil greeting. "Hunter. Mrs. Hunter."

Dale dipped his chin. "Faraday."

Faraday sent his horse prancing, a fancy trot that showed no consideration for the frightened sheep. The two dogs kept close to him, but both were growling, a low, rumbling sound that carried on the breeze.

"You thought any more on that lease?" Faraday said.

"I won't extend," Dale replied, only remembering just in time to add a Southern drawl to his speech. "I need the grazing for my sheep."

"You could run your sheep on the higher slopes and let me have the rest."

"I intend to bring in a bigger flock. I'll need all the grass."

One of the lambs made a playful leap, lost its footing and tumbled down in a somersault. The dogs charged after it, cutting the lamb off from the rest of the flock.

"No!" Rowena yelled. "Stop them! Stop your dogs!"

Faraday put his fingers into his mouth and let out a piercing whistle. The dogs halted, mere yards from the frightened lamb. The rest of the flock huddled together, pressing into a heaving mass. Faraday whistled again. The dogs barked in protest, but turned around and loped back to their master.

Dale spoke with an icy anger. "I'm warning you, Faraday. If I see those dogs anywhere near my sheep again, I'll shoot them. In fact, if I see your dogs anywhere on my land again, I'll shoot them. Do you understand me?"

The man's gaunt face pulled into a sneer. "I thought you had no land. I thought you were hiding behind a woman's skirts, calling it *her* land."

"It's *our* land," Rowena cut in. "Our land, our house, our sheep." She lifted her chin in a haughty pose, product of the best lessons in deportment that money could buy. "And the gun that kills your dogs will be our gun. Does that make it clear enough for you?"

Faraday spat, a gesture as crude as hers had been regal. Making no other reply, he wheeled his horse around and cantered off, the dogs running in his wake. Rowena took a sideways step and huddled against Dale. He wrapped one arm around her shoulders. He could feel her trembling, but during the confrontation she had shown no outward sign of fear, none at all.

"A woman of courage," he said quietly. "I'm proud of you."

She turned toward him and buried her face in his shoulder. When she spoke, her voice came out muffled against his coat. "I want to count them. Make sure they are all there."

"Fine," Dale replied with a resigned sigh. It was a daily routine, and sometimes it took several attempts to complete the count, if the sheep kept milling about. He couldn't wait to get a bigger flock. At least big enough for it to be impossible for Rowena to demand an individual count.

The spring turned into summer. Ruby's foal was born, a long-legged filly that would grow into a beautiful black mare. To Dale's amusement, this time Rowena struggled to find a name. She had tried Jasmin, Delilah, Lilac, and discarded each after a day or two. The horses lived outside now, in two paddocks near the house, and only took shelter at the stables if it rained— which it never did, for the relentless drought had not loosened its grip on the land.

They still rode out every day to inspect their flock of sheep, even though the novelty of it was wearing out. Today the afternoon sun baked down so hot they didn't need overcoats. As usual, they picketed Boston and Louis by the creek. Swallows dipped and dived over the grassy knoll that hid the sheep from view. Dale strode ahead, leaving Rowena to follow. She had a habit of pausing to pick the wildflowers that dotted the hillside. If he waited for her, the inspection of the flock would take all day, including the count.

He could smell the carnage before he caught sight of it. The air was heavy with the stench of blood. Overhead, a buzzard wheeled, waiting to feast on the carcasses. For an instant, Dale was spun back into the past. He lay sprawled on the ground in a rocky canyon, his body riddled with bullets, his blood leaking out of him while jeering men laid bets over how long he would last.

"What is it?" Rowena called out to him.

Dale realized he'd frozen on the spot. He forced his feet to move. He had to get there first, see what lay ahead, assess the situation and use his lawman's expertise to decide how to best protect his wife from any danger that might still be lurking about.

He cleared the ridge. The sight that met him sent anger seething within him. Dead sheep lay in a tangled heap against a line of boulders to the left of the clearing. In the middle of the pasture, a few solitary sheep lay on their side, their fleece matted with blood.

Behind him came the thud of urgent footsteps. "What is it, Dale?"

He eased back down the slope, flung one arm out to halt Rowena's progress. "Stay back. I don't want you to look."

But Rowena fought against his restraining hold. Her motions grew frantic. She clutched a posy of yellow paintbrush in one hand and clawed at his arm with the other. Her voice became shrill with fear. "What is it? Let me see. *Let me see!*"

Dale had no choice but to let her through. After all, he'd promised to treat her as an equal. He lowered his arm. Rowena dashed forward. Then she slowed her steps and glanced back at him, suddenly hesitant, as if afraid to go on, afraid to discover what lay ahead. "What is that smell?" she asked.

"Death."

He saw her throat, so pale and white, ripple as she swallowed. A shiver traveled over the length of her, but she conquered her fear and turned around once more. With stiff legs, forcing herself to proceed calmly, she made her way up to the crest of the ridge. Dale hurried after her, caught up with her and stood beside her as she surveyed the destruction.

"Are they…" She inhaled a sharp breath. Dale saw her nostrils flare, saw her eyes widen. The stench was stronger here, the spring breeze carrying the odors of slaughter toward them. Rowena's hand fisted around the wildflowers, crushing the stems, and the scent of flowers mixed with the smell of blood, as if reminding them of the cycle of death and rebirth that was part of nature.

"…are they all dead?" She finished her question.

Dale surveyed the bowl-shaped area of the pasture. Here and there, he could see movement. A lamb, huddling against its dead mother. A ewe, limping along. Another ewe, lying down, staring at the carcasses with terrified eyes.

"Not all of them," he said. "But most."

"Those dogs…" Rowena's voice was low and harsh. "He let those dogs loose on the flock of sheep."

"We don't know that for certain. It could have been a pack of wolves."

She shot him an angry glance. *Why pretend when we both know it was him.*

"I'm a lawman," Dale told her quietly. "I'm trained not to jump to conclusions until I have reviewed all the evidence. I can't just ride over in anger and accuse a man simply because he is the most likely suspect."

In silence, Rowena made her way to what remained of their flock. Surprised at her willingness to get closer to the grisly sight, Dale followed her. She sank to her knees beside the heap of dead animals and touched the unmarked fleece of one of them. "This is Molly." She stroked the long nose of another one. "And this is Iris."

She glanced back at Dale over her shoulder. He could see the sheen of tears in her eyes. "I used to wish that they would remain still long enough for me to compare them and tell them apart." She turned her attention back to the sheep. "Well, now I can."

Dale helped her up to her feet. "Let's go home. I'll come back with a wagon, sort out the dead from the living and take away the carcasses. Maybe we can use the meat."

"No." Rowena shook her head. "I don't want to eat them."

He took her back to the house, harnessed Samson to the wagon and drove out, the wagon wheels bouncing over the rough trail. He parked at the base of the hillock and began the grim task of sorting through his decimated flock.

Eight sheep remained alive, five ewes and three lambs. The ram was not with the herd but penned up near the house. Dale inspected the survivors, decided they needed no veterinary care. He moved them half a mile north to another pasture and returned to load up the carcasses.

He hadn't decided yet what to do about Faraday. He couldn't accuse a man without evidence. But neither could he simply let it be, brush aside his suspicions. Before leaving, Dale studied the ground, looking for signs. In a sandy hollow beneath the boulders, he found a single paw print, large, like that of a dog, but without claw marks. A mountain lion. Perhaps Faraday was not to blame, after all. He'd consult Spencer. The man might offer some insight to the presence of mountain lions in the area. And he might be able to use some of the mutton so it would not all go to waste.

Spencer's house was a sprawling, single-story log cabin, set halfway up the eastern slope of the valley, high enough to enjoy a view but low enough to avoid exposure to the fierce winds that swept over the crest of the hills. Dale drove into the neatly kept yard. He'd barely come to a halt when Spencer came out of the house, rifle in hand.

"Came to ask for advice." Dale hopped down. He pulled two bloodstained carcasses from the wagon and dropped them to the ground. "What do you think killed these?"

Spencer sank to his haunches and studied the torn throats of the dead sheep. The carcasses left in the wagon showed no visible injury, but Dale had read about that in a book young Okie had lent him. Easily frightened, sheep would flee in panic, unable to stop if they met some obstacle. The line of boulders on the edge of the pasture had been such an obstacle, and the flock had piled up against it, suffocating each other to death.

"A cat. A cougar." Spencer gestured over one of the carcasses on the ground. "See how the rest of the animal is unmarked? A cougar has long fangs to puncture the throat. He likes to kill in a single bite. A wolf has crushing jaws. He likes to hunt in packs. The others will hold the prey down, tearing it apart, while one of them goes for the throat."

Dale nodded. "Obliged." He indicated the wagon. "Could you use the meat? My wife won't have any of it. She named the sheep, treated them like pets."

Spencer's lips quirked into a smile. "She'll learn."

"I doubt it," Dale muttered.

The older man surveyed the load in the wagon. "The meat will keep for another day or two, if the carcasses are gutted and protected from the sun." He gave Dale a guarded glance. "Would you have any objection to feeding Indians? There are women and children starving up on the reservation. They could dry the mutton into jerky and make it last for months. I'd like to take the whole lot over there, if you give your consent."

"I can do better than that," Dale replied. "I can help you gut the carcasses, and if you give me directions, I'll deliver the load for you."

She could scarcely bear it, this groundswell of disappointment and hurt. Rowena stared at Dale who stood by the front door, clad in bloodstained clothing, telling her that the loss of their sheep need not be a disaster without a silver lining.

A silver lining? A silver lining? How could feeding the people who had killed her mother, the people who had taken her mother's scalp to hang as a trophy in some brave's lodge, be a silver lining? It was nothing of the sort. It was rubbing salt in her wounds, if Dale wanted to talk in colloquial sayings.

She could not hide the plea in her tone. "You said that if I ever wanted anything from you, all I needed was to ask. I'm asking now. Please, don't go."

"You'd rather let the meat go to waste?"

"Yes. Burn it. Bury it. Leave it for the scavengers."

"Rowena..." A frown of disapproval wrinkled Dale's forehead. "Be reasonable. The braves who killed your mother might be old men by now. They might no longer be alive. There are women and children starving on the reservation."

"Are you saying the men won't eat? That they'll stand aside and let the women and children fill their bellies while they watch? I don't think that is the Indian way."

"There are human beings suffering because they don't have enough to eat, and you want to stop me from easing their plight. I never expected such cruelty from you."

"Cruelty? Cruelty?" Rowena whipped herself into a fury. Deep down, she knew Dale was right—she was being unreasonable. But the very knowledge that her demands were unjustified, without merit, made her unable to yield, because the only thing supporting her position was her own conviction. "Don't talk to me about cruelty when my final memory of my mother is Indian braves whooping in triumph because they had murdered and scalped her."

Dale's expression hardened. "If I can't convince you, I'll have to ignore you. I'll be back in two or three days." He pivoted on one grimy boot heel and walked away.

* * *

Had this ice age really been worth feeding a few starving Indians? Dale moved his breakfast plate to the other side of the kitchen table, but Rowena slapped her cleaning cloth against the tabletop, barely missing his arm.

"Move over," she ordered.

"I just moved."

"Move again. I missed a spot."

She was using her cleaning like a military campaign. Every time he sat down in a comfortable chair, she insisted on sweeping the floor beneath his feet, dusting the padding beneath his backside, polishing the timber parts of the chair, anything to annoy him.

At other times, she treated him with a cool politeness. They still rode out together every day to inspect their few remaining sheep, but their interactions had become stiff and formal.

At night, he slept alone, for when he had returned from the reservation he'd discovered Rowena had barricaded herself inside the sanctuary of her girlhood bedroom.

He might have thawed the frost between them by apologizing, but why should he apologize when she was in the wrong? He could have kicked down the door to her bedroom and taken what belonged to a husband, but he wanted Rowena to come to him of her own accord. Because she wanted him. Because she liked to sleep cuddled up against him.

But instead of seeking him out at night, she looked at him with the hurt of betrayal in her dark blue eyes. His conscience rioted at the knowledge that she had asked him for something and he had refused. Why couldn't she have picked something easier to give?

To add to his woes, the nightmares were returning. This time it was not the coyote, but the knife fight with Krieger, the soldier who had killed Laurel. Dale dreamed of the flashing blade, of the serrated edge cutting into his chest, seeking to carve out his heart, and he would wake up in the night, shaking, the sheets tangled around him.

After a week he could take it no longer—the lonely nights, the frosty politeness of the days, the feeling that nothing would ever be right in his world again. For all he knew, if he didn't do something, the impasse between them might go on for months—he'd noticed it before: his wife had the ability to hold a grudge.

He made a plan and recruited Spencer to help. When the arrangements were in place, Dale faced Rowena across the dinner table. "Be ready to leave the house at dawn tomorrow. We're going on a trip."

"Thank you for the invitation, but I have too much to do."

His eyes narrowed. "You'll come with me, even if I have to hogtie you and drag you every inch of the way. Be ready at dawn. We're going in the wagon." He dropped his spoon to the table with a clatter and made his exit, leaving Rowena to stare after him.

Chapter Twelve

It didn't escape Rowena's notice that Dale steered the wagon into ruts, so that she kept bouncing against him on the narrow bench. She relaxed her body, making the contact last a fraction longer than necessary before she pulled away. She wanted the discord between them to end, but she didn't know how to achieve it. Even though she accepted that she was in the wrong, her pride wouldn't allow her to apologize. Moreover, she was not ready to let go of her hatred of the Shoshone, however misguided or unjustified the feeling might be.

"Where are we going to?" she asked.

"North."

"I can see that." Rowena hesitated. "Are we going to the Indian reservation?"

Dale gave her a thoughtful glance. "No," he replied. "We are not going to the Indian reservation."

When night fell, they made dry camp. Dale laid out a cold supper of jerky and hardtack.

This is how he must have lived during his years as a lawman, alone, lacking any home comforts, Rowena thought.

Regret filled her, and a touch of shame at her stubborn refusal to take the first step toward a truce. She had no right to make him suffer because he hadn't done her bidding. She opened her mouth but the words of apology caught in her throat. Why did it have to be so hard?

Dale pushed up to his feet. "I'll sort out the bedding."

The sun had disappeared beneath the horizon nearly an hour ago, and darkness was falling, the buzz of insects loud in the silence. A few stars already twinkled in the sky. A gust of wind made Rowena shiver. Not knowing where they were going, she'd put on a blue cotton dress, simple but well-cut, good enough for a visit with officers' wives, in case they were headed for Fort Washakie, where Major Parks had taken the army recruits.

"Ready to turn in?"

Dale was beside her, his hand held out to her. She laced her fingers into his and allowed him to help her up into the wagon, where he had laid out a bed of straw covered with a canvas sheet. Two blankets were spread on opposite sides. Hiding her disappointment, Rowena wrapped herself into one of the blankets. So near, but not together. She gave a long, slow sigh of uncertainty.

"Are you cold?" Dale asked.

What harm was there in a lie? It had worked once before. "Yes."

He reached out, laid his arm across her waist and pulled her toward him. Images of making love beneath the stars filled her mind, but Dale merely held her, letting her share the heat of his body.

"Good night, Rowena."

"Good night." Somehow, she knew that tomorrow

she'd face a test of some kind, a test of courage and wisdom. If she failed, the rift between them might never heal.

Tense with foreboding, Rowena clutched the hard edge of the wagon bench as Dale left the marked trail and brought Samson to a halt in the middle of nowhere. Ahead, she could see nothing but barren land covered in sparse grass and gray rocks. "You said we were not going to the Indian reservation."

Dale hopped down from the wagon. "We're not. Those big boulders mark the reservation boundary. This was easier than getting permission for a number of Indians to leave the reservation land."

He helped her down, his hands curled around her waist. Before he released her, he looked into her eyes and spoke quietly. "Will you do this for me, Rowena? Will you see them?"

Reluctantly, she nodded. Dale released her and went to lift a wooden stool from the wagon. After he had set the stool on the ground, carefully selecting an even spot, he gestured for her to sit down. When she was settled, Dale spread a blanket on the ground in front of her and stepped aside.

Suddenly, it seemed as if the earth itself had come alive. Indians, mostly women and children, stepped forward from between the rocks, from the shadows. Some seemed to simply rise up from the grass, like ghosts materializing from the morning mist.

One of them, a young woman carrying a baby at her hip, separated from the others and walked toward Rowena. Clad in a ragged cotton skirt and a deerskin shirt, she was painfully thin, her hair matted, her cheeks sunken. She halted in front of Rowena, bent to place a small clay pot on the blanket and straightened again. Carefully, she folded aside the piece of blanket that covered her baby and held the child up for Rowena to see.

"Thank you for the life of my baby."

The words came out in halting, heavily accented English. Not waiting for Rowena to reply, the young woman withdrew back into the crowd.

Another woman stepped forward, followed by two children, a scrawny, nearly naked boy, barely old enough to walk, and a girl of around six of seven. The woman laid her hand on the shoulder of each child to bring them to a stop in front of Rowena and bent to place a pair of decorated moccasins on the blanket. "Thank you for the life of my children."

Next, an old woman, toothless, her face lined with deep grooves, came forward with limping steps. Her gift was a small leather pouch with a few glass beads in it. "Thank you for my life." The words were barely comprehensible. It became clear to Rowena that these women spoke no English. They were merely repeating words learned by rote, sacrificing their pride to thank a white woman who had taken pity on them and saved them from starving.

I had no pity, she wanted to shout. Tears welled up in her eyes, tears of compassion and shame, but she blinked them away, aware that Indians preferred solemnity on such formal occasions.

One by one they came, women young and old, some with children and some without. The pile of gifts on her blanket grew, ranging from a deerskin shirt decorated with porcupine quills to a handful of pollen that conveyed a blessing.

Finally, the women clustered to one side. A boy of perhaps fourteen, with a complexion so fair he had to be mostly white, came to stand in front of Rowena, together with an old man using a gnarled branch from a tree as a walking stick. Despite his frail body, the old man walked with the pride of a chief with ancient traditions behind him.

"My grandfather speaks no English, so I'll translate for him," the boy said.

The old man fastened his black eyes on Rowena and spoke a few guttural words.

"My grandfather thanks you for your gift to his people. He hopes you are pleased with the gifts they have given you in return."

Rowena nodded. "Tell him I shall treasure the gifts of his people."

The young man passed on her comment, and the chief replied, haughty and regal. The boy could not hide the startled flicker on his face, but when he translated his voice remained bland. "My grandfather has learned what happened to your mother. He says he knows of an Arapaho brave with the scalp of a flame-haired woman in his lodge. If you like, my grandfather will fight the brave for the scalp, so you can get back your mother's hair and put it in her grave, make her body complete in the afterlife."

Rowena clasped her hands together in her lap. At the mention of her mother's fate, grief and anger surged within her, but quickly ebbed again. It was in the past. Nothing to do with this ragged collection of Indians, a nation who had lost their land, their freedom, their way of life. She contemplated the old man, as fragile as a dried-up twig. He could fight no brave. He couldn't even fight her.

"Thank your grandfather, but there is no need. It no longer matters."

The boy translated. The old man gestured at Rowena and spoke again.

"My grandfather says, white women don't value their hair?"

"Tell him..." She felt a twitch at the corner of her mouth and had to bite her lip to bring the flash of amusement under control. "Tell him that white women value their hair very much while they're alive. After they are dead, they no longer care."

The old man replied. When his grandson started to translate, the chief held up his hand to demand silence. Slowly, each word measured, he said, "White... women...wise."

No longer feeling the need to hold back a smile, Rowena nodded. "Thank you. I wish your nation well. May the drought end soon and there be many buffalo roaming the prairie, so that your people never need to go hungry again."

The Indians turned away and walked off. By now, the sun had risen, and the bright light revealed their ragged poverty in every detail.

Who am I kidding? Rowena thought bleakly. *The drought shows no signs of ending and the buffalo have all been killed by wealthy tourists who shoot them from the train windows for sport.*

The sky was a blue dome above, the sun hot, the breeze cool, the prairie ablaze with wildflowers. It would have been a lovely day for an outing but Rowena's agitation kept her from enjoying the journey home. She barely had the courage to look at Dale. He had bundled the blanket with the gifts from the Indian women into the wagon, and he had helped her up, but since then he had spoken not a single word. It was clear he was not going to help her.

"I'm sorry," she finally said. "I was wrong."

"I know."

"I felt betrayed... You said I only needed to ask..."

"I know."

She stole a peek at him. "At least the house is spotless now."

Dale sighed. "I know."

From that moment on, the silence between them grew easier in texture. Here and there, they broke it with small, inconsequential comments.

"Did you see the skylark?"

"What was that? A prairie dog?"

When they got home, Rowena offered to cook while Dale unhitched the wagon and took care of the horse.

"What about these?" He indicated the gifts bundled into a blanket.

"Leave them in the barn for now. I'll sort through them tomorrow." She valued the items, but she expected that she would value them even more once she could be sure they were free of bedbugs and fleas.

In the kitchen, Rowena did her best with a chunk of beef and a tin of carrots, but her nerves eroded what little skill she possessed. When she heard Dale's footsteps in the hall, she dished out the food.

He sat down and studied his plate. "What is this?"

"Beef stew."

He stirred the charred pieces of meat and the carrots

hardened into pellets with his spoon, then took a cautious mouthful. "It tastes all right."

For a while, they ate in silence, the strain between them as suffocating as the oppressive thickness in the air that precedes a thunderstorm.

"Are we going to get more sheep?" Rowena asked finally.

"The Shoshone say it's going to be a harsh winter. Perhaps we should wait until spring, so we don't need to nurse the flock through snowstorms." He looked up at her. "What do you think?"

Her gaze collided with his. His eyes were green, so green. And the scar on his face was so familiar, she could close her eyes and in her mind trace her fingers along the length of it. He hadn't shaved, but from the droplets that glinted in his hair she knew he'd had a wash at the outside well, like he did most nights, to leave the bathing room free for her. She felt her chest tighten.

I've missed you, she wanted to tell him. *I'm sorry I was foolish and stubborn. Will you love me? Will you ever love me?*

She recalled the hand-carved ornamental stones up in the graveyard, a monument of Mr. Reese's devotion to his wife. What did it take to make a man love a woman so? Were some men born with the capacity for such depth of emotion, while others would always lack it? Or could a woman, the right woman, inspire such devotion in any man?

But she held her tongue. Once before, she had spoken of love to a man, and he had trampled all over her feelings. "I think you are right," she said. "It's best to wait until next spring. Do the same as we did this year, get a mix of ewes and lambs, but more of them."

Dale finished his stew and got to his feet. "I'm off to bed. Good night."

And with that, he walked out of the kitchen, not looking back.

No invitation, no plea, no command. No *Will you come and keep the coyote away?* Nothing to ease her back into how things had been between them before she chose to shut herself away from him. The message was clear: *You broke it. You fix it.*

Nerves thrumming, Rowena cleared up in the kitchen and had her evening wash. She went up the stairs into her white-furnished bedroom and changed into her prettiest nightgown, a fine lawn cotton shift, trimmed with lace at the collar and at the end of the sleeves. Cold in her bare feet, she stood in front of the mirror and studied her reflection in the light of a single candle burning in a brass holder.

Coward, she told herself. *If you don't go to him, you're a coward.*

In her mind, she practiced her entrance. *May I get into bed with you? May I join you? Can I come and keep you company?*

She frowned at her image in the mirror. Surely, a wife didn't need permission to join her husband in bed? It was her right by law. A duty, in fact. And she would exercise that right. Fulfill that duty. At once, before she lost her courage.

Dale lay in bed, listening. Would she join him? He heard the creak of a floorboard in the corridor first, before he felt the cool draft as the door flew open, with enough force to slam against the wall. Tense and still, he listened to the sound slowly fade away.

Leaving the lamp burning would have revealed he was waiting for her—waiting and hoping—so he had extinguished the flame, and darkness filled the room. After what felt like an eternity a single point of light appeared through the open doorway. A candle, with a hand cupped around the flame. Then the rest of his wife flounced into sight. With a determined thud of footsteps, she strode over to the bed, so hastily the candle almost fluttered out with every step, despite the protective shield of her hand.

When Rowena reached the bedside, she held up the candle to cast the light over him. "Move over," she said, and to emphasize the command she made a shooing motion with her free hand. "I'm getting into bed with you."

Triumph coursed through Dale, triumph and relief. He scooted backward on the thick feather mattress, to make space beside him. He held up the edge of the bedding. Rowena placed the brass candleholder on the nightstand and bent to blow out the flame.

"No," he told her. "Leave it burning."

She glanced back at him over her shoulder. He could read anticipation and excitement and even a hint of victory in the small smile that hovered around her mouth. She made no reply, merely turned around and slipped silently next to him beneath the covers.

Dale bundled his wife into his arms. The feel of her supple body against his. The faint scent of her soap. The way her hair tickled his skin. The sound of her breathing when she fought a burst of nerves. How could everything about her have become so familiar in the space of a few short months? How could it feel like a piece of him was missing when she was not by his side?

Dale framed his wife's face in his hands and looked

into her eyes. The candle burning behind her left her features in shadow, but he could read her expression anyway. He thought he saw echoes of what he felt, and that gave him the courage to speak.

"I've missed you."

"I've missed you, too."

"Don't ever do that again. If you want to fight, fight. Shout and yell. Slam doors and throw things. But don't ever freeze me out again like that."

He kissed her, a fierce, possessive kiss. His heart was hammering so hard he felt the room might echo with the sound. While he'd been waiting, wrought with uncertainty and doubt, he had thought it would be enough to hold her, to feel her against him, to reassure himself that he had not lost her. But now the need to possess her, to stamp his ownership, burned like a brushfire through him.

Closing one hand over the rounded swell of a breast, Dale rubbed and tugged and caressed, his fingers feeling the supple shape through the fabric of the nightgown. Rowena arched her spine to meet his touch. She made a small sound, a cry of abandon that he captured with another hungry kiss.

Before, she'd welcomed him at night, but now she met his passion with her own. Tongues dueled, teeth clashed. Her hands raked into his hair, holding him in place. Unable to wait, Dale curled his fingers over the lace collar of Rowena's nightgown. He rolled half on top of her, his leg thrown across hers, pinning her down. His arm tensed, ready for one big downward tug that would tear the garment open.

Beneath him, Rowena wriggled. Her hands left his

hair and curled around his wrist, stalling him. "No…"
Her voice was a breathless whisper. "Don't…"

Don't. Dale froze. It felt as if his heart had stopped
beating. As if his blood had stopped moving in his
veins, his lungs had stopped breathing. As if every
clock in the world had stopped. As if the world itself
had ended, with those two small words of rejection.

No. Don't.

He forced himself to meet Rowena's eyes. There was
no fear in them, no recoil or hesitation, only the misty
haze of passion. Her skin was flushed, like velvet in
the soft glow of candlelight. Her hair, rich brown with
coppery glints, fanned over the pillow like a carpet of
autumn leaves. Her lips were parted, glistening from
his kisses. And then that lovely wide mouth that he
could never kiss enough curved into a grin of mischief.

"This is my best nightgown."

The dawning of understanding came in stages, like
a trickle of water falling on a parched land, reviving,
restoring life. All those clocks in the world that had
stopped began ticking again. His lungs filled with air,
his heart resumed beating, his blood flowed through
his veins again.

Somewhere inside him a kernel of humor grew and
grew, until it burst through. With an easy chuckle, Dale
eased the grip of his fingers around the lace collar of the
garment that had slowed him down. And perhaps it had
been a blessing in disguise. Once before, he had taken
his pleasure too fast, too hard, and left his wife to go
to sleep unfulfilled. He would not let it happen again.

As if reading his thoughts, Rowena released her
stranglehold on his wrist and reached up to trace the

scar on his cheek with her fingertips. "There is no need to hurry," she told him softly. "We have all night."

A smile on his face, Dale searched for the tiny pearl buttons at the lace collar of his wife's nightgown and slipped free the first of them. Letting his fingers linger, he stroked the soft skin on Rowena's neck, felt the rapid beat of her pulse in the hollow between her collarbones.

There was no need to hurry. They had all night.

And he intended to make every minute count.

Chapter Thirteen

Rowena put away the milk and the meat before she opened the envelope that Faraday's ranch hand had delivered with the twice-weekly supplies. Inside the envelope she found a scribbled note and a stiff vellum card with a printed invitation.

She had to read the text twice before the message sank in.

"Dale! Dale!" Flapping the invitation in one hand, she hurried outside, round the back to where the foal and the mare grazed in a small corral. Mr. Spencer's Indian trackers had already hunted down the mountain lion, but they preferred to keep the foal close by, just in case.

"Dale, you won't believe this!" Panting, she came to a stop.

Dale was bent over, cleaning the mare's hooves. He merely grunted in reply. Too impatient to wait for him to finish the chore, Rowena blurted out her news. "Faraday has sent us an invitation to a ball in Cheyenne. A fund-raiser for the statehood campaign. His eldest son's employer, Insurance Company of North America, is sponsoring the event. Faraday can't go, but he has asked if we would like to use the tickets."

The worn flannel shirt stretched across Dale's shoulders as he bent to set the hoof of the mare back against the ground. He straightened, pushed back his hat and wiped his forehead with his sleeve. "A ball? In Cheyenne?"

"Yes." She frowned at him. "Why would he invite us? Could it be a trap?"

Dale shook his head. "No. In truth, I've been expecting some kind of a friendly overture. Faraday knows I've been talking to Spencer. He doesn't want to be left at a disadvantage. Offering the tickets to us will cost him nothing, and I very much doubt he could afford to go himself, with the train fare and the overnight stay."

"Could we…could we go?"

"It's a long way."

Her mouth opened and closed. She wanted to go, so badly she ached with it. But she couldn't bear the prospect of asking for something and having her request turned down again. "My lovely evening gowns… I never get a chance to wear them…"

"You'd travel all the way to Cheyenne just to wear a pretty gown?"

"And to sightsee. When we came through last time, I was too nervous to pay attention to my surroundings. And we had no money."

Dale's mouth tipped into a crooked smile. "Wedding night nerves. I remember."

She lifted her chin, amusement and a touch of smug pride in her expression. "From what I recall, I managed quite well, thank you very much."

With a few lazy steps, Dale closed the distance between them. He wound his finger into a strand of hair escaped from her upsweep and tugged at it, drawing her toward him. "We could have a second honeymoon. See if we can improve."

She could smell the horse and hay on him, could feel the heat of his body. Her heart was beating very fast. He was making her forget why she had sought him out, but the mental image of them gliding together across a dance floor reminded her, and she could not hold back the words. "Can we go? Please?"

"Yes, if it matters so much to you. I have business to take care of in Cheyenne anyway."

"Thank you." Bouncing up on tiptoe, Rowena wrapped her arms around his neck and gave him a big, smacking kiss on the mouth.

Dale chuckled and disentangled himself. "I'm sweaty and dirty. Save it for tonight."

With a smile and a wave, Rowena left him to his tasks and hurried back inside. There'd be music, an orchestra. At school, she had learned to play the piano. She had shown great aptitude, but the lack of an instrument at Twin Springs deprived her of the opportunity to enjoy the skill.

Upstairs, she riffled through the dresses she had unpacked from her trunks. Her jewelry had been safe, too, in a leather case beneath the clothing. Once again, she fought a burst of curiosity over the big inlaid chest that Reese had left behind, with his late wife's belongings. Like those other times, she conquered the urge to peek inside.

Crossing the room to the dressing table with a mirror, Rowena draped her mother's gold-and-sapphire necklace against her throat. With a touch of sadness, she inspected the single matching earring. Too grand for everyday wear, her mother had worn the earrings anyway, and when she'd been killed by the Shoshone one of them had gone missing. Either it had got lost in the sand by the river, or it now hung from the earlobe of an Indian brave. With a sigh, Rowena put the earring away. Lost is lost. Dead is dead. Time to forgive and forget.

The splendor of it! Rowena kept turning her head, taking in the crowded ballroom. Electric lights hummed in the ceiling. Electric lights, in a private residence!

"Don't gawk," Dale whispered into her ear.

"How could I not?" she whispered back.

They'd arrived in the afternoon, and she had enjoyed the comforts of their room at High Meadows while Dale went out to take care of errands. Tomorrow, she would make the most of the opportunity to look around Cheyenne, the city the newspapers called the Paris of the West, a fashionable playground for the rich.

"There's Major Parks," Dale said. "I had a message at the Western Union office that he wants to see me. Do you mind if I go over and find out what he wants?"

"Not at all," she replied with a quick smile. "I'll be happy gawking."

Dale walked away. She followed him with her eyes. Lean, with wide shoulders and narrow hips, he carried his clothes well. He must be one of the handsomest men in the room, she thought with pride, even though he wore an ordinary suit in black broadcloth, instead of a fancy evening suit or a military uniform, like some of the other men.

With a flare of uncertainty, Rowena cast a critical eye over the ladies gossiping in groups. The artificial light gave a sickly pallor to those with a very pale complexion, and brightly colored dresses looked too dazzling. The slight tan that marked her as a farm wife might be flattering, after all, and her gown—silver satin trimmed with midnight blue—had been a good choice. Fortunately, the fashions had changed little since she had acquired her Boston gowns, although the bustles gathered at the back of a dress had grown bigger.

With a sigh, Rowena relaxed. She'd hold her own. Once Dale returned to her side, they would seek out a representative of the Insurance Company of North America, thank him for the chance to attend. Right now, the orchestra on the balcony was playing Mozart, but later there would be dancing. She could already imagine herself gliding around the ballroom in Dale's arms.

A group of young men talking too loudly jostled around the punch bowl, blocking access to everyone else. Rowena craned her neck for a better look. If there was going to be an altercation of some sort, she was curious to witness it.

Her eyes fell on a head of golden hair, on a patrician profile. It felt as if her heart had stopped beating. *It can't be...surely it can't be.* But it could. And it was. She must have made a sound, for people turned to look at her. And then Freddy turned, too, and their eyes met.

He had changed in the three years since they'd parted. His features had grown puffy, and there was a new slackness to the line of his jaw, but he still presented a picture of masculine elegance. At first, Rowena could read joy in his expression. In the next instant, the pleasure of recognition vanished and an ugly sneer took its pace. He put down his drink, said something to his companions and forged a path toward her through the crowd.

The distance between them allowed Rowena a moment to steel herself against the reunion before they stood face-to-face. Freddy came to a halt before her, swaying on his feet in a manner that revealed he had already consumed too much punch.

"Rowena, what are you doing here?"

No courtesy of a greeting. Only the discourtesy of using her given name. If overheard by others, the familiarity might be enough to tarnish her reputation.

Before she could gather her wits and find a way to defuse the situation, Freddy went on, "Of course, you live in Wyoming. How could I forget?" His brows lifted in disdain. "Tell me, how is the cattle business? The huge herds roaming on your father's endless land?"

"My father is dead. And I am married now. It's Mrs. Hunter to you."

"You are married?" For an instant, the world-weary mask on Freddy's face slipped to reveal some inner pain. Then he rocked back on his feet and smirked at her. "So, you finally found some man who wanted those miserable acres of yours enough to marry you. Or did you lie to him, like you lied to me?"

"I never lied to you."

"You didn't?" His face puckered in an exaggerated frown of concentration. "What was it you said? Oh, yes." His voice rose in a shrill imitation of a female. "*'I spent hours trying to count the cows but there were so many I never managed it.'* And what else? Oh, yes. *'We rode to the boundary of the ranch and it felt like traveling to the end of the earth.'*" He shook his head, an angry gesture that conveyed a bitter accusation. "No, you never lied to me."

"I was talking about my childhood, describing the ranch through the eyes of a child."

"Tell me." Freddy's demeanor gained a trace of cruelty. "How did your husband react when he saw the ranch?" Not allowing her a chance to reply, her former fiancé took a step back and swept a bold, sleazy look up and down her body. "Or did you use your feminine charms to make sure he married you before he had a chance to discover the truth? In that case, you did a better job of locking him in than you did on me."

Shame burned on Rowena's cheeks. He was making her sound like a slut, a whore. She wanted to say something to contradict him. To make sure all those people overhearing the conversation would understand he was talking out of spite, his remarks unjustified.

But there *was* a grain of truth to it. She had wanted to consummate the marriage with Dale before he set eyes on Twin Springs. She couldn't sweep Freddy's comments aside as lies, but neither could she pick his words apart to point out the untruths, for a lady could not talk about such intimate details, at least not in public.

Tears pricked behind her eyelids, tears of shame and humiliation and disappointment. She had looked forward to the trip, to the ball, to a festive night, and it had all turned to poison. Clenching her beaded reticule in her hands, she gathered the shreds of her pride.

"It has been a pleasure to see you again, Freddy. Give my best to your family."

She turned and fled. Unable to see ahead, she crashed into something solid and unyielding. Strong hands curled around her upper arms and halted her progress. She looked up and saw Dale looking down at her, concern in his eyes.

Dale, oh, Dale, she wanted to cry. *Take me away from here.*

"Is that belligerent young pup your former fiancé?" The sharpness of Dale's tone told Rowena he knew something was wrong, but she had no means of figuring out how much of the conversation he might have overheard.

"Can we leave?" she pleaded. "Now, at once?"

Dale shook his head. "No. By the look of it, you have some unfinished business, and I didn't marry a coward." He spun her around by the shoulders and nudged her into motion, sending her right back toward Freddy, who was now surrounded by his friends, the way an executioner might be surrounded by a jeering crowd.

She could not speak. Her knees threatened to buckle beneath her. Maybe she could close her eyes and pretend to succumb to a swoon. Hiding behind such subterfuge was a lady's privilege, after all.

"Well, *cherie*, aren't you going to introduce me to your friend?"

She heard Dale's calm, steady voice beside her. Unlike at school, when she'd felt an outsider among the wealthy girls, she was not alone. Rowena drew a shaky breath and steadied her voice. "Dale, I would like to introduce you to Frederick Livingston, an old friend from my school days in Boston. Freddy, this is Dale Hunter, my husband."

Dale gave a tiny bow, in the style of a Southern gentleman. "Pleased to make your acquaintance, Livingston."

"Hunter." Freddy's nod was haughty, superior.

"What a stroke of luck," Dale went on. "I've just received a gift from my mother to my bride. We didn't have any of Rowena's friends at our wedding, so it seems fitting to have one of them to witness the occasion." He reached inside his jacket, pulled out a small velvet box and clipped it open. "Your engagement ring, *cherie*. Sorry for the delay in getting it sent out. Major Parks delivered it in person."

Fascinated, Rowena peeked into the box. The biggest diamond she had ever seen nestled against the black velvet, sparkling under the steady glow of the electric lights.

"That's a fancy piece of glass," Freddy said, but his voice lacked its former belligerence.

Dale's eyes narrowed. "It's a diamond, as flawless as my wife's beauty. I guess with all your family heirlooms sold off years ago and replaced with paste, you lack the ability to tell the difference."

Freddy was spluttering now, going purple in the face, but Rowena paid him no attention. Dale's words about the Countess of Clairmont and her grisly end sent a shiver of apprehension through her. She stole a glance at her husband. "Did she...? Did she...?"

Dale gave her a reassuring shake of his head. "Did the countess go to the guillotine wearing the ring? No, she did not. She hid all her jewels in the garden of the family chateau long before. Her young nephew, my great-great-grandfather, a boy at the time, kept his head—both literally and figuratively—and recovered the jewels later."

Dale took out the ring and slipped the empty box into his pocket. "Well, give me your hand, *cherie*. This is meant to go on your finger, to mark that you belong to me."

The room had hushed to silence now, with everyone listening, only the music playing softly in the background. Spellbound, Rowena held out her left hand.

Dale eased the ring over her third finger, next to her plain wedding band. "See?" he said softly. "It's a perfect fit. Like the slipper for Cinderella."

But Freddy was not quite done yet. He burst into a crude gust of laughter. "You think of yourself as Prince Charming, Hunter? Whatever gave you the idea?" He drew a line along his cheek, marking the position of Dale's scar. "More like the beauty and the beast."

Dale pretended to give the question careful consideration. "Do I think of myself as Prince Charming? No, not at all. It must be my mother who thinks I'm a prince among men. But then, every mother likes to believe the best of their son. I'm sure yours does, too, as misguided as she may be."

When Freddy struggled for a reply, Dale made an airy gesture with his hand. "You might have heard of my mother, Madeline Hunter? Hunter Ironworks? Hunter Steel? Hunter Locomotives? Mother likes to think she is notorious, the way she took over the running of the companies after Father died. A woman holding her own in a man's world."

"Your mother is Madeline Hunter?"

"Yes. Unless I was a changeling."

"But why did you…" Freddy's brow pleated in confusion. "Why did you marry a woman lacking in wealth or connections? You could have had anyone."

Dale replied with a bright smile. "Precisely. And I chose this one." He leaned forward and lowered his voice, as if speaking in confidence, but Rowena knew that every word would carry around the ballroom. "See, Livingston, some men are too cowardly to defy domineering parents, and some men have to marry to fill the empty family coffers. I was lucky enough to be free to follow my own wishes."

Someone on the organizing committee of the ball must have alerted the orchestra to the fracas, for the mellow notes of the Mozart violin concerto came to an abrupt end. After a couple of discordant notes, the first bars of a waltz flowed over the crowd.

Dale put his hand out. "Will you dance with me, *cherie*?"

Rowena slipped her hand into his. As they whirled around the vast expanse of the parquet floor that had quickly filled with couples, she blinked away the mist of tears. "Why was he so vile? Why does he hate me so?"

"He doesn't hate you. I think he may have been in love with you, but he was too cowardly to defy his family. It is himself he hates, his own weakness that caused him to give you up against his will, but it is easier to take it out on you."

"Can we leave?" The weight of curious stares made her body feel stiff and clumsy. She hated scenes, hated the hushed whispers she knew were about her. Despite Dale's gallant intervention, she couldn't help feeling that the evening had been ruined.

Dale tightened his arm around her and spun her in a tight turn. "No," he told her. "We must stay. If we go home, it will leave him free to spread his lies and innuendo. Don't let him win. The way to beat him is to stay and let him see what he lost when he let you go."

Dale danced with his wife, but at the same time he kept an eye on that belligerent young pup, Livingston. The scalawag was talking to his friends, gesticulating, glancing over to the dance floor with an increasing air of glee. From the crafty look on Livingston's face, Dale guessed the young man must have stumbled upon another way to renew his attack.

And Dale could guess what that line of attack might be. He should have kept his mouth shut. Or at least he should have kept his mother's name out of it, should never have mentioned the family business. But he had seen the hurt on Rowena's face, and he had used every means at his disposal to protect her, even at the risk of giving away a connection to his past.

For nearly an hour, they were left in peace, while Livingston sought extra courage from the punch bowl. When the orchestra took a break and the dancing couples ceased their spinning, the young man ambled over. He shook his head and spoke with a feigned look of concern.

"I don't know how you can sleep at night, Rowena."

Don't fall for it, Dale pleaded in his mind.

But of course she did. Too well brought up to ignore a comment addressed to her, Rowena replied, "What do you mean?"

Livingston was shaking his head. "I mean, don't you lie awake at night, fearing that a knife will slice into your belly?"

"I…" Rowena hesitated, stole a glance at Dale. He could see confusion in her eyes, confusion and fear, and the dawning of understanding. When she spoke, her voice was small and tight, betraying her doubts. "I don't know what you are talking about, Freddy."

Livingston gloated in triumph. "That you are sleeping beside a murderer, of course. Dale Hunter killed three men in cold blood. Shot two of them—in the back, I wager—and gutted the third one like a fish.

He avoided the hangman's noose by going into hiding. Spent ten years on the outlaw trail, robbing stagecoaches and banks."

Dale could feel Rowena stiffen by his side. She wasn't turning to look at him, at least not yet. *Don't ask me if it is true*, Dale prayed. *Not here. Not now.*

And his prayers were answered. Rowena lifted her chin in a haughty gesture. An utter calm seemed to have settled over her, but Dale knew it was all those etiquette lessons taking over. Barricading her mind against the information, against the need to separate the truth from the lies, Rowena was merely seeking a way out without allowing the scandal to escalate.

"I very much doubt my husband is guilty of such atrocities. He was employed as a federal marshal, after all. Any violence must have been committed in the line of duty, to protect women and children and make this country safe."

Livingston's coarse laughter rippled around the room. "You fool. He was an outlaw until a few years ago, when his mother got him a pardon. They say Madeline Hunter used her connections in Washington." A sly grin spread on Livingston's face. He leaned closer to Rowena and lowered his voice. "But we all know about a woman's connections, don't we?"

Dale took a step forward. "Livingston, I'm warning you. Rein in your tongue."

Ignoring him, Livingston straightened, swaying on his feet, and shouted at the top of his voice, "Flat on her back, she must have been when she used her influence to buy her son's freedom. Flat on her back, like a two-bit whore."

Dale let his arm swing and relished the impact as

his fist crashed into Livingston's jaw. The young man toppled backward. People had already scurried out of the way, and Livingston landed on the polished parquet floor without careening into anyone else.

When Livingston lay in a sprawl, Dale bent over him and grabbed him by the front of his fancy evening coat. "Not a single word more, Livingston, unless you want to wake up one night and feel the blade of my knife carving out *your* entrails."

Livingston paled. Dale flung him back down to the floorboards, straightened and turned toward Rowena. She was standing very still, like a statue. Her face was totally without expression. Only her eyes seemed alive, and they were flickering over him—his chest, his belly, his legs. Every part of his body where scars—now hidden from sight by the pristine white shirt and the black broadcloth suit—bore evidence of his violent past.

"Rowena…we need to talk."

She nodded, too distressed to speak. The fingers of her right hand were toying with the rings on her wedding finger, nervously twisting the gold bands around, as if already preparing to remove them. Dale felt the tension drain out of him, giving way to a sense of defeat. He'd always known that nothing could be settled in his marriage until he had told Rowena the truth about his past.

But although down on the floor, Livingston had not given up the fight.

"See that?" the young man yelled. "Hunter assaulted me, in front of witnesses. Someone fetch the sheriff." He wiped the back of his hand across his mouth, studied the streak of blood. When he looked up at Dale, his features distorted with hatred, but then a cunning smirk lit up his face. "That's right. Fetch the sheriff! Maybe there never really was a pardon at all. Maybe there's still a warrant out on him."

From the corner of his eye, Dale could see Major Parks set into motion and clear a path through the crowd. Managing to catch the older man's attention, Dale shook his head. Major Parks frowned in protest but he halted his advance. If, as Dale suspected, there was something between his mother and the major—who had been involved in his pardon, even if merely in a limited capacity—anything the major did now to help would only provide another ingredient to the already thick brew of scandal.

"You were right," Dale said to Rowena. "We should have left."

He ushered her out of the ballroom. People parted to make way, staring at them in curious silence. Outside, darkness had fallen, but the electric lights in front of the mansion created an island of daylight.

"We'll go to the station," Dale said. "There's a night train back to Rawlins."

"But our things…they are at the hotel."

He took the first step of telling her the truth. "My certificate of pardon is at Twin Springs. I want to go home, before anyone gets the bright idea to throw me in jail."

Chapter Fourteen

While they rolled across the flat prairie, the night painting the train windows black, Dale told Rowena about his past. In a deadpan voice, all his emotions locked away, he described every single act of violence, every breach of the law.

He told her about Laurel, how he had tracked down the men responsible.

The sergeant was already dead, sparing Dale from deciding if the small spark of compassion the man had shown toward Laurel was deserving of mercy. The next two, he had dispatched with a bullet. Each time it had been a fair fight, with the other man drawing first. But he had drawn faster and aimed better. The final man, Krieger, had thrown away his pistol and pulled out a blade. Dale had followed suit, and the victory had almost cost him his life, leaving his chest and abdomen webbed with scars.

He told Rowena how a warrant for murder had forced him into hiding. In the outlaw camp, he'd acted as a quartermaster, hauling in supplies. He had never robbed a stagecoach or a train. Until the final year, when all but one of his associates had been killed and he had become a member of the Red Bluff Gang. It was breaking away from those violent men that had left him wounded, for the coyote to finish, and had ultimately earned him his pardon.

Throughout it all, Rowena made no comment, asked no questions. She merely listened, occasionally nodding. Her face, normally so expressive, had turned into a pale mask. Only her eyes, wide and fearful, betrayed her anguish.

When Dale finished talking, he felt mentally drained. He needed space around himself. Space for the nightmares he already felt stalking at the gates of his mind. If he failed to stay awake, it would feel as if he had tumbled into hell. He didn't want Rowena to see it. Didn't want her to be drawn into that aura of violence.

He got to his feet. His limbs weighed like lead. His scars ached, as if reliving the memories had torn them open again. "I'll find another compartment. It's already past midnight but you might be able to get a couple of hours of sleep. I'll come back and wake you up in good time before we get to Rawlins."

Call after me, he thought as he pushed open the door into the corridor. *Tell me not to go.*

But although he could feel her eyes following him, Rowena made no sound.

When they got off the train in Rawlins, storm clouds covered the sky, blotting out the faint dawn light. Rowena waited at the railroad station while Dale went to the livery stable to fetch their horse and wagon.

Her mind rattled as empty as a pauper's cauldron. Every time she tried to organize her thoughts, they slipped away from her, like a flock of birds scattering. She was a coward, but she already knew that. In the past, she'd run away. Now she was shutting her mind, as if she could escape from her own reactions, her own thoughts. Wasn't that what she had once told Dale—that she was running away from herself?

He helped her up to the wagon, this man who was her husband but also a stranger. The wind was gathering force now, howling across the prairie. Even if she had wanted to talk, conversation would have been impossible. After a mile, the skies opened. Her skirts blew and flared around her, the silver satin gown, piped with midnight blue, now ruined. The rain lashed at them, soaking them in seconds. The wind tore off her bonnet and made her evening wrap flap around like a washwoman's cloth, the wet fabric slapping at her body.

Dale halted the wagon, searched out a tarpaulin and wrapped them both into it. She huddled against him beneath the cloth as he drove the wagon through the storm. She could feel his warmth, the strength in him as he controlled the horse frightened by the lightning and the thunderclaps, but it no longer gave her the sense of safety she had felt when she curled up against him in bed at night.

The rain, the wind, the thoughts she refused to face, they all sapped her strength. By the time they stopped for the night, Rowena could barely stay awake. Side by side, they settled down on the wagon bed, sheltering beneath the canvas, together but alone.

When they got to Twin Springs, Dale stacked the huge fireplace in the parlor with logs and got the flames roaring. "I'll heat water and bring out the bathtub. You can have your wash by the fire."

He returned outside to take care of Samson, then came back and filled the tub for her. Rowena huddled in a chair by the fireside, the soaked gown clinging to her skin, clouds of steam rising from the fabric where the skirt hung too close to the flames.

Dale put out his hand. "Let's get you out of those wet clothes."

She shrank back from him. "No!"

His arm fell. In his eyes she could see anguish. A small crack appeared in the armor she'd built around her emotions. "You should have told me…"

"I know. But I wanted a chance for things to be perfect between us. Not just one night, but forever."

"It felt like a betrayal…to find out, in front of all those people…with Freddy gloating…with everyone staring."

"I'm sorry I didn't tell you before. But now you know everything."

Her anger stirred. "You say I know everything, but how can I be sure? You had a whole hidden life, a hidden past. I thought you had been wounded in the line of duty, but it was a lie. I thought you were a lawman, but you were an outlaw. Is there more? Are there women you've left behind, children I don't know about?"

"No one but you. Ever."

Unable to accept the reassurance in his words, Rowena curled up in her seat. It felt as if she had been broken into pieces inside.

Dale crouched to add more wood to the fire. He spoke quietly, the hiss of sparks and the howl of the wind outside almost drowning out his words. "I can't change my past, Rowena. It will always be there. You know what kind of man I've been, but I hope that in the past three months I've shown you what kind of a man I am now."

He got up and faced her, arms hanging down his sides, a vulnerable pose, as if he expected to receive a blow. "After I took the meat to the Indian reservation, you put up a wall between us. I won't go through that again. Not for a month, not for a week, not for a single day. Either you accept me as I am, or we go our separate ways." He stepped closer to her, leaned down and slipped his fingers beneath her chin, making her look up at him. "I'm going to have a wash in the bathing room, and then I'm going upstairs. Either you'll sleep in my bed tonight or I'll ride out in the morning."

Dale lay awake, listening. A lamp burned on the nightstand, casting a soft glow over the room. Outside, the storm raged. Fierce gusts of wind slammed into the building, making him imagine the creak of footsteps even when there had been none.

Instead of an ultimatum, he should have given her time. Let her get used to the idea of his past. But even as he racked his brain for how to take back the words without sacrificing his pride, he knew it to be futile. He had meant what he said. He couldn't go through it again, that cool rejection that made him feel as if he had lost everything once again.

What was that?

Braced up on his elbows, Dale listened. Surely, those had been footsteps? But then the soft pattering sound ceased. For what felt like an eternity he stared at the door to the corridor, not breathing, not moving. Even his heart seemed to have ceased beating.

Then the door inched open. One bare foot peeked into view, followed by the flowing hem of a nightgown.

She should be wearing socks, Dale thought. *Her feet will get cold.*

Rowena halted by the entrance and pushed the door closed behind her. She was carrying a candle, and in the flickering light of the flame Dale could see her face. She looked beautiful and brave and gentle and dignified. During those lonely years in the outlaw camp he'd dreamed of a woman, and she was the fulfillment of all those dreams. Whatever happened between them now, there could never be anyone else.

A sudden flare of the draft extinguished Rowena's candle, and Dale could no longer see her features, could no longer see the play of expressions that so easily gave her emotions away. But the way Rowena stood still by the doorway suggested that she wanted to make a declaration of some sort. Never in his life had Dale understood that words could wound a man, cut him down as effectively as a bullet or a blade.

"I once asked you what you thought of Twin Springs. You never replied."

His brows drew together. He tried to remember such a question, tried to remember the circumstances, so he could give the right answer, but his memory failed him. "It's a good, solid house. The land might not be the best, but it is well suited for sheep."

"You married me for the ranch. Are you satisfied with your bargain?"

"I'd be satisfied with my bargain even if you come without a single acre of land."

Dale thought he heard a gasp of surprise, but it might have been the storm outside. Again, he strained his eyes to see Rowena's face. The glow of the lamp was too faint to reach that far and he couldn't make out anything but the pale outline of her features as she went on talking.

"You grew up with wealth and glamour. You have money that is yours for the taking. I heard you say it. Hunter Ironworks. Hunter Steel. Hunter Locomotives. One day you might wish to return to that life. I don't want to be part of a family that rejects me, or live in a world where I will always be an outsider."

He wanted to tell her that his mother would welcome her. That he would never take her anywhere she didn't want to go. That he would never allow anyone to treat her like an outsider. But it would be impossible for him to give such guarantees. Instead, Dale was forced to search his own mind, formulate ideas he had never cared to analyze before.

"My father freed the slaves long before I was born. Although I lived on a plantation, I never felt the loss of a lifestyle. Only the loss of a home. And a home is people as much as it is a place." He paused. "In my travels as a lawman I've stayed on many small ranches, run by a husband and wife. It's a good life. Perhaps the best life I have seen. This is the life I want. A life with you."

The white nightgown fluttered as Rowena took a step toward him and spoke quietly. "When I first saw you, I knew you were the kind of man who could help me take back Twin Springs. A fighting man." She took another step forward. "I married you because you were tough and strong and capable of defeating your enemies. How could I now condemn you because you possess those very qualities, the qualities I needed you to have?"

She'd been holding the extinguished candle in her hand, and now it clattered to the floor. She ran toward him, and Dale opened his arms. Instead of getting in with him beneath the covers, Rowena sank to her knees by the bedside. She lifted one hand, traced the web of scars on his chest, her gentle touch gliding over his skin. Bending her head, she brushed soft kisses where the puckered white lines cut across his heart.

"I'm sorry," she said between kisses. "I'm sorry for everything you have lost...your home...your family... your childhood...years of your life..."

When she raised her head and looked at him, Dale could see the sheen of tears in her eyes. In that moment, it hit him, a swell of emotion so powerful it felt as if he might not be able to contain it but his very heart would burst wide-open.

He loved her. He loved her. Perhaps he had loved her from the first moment he set eyes on her at the jail in Pinares. He reached out to pull Rowena up beside him, but she leaned away from him and shook her head. "Lie back," she told him. "Let me."

Dale obeyed. As the storm raged outside, Rowena traced his scars with her fingertips. Leaning over him, she kissed each one of the flaws and imperfections that mapped out his violent past, as if to tell him they didn't matter, that she accepted him as he was, for what he was, for what he had been.

While he had lain alone in bed, waiting, terrified that she might not come to him, Dale had ached to hold her, feel the closeness between them, the closeness he feared he might have lost forever. Now he needed more. He wanted to feel her passion, feel that ultimate joining that proved she belonged to him and no one else. He curled his hands around her waist, lifted her up to straddle him. "You do it. You dictate the pace."

At first, Rowena stared at him, wide-eyed. But she did not protest. With an awkward, hesitant motion, she sank over him and paused there, uncertain how to continue. Dale could feel her close around him. He wanted more. More and more and more.

"Do it," he said. "Love me."

Rowena rose above him, sank down again. As she found a rhythm, her body took over. She closed her eyes, tipped her head back and began to move with abandon. On her face, Dale could see the strain of tension as she sought that elusive completion.

He waited, tried to make it last. Just when he thought he could hold back no more, Rowena bowed over him and cried out, eyes closed, mouth open, her head tipped back. He could feel the tremors that rocked her and gave in to his own release.

"Look at me, Rowena. Open your eyes."

Her lashes lifted. Their eyes met and held. And then, at that magical moment when shared pleasure ought to have sealed their togetherness, her gaze veered away. Even as Dale shuddered in the throes of completion, he could feel the distance, the mental separation between them. And he understood that although Rowena had chosen to accept him as her husband and wanted him to stay, when she looked at him she saw a killer, a man to fear.

Life settled into a pattern. They both behaved as if nothing had altered between them, but Dale couldn't ignore the shadow of anxiety he could see in Rowena's eyes whenever she looked at him. More and more often, she made some excuse to remain in the house when he rode out to inspect the sheep. It seemed to Dale as if his wife's previously robust health had suddenly given way to a range of minor ailments. Today, it had been a bout of nausea.

And perhaps it was for the best that she had chosen to stay at home this morning, Dale thought when he caught sight of Faraday cantering toward him. The pair of dogs raced behind his big sorrel horse. When Dale pulled his dun gelding to a halt, Faraday almost crashed into him. Mud flew up beneath the sorrel's hooves as the horse came to a sudden stop. The dogs yapped and growled.

Frowning, Dale studied his neighbor. Dressed in a fraying shirt and dirt-crusted trousers, unshaven, with straggly hair poking out from beneath his battered hat, Faraday had the look of a vagrant.

"When will you sign the lease?"

"I've told you. I'm not extending."

"You've got to. Man, you've got to."

A flicker of pity made Dale soften his reply. "I'm sorry, Faraday. There is nothing you can do to change my mind."

"Nothing?" Faraday's voice rose. "You said it is your wife's land. *She* can change your mind. I'll *make* her change your mind."

Every trace of pity vanished. "You leave my wife out of it, Faraday."

The older man's expression grew crafty. "She'll listen to me."

Dale felt a surge of icy fury, the kind that had sustained him through the years when he'd given up the last of his childhood and all his youth to avenge Laurel's death. "I'm warning you, Faraday. You go anywhere near my wife and I'll kill you, as surely as night follows day."

"You can't stop me. You can't stop me from taking what I want." Faraday's eyes bulged in his head, making him look like a madman. Spittle gathered at the corners of his mouth. He muttered to himself, oblivious to his surroundings. "Tried to stop me…didn't mean to…"

Dale fought the grip of fear. Faraday had ridden in from the west, but he could have made a detour, could have already been to Twin Springs. "You didn't mean to do what, Faraday?" Dale nudged his horse closer, every nerve taut. "What have you done?"

For a moment longer, Faraday continued his incoherent mutter. Then he gave a muffled cry. A shiver rippled over him, as if he'd woken up from a nightmare. Appearing to pull himself together, he straightened in the saddle and controlled the horse spooked by his nervous ramblings. When he spoke again, his voice had returned to normal. "I need that lease, Hunter. I must have it, or I'll be ruined."

After Faraday had wheeled his big sorrel around and ridden off, Dale put his heels to the flanks of his gelding and set off for home. The horse's muscles flexed and strained beneath him, the wind whipped into his face, the landscape flew by. Every second that went past his fear escalated until nothing mattered except getting to Rowena.

At Twin Springs, he vaulted from the saddle and stormed to the front door.

"Rowena! Where are you? Are you all right?"

His wife came in from the parlor, a threaded needle in one hand and some flimsy garment in the other. "Why are you yelling like that?" she complained. "Good heavens, it was only an upset stomach. Must be because I've been doing the cooking recently."

"Faraday wasn't here?"

"No." Her reply was calm, but the way she gripped her mending betrayed her unease. Dale wanted to bundle her into his arms and tell her that he'd never let anyone harm her. But to keep his wife safe, he might be forced to kill Faraday. The man's mental balance already teetered on edge. One day soon, it would give way, and Dale would be left with no choice. He'd have to let out that ruthless killer inside him, let Rowena witness what he had once been. And that might cause the anxiety in her eyes to turn into horror.

For two days, Dale wrestled with the dilemma. How to keep Rowena safe without having to kill Faraday? He could only think of one way. And that meant taking the final step of making peace with his past.

Unwilling to leave his wife alone, he escorted her to attend the ladies' sewing circle in Clayton. While Rowena spent the afternoon gossiping, with the pretext of making a wedding quilt for the barber's eldest daughter, Dale took the opportunity to send another telegram to his mother.

Need help. Must buy out difficult neighbor. Send unlimited funds.

He waited for a week, to allow enough time for an express message to deliver a gold shipment to the bank in Rawlins. He used the delay to move the ram out with the ewes and lambs, and to fence in another paddock by the creek where the horses could look after themselves for a few days.

Then he told Rowena that he needed to make a trip

to consult other sheep farmers. The lie grated in his gut,
but if he revealed he was going to Rawlins, she might
ask to come along. It was safer for her to stay behind,
and further, he did not wish to reveal his plans, in case
his mother refused to provide the funds. During his absence, Rowena should take the opportunity to visit her
friends in Clayton. Dale left her with Sharon Madigan
and her husband, with orders that she must remain there
until he returned.

"Nothing? Nothing for Dale Hunter? Nothing at all?"
Dale stared at the young man through the glass parti-
tion of the teller's cage at the bank in Rawlins. "Are
you sure?"

"I'm absolutely certain, sir." Slight with fuzzy blond
hair covering his chin, the teller was little more than a
boy. Probably the banker's son.

"Can I talk to someone in charge?" Dale asked.

"Certainly, sir." A surly note entered the young man's
tone. "But it won't change anything." He vanished into
the back. A moment later, a fair-haired man in his fifties walked out of the office and settled into the wooden
chair behind the counter.

"We've had no wire transfers in your name, Mr.
Hunter. In fact, we've had no substantial deposits of
any sort." The man cleared his throat, leaned closer and
lowered his voice. "There is a gold shipment expected
this morning, but it will be accompanied by the owner.
An important businessman from the East."

"I see."

Dale left the bank. His steps were weary, his mood
grim. Had his mother finally given up on him? Served
him right. Madeline Hunter had cashed in every favor,

used every connection to get him a pardon, the chance of a new life, and what had he given her in return? Three years of absence. Three years of silence.

His steps took him to the railroad station. At the platform, people were craning their necks, staring along the eastbound tracks. Dale joined them. The morning sun was still low, and he adjusted the brim of his hat as he strained his eyes into the distance. Like the rest of the crowd, he could feel the slight vibration in the ground, could see a wisp of steam floating into the bright blue sky. He listened to the snippets of conversation around him.

"Half an hour ahead of schedule."

"Impossible. Trains are usually late."

"They never come early."

The plume of steam thickened, the vibration of the rails grew stronger. A dark dot formed on the horizon. The voices around him grew in excitement.

"It's not a train! It's just the engine!"

"A robbery!"

"The cars must have been uncoupled, left stranded."

"Get the sheriff! Get the doctor!"

"Form a search party."

"Bring water and blankets and clean dressings."

"Get ready to ride."

As the crowd stirred and shifted, preparing for action, a shiny new steam locomotive chugged in along the rails, slowed its pace and pulled to an orderly halt next to the platform.

A door opened, and a small woman clad in a dark blue silk gown, now streaked with soot, hopped down. Behind her, two of the biggest men Dale had ever laid eyes on unloaded a huge steel chest. Two more men followed, each carrying a revolving shotgun, in addition to a double rig of pistols on a gun belt and a rifle slung over their shoulders.

Madeline Hunter came to a halt and swept a look over the platform. When she spotted Dale, her expression grew tender. She gathered her skirts and hurried toward him.

Dale felt as if he'd been spun back through time, to those carefree days when he was a child. She had cured his hurts, shared his secrets, loved him without question. But with every step she took toward him, years seemed to flash by, with blame and guilt pushing them apart. Had it really been that long? She looked so small, so vulnerable. He had forgotten about time taking its toll. By the time Madeline Hunter came to a stop in front of Dale, he had conquered the initial shock of seeing her for the first time after she had visited him in hospital, when he had been so close to death he could barely remember the occasion.

"Mother," he blurted out. "What are you doing here?"

"You said you needed me." She reached up and laid a hand against his cheek, her reserved nature and lady-like manner preventing more exuberant public shows of affection. "For fourteen years, I have been waiting to hear those words. How could I not come?"

Dale curled his fingers around his mother's wrist. Her bones felt fragile. He studied her face. She was still beautiful, but he could see lines around her eyes and strands of gray in the jet-black hair they had in common. A million words churned inside his head, a million explanations and apologies. He only managed a grunt, his throat tight with emotion.

His mother blinked away tears. Appearing to understand that he needed time, she turned to the men in charge of the steel chest. "Let's get this to the bank."

"How much did you bring?" Dale asked.

"A quarter of a million." She glanced at him. "You said unlimited funds."

"I need to buy a ranch. Not half of Wyoming."

She laughed. There was lightness in the sound, a ring of true happiness. The pressure of guilt and doubt inside Dale eased. "How did you get here so fast?"

"There are benefits in owning a company that manufactures locomotives. The hardest part was finding towns with a spur rail, so we could overtake trains." She took his elbow and ushered him along. "Let's go and deposit your gold at the bank. I want to get going, so I can meet my new daughter-in-law."

Chapter Fifteen

Rowena folded silk ribbons in the display. Working in the store seemed a good way to pay back Sharon's hospitality. And it kept her mind occupied. However, nothing could stop her from thinking about Dale.

How could she love such a man? A killer. An outlaw. But she did. The seeds had been sown during those lazy afternoons in her jail cell, and the feeling had grown ever since. And then, when Dale stood up for her in front of Freddy and his jeering friends, that love had bloomed like a flower bursting open in the sunshine. The next hour, when they whirled on the dance floor, had been the happiest in her life.

The way she'd learned about Dale's criminal past, ugly words spilled out in public, had been a shock. And it had been an even greater shock to discover that love could not be put out, like extinguishing a candle. Love remained, even against one's will.

She should have let him go. Let him ride out. If the range war escalated again, Dale might have to kill. He'd be plunged right back into that world of violence he'd worked so hard to leave behind, and it would be her fault. And if he chose not to fight, he might end up dead, and she couldn't bear the idea of Twin Springs costing the life of yet another person she loved. There was no solution. No solution at all. Only the coward's way of running away again, and she was through being a coward.

The bell above the door jangled. Rowena put away the crimson silk, like a river of blood, and looked up. It was Mr. Faraday. He'd been in town the day before—she'd seen him through the display window, but he hadn't come inside. Yesterday, he'd been unshaven, in dirty clothing, but today he had made an effort to tidy up his appearance.

"Miss Rowena. I wish I'd knowed you were here."

"I'm helping out, just a few days. What can I get you?"

"I have something that belonged to your mother. An earring. Gold, with white and dark blue stones. I found it by the river, half buried in the sand. If I knowed you were here, I'd have brung it over."

Mama's earring! It must have been washed downstream to Faraday's land. Yearning seized Rowena. If she could make the pair complete again, it would be a connection to her mother, something she could cherish. "Could you bring it in tomorrow? Please, Mr. Faraday."

The man pushed back his hat and scratched his lank hair. "I'm kind of busy, Miss Rowena. Don't have much time. With the poor grass, I need to keep moving my herd around."

"But you were in town yesterday."

"Forgot a few things." He glanced at her, a shifty flicker, not quite meeting her eyes. "Now, if you could spare the time to ride home with me, I could let you have it tonight. One of my ranch hands could escort you back before dark."

The idea of being alone with Faraday sent a shiver of alarm over Rowena, but she pushed her misgivings aside. She was not a coward. What could he do to her? Hold a gun to her head and demand that she sign the lease? Fine, she'd sign. That might be the easiest way to defuse the situation anyway, at least for a while. Dale would understand.

Rowena craned forward on the wagon bench, studying the buildings ahead as they pulled to a halt. It had been nearly ten years since she'd last seen Faraday's ranch. Nothing she could see matched her recollection. The yard looked unkempt, the house ramshackle. Upstairs, a few broken windows had been boarded over. There was no sign of anyone about. She shouldn't have come. At least she should have insisted on taking her own horse, a means to escape. Now it was too late.

"Miss Rowena." Faraday held out a hand to help her down.

She pretended not to notice his outstretched hand and climbed down unassisted. Her skirts tangled with the wagon tongue. She yanked the garment free and heard the fabric rip.

"Don't fret yourself, Miss Rowena."

"Where is everyone? Who will drive me back into town?"

"Come." Ignoring her questions, Faraday led the way toward the house.

Rowena surveyed her surroundings. It was no use. The land was flat, offering no hiding place. The summer temperatures would allow her to survive out of doors, but if she tried to run, Mr. Faraday would find her. She followed him inside, caution thrumming in every nerve.

The house smelled musty, unused. As they passed the kitchen door, the rancid odors of rotting meat nearly made her retch. On the way up the stairs, their footsteps stirred up clouds of dust.

"Where is everyone?" she asked again.

"There is no one, Miss Rowena. My sons are dead or gone, and I can't afford to pay hired hands."

"But you said…" She let the words trail away. There would be no ranch hand to escort her back into town. Too excited by the prospect of recovering Mama's earring, she had acted rashly. Only now did she notice the strange glint in Mr. Faraday's eyes, the nervous tick in his jaw, the tense, jerky movements of his limbs. Mr. Faraday must be losing his mind. She must act normal, humor him while she figured out a way to extricate herself from the situation.

Mr. Faraday opened a door. "This way."

The room ahead was in darkness. It must be the one with boarded-up windows, Rowena thought. She halted, tried to retreat, but a rough hand closed around her arm and shoved her forward. Nearly stumbling, she lurched across the threshold.

Behind her, the door slammed shut. In the faint light that shone through the gaps in the timber nailed across the windows, Rowena could see the glass was not broken. Shuffling her feet, in case there were any obstacles on the floor, she made her way across the room. Past the narrow bed and the washstand that were the only furniture in the room.

Beneath the window, she found a smattering of sawdust, so fresh it still smelled of pine resin. It appeared the room had been turned into a prison. On the day before, Mr. Faraday had been in town. He must have spotted her behind the store counter and he had concocted a crazy plan to take her hostage.

She hurried back to the door and pummeled it with her fists, so hard the door rattled on its hinges. Pain shot up and down her arms, but she kept up her frantic pounding. "Let me out! Let me out!"

"Calm down, Miss Rowena. I mean you no harm. I'll ride over to Twin Springs and leave a note for your husband, tell him that he can have you back when he signs the lease."

"I'll sign the lease. Let me out."

A burst of laughter boomed through the door. "A woman's name on a piece of paper is worthless. It's your husband who has to sign."

Rowena let her hands drop down to her sides. She was stuck, a prisoner in the house of a man whose sanity was crumbling. How long would it take Dale to get back from his trip? What would he do? She fought the surge of panic. Would he sign the lease, resolve the situation with peaceful means? Or would he embrace the violence he had tried to leave behind? If he did, it would be her fault. Her careless actions would force him to become the killer he had once been, and it might plunge him right back into that world of nightmares.

When there was no sidesaddle and a lady-trained horse available in Rawlins, Dale's mother bought a fancy buggy and a smart, high-stepping bay mare. It would be a wedding present for her new daughter-in-law, she said.

They drove out of town before midday, with Dale's

saddle horse tied behind the buggy. He'd forgotten about his mother's boundless energy. Despite the long journey in a locomotive, Madeline Hunter looked immaculate, every hair in place, her blue satin gown brushed clean and the worst of the soot stains removed.

She kept up a light chatter, until she seemed to run out of words. The silences grew longer. Finally, she spoke in a low voice. "Why, Dale? Why did you cut me out? Why did you not let me be part of your life? If you wanted a ranch, I could have bought you one three years ago, any property you chose."

"How could I accept anything from you? Every time you looked at me, I could see resentment in your eyes. I knew what you were thinking. You were blaming me for letting Laurel die. For hiding behind a tree while she was being raped and murdered."

"How can you say that?" his mother wailed and grabbed his arm. "Stop the horse. It's high time we had this conversation, and I want your full attention."

Dale brought the mare to a halt. His mother twisted sideways on the bench to face him. "How can you suggest that I would have preferred to lose both my children instead of only one? If you had not hidden, those soldiers would have killed you. You know it. I know it. Laurel knew it."

"But I did nothing to help her. Nothing."

"You survived. That was the best you could do. All you could do."

"If that is what you think, how come you barely look at me?"

His mother emitted a small, choked sound. Her face crumpled, those faint lines suddenly turning into deep grooves that made her look tired and worn. She shook her head and blinked away tears. "It is my guilt you see when I look at you. I knew what you were planning. Every day, I watched you practice with a gun or a blade. You were a child, twelve years old, and I let you become consumed by hatred."

"You could have done nothing to stop me."

"I could have tried! I could have tried!" She was weeping now, tears running down her face. "But I didn't. You were a child, and I let you become the instrument of my revenge. Every time you disappeared and came back looking a bit more hardened, a bit less human, I knew you'd killed one of those men and I felt a gloating sense of justice. *It's for Laurel*, I told myself. And all along, I was sacrificing you. My guilt is because instead of helping you to heal and to forget, I let you remember. And you paid the price for it."

"Mama…don't cry."

Sobs racked her slender frame. Dale couldn't remember ever having seen his mother reveal her emotions like that. Even when her husband died, even when her daughter died, when her home was burned to the ground, she had hidden her grief behind a wall of reserve.

"Don't tell me I can't cry," she said and rubbed her eyes. Her nose was red, her eyes swollen, every trace of vanity and restraint forgotten. "When you were small and skinned your knee, you'd run into the house and cry against my shoulder. It's my turn now."

Awkward, Dale put his arms around his mother and patted her back. She pressed her face to his shoulder, the flow of her tears soaking his shirt.

"Mama, I'm sorry," Dale said softly. "I'm sorry I couldn't save Laurel."

"I know. But I wouldn't have wanted you to do anything different. It would have been easier for you to die with her than it has been for you to live. I am grateful that you had the courage to survive."

Rowena needn't have worried she'd starve. After Mr. Faraday returned from leaving his message to Dale, he banged pots and pans in the kitchen, and an hour later he came to let her out of her makeshift prison. In the dining room, cobwebs hung from the ceiling, but her host had made an effort with a clean tablecloth and crockery.

She picked at her food. Mr. Faraday ate in gloomy silence. Afterward, he let her use the convenience before locking her in her upstairs room again. Rowena walked with stiff, cautious steps, careful not to reveal the fork she had managed to secrete away in her skirt pocket.

They were using the back stairs now, a narrow, poorly lit passage intended for servants. During the night, she had heard banging and crashing. She'd been terrified, but this morning she had learned the reason for those strange noises. The main staircase was blocked with discarded furniture, as if someone had cleared most of the bedrooms by throwing the contents down the stairs.

The next day, Mr. Faraday brought breakfast and lunch to her room. In the evening, he fetched her downstairs to dinner. Rowena walked behind him along the narrow staircase, her fingers curled around the stem of the fork. How hard would she have to strike between his shoulder blades? He was wearing a leather vest on top of his shirt. It would require great force for the tines of the fork to penetrate the layer of rawhide.

She eased her grip on the solid silver utensil, a relic of more affluent times. Dale ought to be back tonight. He'd ride over, sign the lease. Give Faraday what he wanted. Peaceful way was the best. *Coward.* The accusation whispered through her mind, but she closed her ears to it and concentrated on observing the man across the dinner table.

"Mr. Faraday, where are your sons?"

"Andrew is in Europe. Wants to be an *artist.*" He pronounced the word as if it involved sin. "Simon is in Philadelphia, working for that insurance company. He wants nothing to do with ranching." Mr. Faraday looked up from his untouched plate. "Edward was the only one who loved the land the way I do. And now he is dead." His eyes burned with fervor. "I can't lose this place, Miss Rowena. My wife and my son are buried here. The small piece of ground where they lay is all I have left of them."

Pity swelled in her, blotting out her fear, blotting out the anger. "I'm sorry, Mr. Faraday," she said softly. "I'll talk to my husband when he gets here. I'll make sure he signs the lease." She sighed, sinking deeper into the padded chair. "Just like you miss your wife and son, I miss my mama. It was a cruel trick to pretend you had found her earring."

Faraday's eyes bulged. His nostrils flared. His breathing grew harsh and his upper lip curled, exposing his teeth, like a wolf baring its fangs. "I did find it."

"Oh, Mr. Faraday, why didn't you say so before?" Rowena jumped to her feet. If the table hadn't separated them, she would have embraced the man, even though the signs of his mental decay frightened her. "Please, can I have it? Can I see it?"

For a while, Faraday didn't move. Then, as if in a trance, he pushed up to his feet. He left the table and walked toward the door. He didn't invite her to follow. He ignored her, as if she had ceased to exist.

Her heart thundering so hard she could feel each thud against her ribs, Rowena set off after him. On tiptoe, she followed him through the rear hall. Up the gloomy, windowless back stairs. Across the landing. Into a large bedroom. Here, the furniture remained in place, ornate antique pieces that must have once cost a fortune. The last rays of the evening sun through the window illuminated the dust, the cobwebs, the black dots of mouse droppings on the floor. The room appeared to have been unused for years.

Faraday's gaze slid toward a mahogany cabinet in the far corner.

Rowena could barely contain her eagerness. "There? In the cabinet? Please, get it for me, Mr. Faraday."

With jerky motions, as if fighting against a current, her host walked over to the cabinet and crouched in front of it. He pulled a watch from his vest pocket and used a key hanging from the chain to unlock the cabinet. With an air of reverence, he lifted out a small wooden box decorated with ivory inlay and set it on top of the cabinet.

Rowena wanted to run closer, but something held her back. Her legs gave beneath her and she sank into the fraying armchair near the entrance. Confused thoughts, half-formed crazy ideas, tumbled around in her head, too terrifying to accept.

Mr. Faraday bent over the inlaid box and blew away the layer of dust on top. He selected another, smaller key on his watch chain, unlocked the box and lifted the lid.

For a second, he stared at the contents. Because he stood with his back toward the room, Rowena couldn't see his expression. But she could see his arm move, could see his hand dip into the box. When he turned around, something glinted between his thumb and forefinger.

Once more, Rowena jumped to her feet. She rushed over, met him halfway. Her eyes became riveted on the glittering diamonds and blue sapphires set in yellow gold he held between his fingers. "It is…it is Mama's earring…"

Faraday stared at the jewel, mesmerized.

She put out her hand. "Let me see it."

For a while, they stood frozen, as if locked in a combat of wills, her hand hovering beneath Faraday's calloused fingers. Then he dropped the earring in her palm. Rowena bent her head to inspect it. Echoes of past grief mingled with the delight of discovery in her mind.

"It's not tarnished at all." She touched the jewel with a gentle fingertip to turn it over in her palm. The sapphires and diamonds sparkled in the setting sun. "Mr. Faraday, how did you clean it?"

When no reply came, she glanced up at him. Her host was back by the mahogany cabinet. He was staring into the open box, a look of morbid fascination on his face.

A layer of dust on the box. As if it hadn't been touched in years. *No sign of tarnish on the earring.* As if it had never been buried in the sand—at least not for almost two decades.

Those confused, half-formed ideas she had tried to ignore took on solid shape and shot like a burning arc through Rowena's mind, even more terrifying in their clarity. She fisted her hand over the earring, gripping so hard the prongs of the setting cut into her palm.

She didn't want to face it. Didn't want to know. But how could she *not* know.

"Do you have something else in there?" Each word came out strained, like a thorn in her throat. When Faraday didn't move, when he merely kept staring into the box, the need to know spurred Rowena into action. She rushed over to the cabinet, her shoes clattering against the floorboards, dust flying up in puffs, and she craned to peer over Faraday's shoulder.

Before she could see into the box, Faraday slammed the lid shut. He seized the box away and clutched it to his chest. "Don't look! Don't look!"

"Let me see!" She tried to wrench the box away from him. The earring slipped from her fingers and fell to the floor, where it rolled and rattled around like a gambler's die.

Oblivious to the loss of the jewel, Rowena clawed at the hard wooden edges of the box with her fingernails, trying to pry open the lid. Her elbow jabbed at Faraday's gaunt ribs. Her shoulder slammed against his sunken chest. Using all her strength, she twisted and pulled, fighting for the control of the wooden box.

With a cracking sound, the hinges gave way and the lid snapped away. Something fell out of the box and tumbled through the air, like the flicker of a sorrel horse's tail. And then it lay down on the floor, almost hidden in the shadows, but she could recognize it for what it was—strands of long, red hair, brittle with age, and faded to the color of rust.

"I told you not to look!" Faraday was screaming now. "I told you not to look!"

Unable to move, unable to think, Rowena stared

down at her mother's scalp. "But they said…they said it was Indians…the Shoshone…"

"I never meant to kill her. I never meant to kill her!" Faraday's eyes were rolling in their sockets, his body shaking. "I only wanted to kiss her. But she fought against me, tried to push me away. She slipped and hit her head on a rock." He covered his face with his hands, as if to shut out the visions of the past. "It was an accident. I feared nobody would believe me, so I chanted like the Indians and took her scalp. I never meant to kill her!"

Dazed, Rowena shook her head. All those years of hating the Shoshone, blaming the Indians for her mother's death. No one had ever suspected any different. She recalled the old chief who had talked about an Arapaho brave with a long flame-red scalp. But that scalp must have belonged to some other woman. Someone else's mother, sister, wife, daughter.

She stared at Mr. Faraday and spoke haltingly, the information too enormous to take in. "You… It was you all along… You killed her."

Faraday uncovered his face. He squared his shoulders, the memory of past authority stamped in his ramrod posture. "You can't tell. I'll be ruined."

Up to that moment, the shock of revelation had dulled Rowena's reaction. It had been so long ago the truth didn't seem to matter anymore. It wouldn't change anything. But now, Faraday's selfish demand whipped her into anger. Did he expect her to hold her silence? To forgive and forget? He'd killed her mother. And he expected her to protect him.

She faced him, disgust and loathing in every gesture. "You have to go to the sheriff, Mr. Faraday."

"No! You can't tell." He took a step toward her. He was panting now, his breath coming with a wheezing sound. His eyes darted wildly, unable to focus. Saliva trickled from one corner of his mouth and dripped to the front of his wrinkled shirt.

Rowena recoiled a step. Then another.

Faraday followed. He tossed the broken box aside. It smashed against the floor, the sound as sharp as a gunshot. Faraday lifted his hands. The bony fingers flexed and curled in the air, like the claws of a predator. "You can't tell," he screamed, spittle spraying in the air. "You can't tell!"

Rowena whirled about and ran. Behind her, she could hear the crash of furniture, followed by the thud of footsteps. She burst into the corridor, raced down the hallway. The footsteps chased her. Their beat grew faster, the sound louder. He was gaining on her.

When she reached the landing, she hurtled toward the stairs. Her skirts were flaring and flapping around her legs, slowing her down. She felt a sudden jerk as Faraday reached out and grabbed at the bustle gathered at the back of her gown, attempting to jerk her off balance. She stumbled, fell forward, spun around and crashed against the balustrade of the galleried landing, the layers of petticoats softening the impact.

Faraday loomed over her, so close his boots tangled with the hem of her skirts. The smell of his rancid breath filled Rowena's nostrils, nearly making her retch. And then she was spared from the repulsive odor, because a pair of gnarled hands wrapped around her neck and squeezed down on her throat, cutting off her air.

Chapter Sixteen

Dale knew something was wrong the moment he pulled the buggy to a halt outside the entrance at Twin Springs. They had camped overnight by the trail, with his mother sleeping curled up on the padded bench of the buggy. He was going to drop her off first, and then he would ride into town and alert Rowena to her arrival. This way, his mother would have a chance to rest and freshen up, and Rowena would have an opportunity to get used to the idea of a mother-in-law before the two women came face-to-face.

But to his consternation, the front door of the house stood carelessly ajar. The setting sun cast long shadows on the ground, and among them Dale could see the imprint of a man's boot, right by the threshold, hinting at the presence of an intruder. It comforted him to know that Rowena was safe in town, visiting with friends.

"Stay here," he ordered his mother, even though past experience warned him she wouldn't obey. He jumped down and drew one of his Colt Peacemakers out of the holster. The pair of plain, serviceable weapons had replaced the silver-handled family heirlooms he'd carried during his outlaw years.

On soundless feet, he crept toward the entrance. He pushed at the door until it swung open with the faint creak of hinges. Silence. Utter, complete silence. Instinct, developed from years of living with danger, told him it was the silence of emptiness.

Behind him, Dale could hear the rustle of skirts, the groan of buggy springs, the soft patter of light feet. True to form, his mother was ignoring orders. With a quick backward look and a wave of his arm that gave her permission to follow, Dale went inside. A sheet of paper hung from a nail hammered to the parlor door. He eased over, careful not to damage any evidence the intruder might have left behind. His eyes skimmed over the bold letters.

Got your wife.
You can have her back when you sign the lease.

No salutation, no signature. Neither was necessary. Dale tore the ransom note free and gave it a closer inspection. The letters were uneven, printed with a trembling hand. Smudges blurred some of the pen strokes, attesting to Faraday's state of agitation, his crumbling sanity.

A man became unpredictable when he lost his mind. He should have been more careful, Dale realized. He shouldn't have allowed Rowena out of his sight. A grim sense of the past repeating itself, like an endless cycle that would go on and on, as long as he had someone to love, swept over him, filling him with an icy dread. Beside him, his mother was prattling on, asking about the house, her new daughter-in-law, about the ranch. Questions that soon might have no purpose.

Dale crumpled the ransom note in his hand. "I have to go."

"But what…?" Sensing his fear, his mother fell silent, her dark brows gathered into a worried frown.

Dale strode to the steel gun cabinet in the corner of the parlor. He unlocked the door, pulled out a rifle and a box of shells and held them out to his mother. "You know how to load. If there is any trouble, don't hesitate to pull the trigger."

Madeline Hunter accepted the weapon without protest. During the war she had lived through too many attacks, too many ambushes, too many hostile confrontations not to know when it was best to obey without question. But Dale wanted to make sure. He thrust the ransom note at her. Already on his way out, he called back at her, the solemnity of a promise and the hard edge of command in his voice. "I'll bring her back. I want you to be here, waiting, in case she needs the kind of care that is better delivered by a woman."

The ground thundered beneath him. Rocks and grass and earth passed in a blur as Dale searched the terrain ahead, guiding the horse along the fastest route. Fortunately, Louis had already been saddled, tied behind the buggy. The gelding was tired after the trip to Rawlins, but it helped that on the way back he had not carried a rider. Dale crouched low in the saddle, his body rocking with the motion of the horse. He emptied his mind, seeking that lonely space inside his head where he retreated when he knew he might have to kill.

He'd met men—soldiers, outlaws, bounty hunters—

who had spent too much time in that lonely place, accepting the violent impulses people normally kept shut away. Those men had lost some of their humanity and never found a way out again.

The same might have happened to him. He had come back slowly, in stages. In the months at the hospital. During his years as a federal marshal. And Rowena had helped him to shed the last of the darkness, overcome the nightmares. But if Faraday had harmed her, Dale would kill him. He would do it slowly and without mercy, and feel no remorse.

The ranch loomed ahead, a ramshackle collection of log buildings weathered to silver. The sun had dipped beneath the western slope, leaving the yard in shadows. Dale had only seen Faraday's home from a distance before. Now, as he drew closer, the aura of decay startled him. Hole in the barn roof. Boarded-up windows in the house. Rusty well. Pump knocked down and useless. Fence posts that had snapped and fallen away like rotten teeth.

A spark of that hard-won humanity flickered within Dale. If he had known the true extent of Faraday's ruination, he might have shown compassion. Let Faraday have his lease for another year. However, a concession to Faraday might have ended the truce with Spencer, and Dale had regarded the polite Southerner the more dangerous of the feuding pair—an assessment he now understood to be a mistake.

He vaulted from the horse before it had come to a stop and stormed to the entrance. The front door was made from dressed logs, thick enough to stop a bullet from a rifle, and trimmed with iron fittings. Dale could see marks where gunfire, or perhaps arrowheads, had slammed into the timber.

He wanted to burst in and call Rowena's name, but experience had taught him to approach such situations with caution. He tried the wrought-iron handle. It turned. He inched the door open. Too late, he felt the resistance on the other side. He flung the door wide and flattened himself against the outside wall, waiting for the crashing noises to subside.

When only a faint rattle remained, he leaned across the threshold to peer inside. It had been a rickety wooden chair, stacked with tinned goods and glass jars full of pickles and preserves. Red and yellow and green puddles, thick and sticky, spread over the floorboards, like molten lava. The acid odors suggested the preserves were old, no longer fit for consumption.

Dale picked his way past the mess, his eyes flickering between the floor and the foyer ahead. He didn't want to trip up on the scattered tins and bits of broken glass, but neither did he want to let Faraday sneak up on him.

When the entryway opened up to a soaring, two-story foyer, he heard a wheezing sound. Two different sounds. Like a duet. A thin, terrified rasp. And the heavy, hissing sound of someone breathing through their nose, with their teeth clenched and their lungs heaving.

Dale looked up to the direction of the sounds. The image imprinted on his brain like the magnesium flash that creates a photograph. On the galleried landing, Rowena was bent backward over the balustrade. Her elbows stuck out and her hands clawed at her throat, trying to loosen the hold of the bony fingers wrapped around her neck.

Not a tall man, Faraday was standing in a crouch to create an angle that added to the pressure of his thumbs against Rowena's windpipe. His position, combined with Dale's limited line of vision from the foyer below, kept Faraday hidden. Dale didn't have a shot. Even with his skill as a marksman, the risk of hitting Rowena was too great.

"Let go of her, Faraday. I'll sign the lease."

The man showed no reaction. No response, no easing of pressure around Rowena's neck. Faraday must have tumbled into insanity, beyond reason. Dale felt the familiar jolt of battle readiness. His blood hammered in his veins. His body grew taut, making him feel as if his strength had increased hundredfold. His vision sharpened.

Sleek and agile as a mountain lion, he took two steps toward the stairs—and came to an abrupt halt. Halfway up the curving staircase, furniture, some of it smashed into pieces, had been stacked to form a barricade that almost reached to the ceiling. If he tried to ram his way through, most likely he would send everything tumbling down and be buried among the debris. There had to be a back staircase, but he had no time to search for it.

"Can you hear me, Rowena? Nod if you can!"

She moved her head. Her upsweep had been near to collapse, and now the ivory pins slipped free and rained to the floor. Like a river of mahogany, her hair cascaded past her shoulders, forming a thick cloak that shielded Faraday even more effectively from view.

"When I start shooting, don't move, Rowena! Don't move at all!"

The river of mahogany rippled with another nod.

Dale took aim, shot the iron chain on the candelabra that hung from the ceiling. The candelabra clattered down, like a windmill, metal spokes spinning in the air. When it hit the floor, the glass globes shattered, showering fragments of frosted glass around the foyer.

There was no reaction from Faraday. None at all. Rowena was still on her feet, her fingers clawing against Faraday's hold. The wheezing sound of her breathing was becoming more urgent, more desperate. If she stopped breathing altogether, Dale knew he would only have a few short minutes to get to her and revive her before she suffocated to death.

Frantic, he surveyed the foyer and the galleried landing above. From where he stood, he had no shot. It would take too long to climb over the barricade or to find the back stairs. His only chance was to rattle Faraday. Make him flinch, just enough to get a shot at the edge of his arm…at his shoulder…at his elbow. Even a minor injury would ease his grip around Rowena's throat, and she could get in a few breaths of air.

Dale shot at the brass dinner gong suspended from a wooden stand in the foyer. The bullet sent the huge metal plate swinging against the wall. The clanging echoed around the room, like the bells of doom, but Faraday seemed oblivious to the sound. Dale fired both his pistols into the furniture stacked on the stairs. Like a mudslide, the pile of timber lurched and tumbled, cracking and snapping as it settled into a new formation, but Faraday still showed no reaction.

Shuffling backward, Dale flattened himself against the foyer wall. A man who lived by his guns learned to count his shots. When his pistols were holstered, he kept the hammers on an empty chamber, which gave him ten shots. He'd used four. Six left.

Up on the landing wall, behind Faraday, hung a large portrait of a young woman, wearing the kind of wide crinoline dress that had been fashionable thirty years ago. Dale shot a hole through the woman's left eye. Although he could see little of Faraday, he saw Rowena shift, and he knew Faraday must have caused that tiny motion. Dale shot a hole through the woman's right eye. "I have four bullets left, Faraday!" he called out. "Her forehead." He squeezed out a shot. "Her mouth."

Two bullets left. And still he had no shot. "Her heart," Dale called out. "If she was ever fool enough to love you, every memory of that love will die when I put a bullet through her heart."

When Dale fired, Faraday could not resist the urge to look at the portrait on the wall behind him. For a fraction of a second, his gaunt body twisted, bringing part of his left arm into Dale's line of sight.

Don't move, Rowena, Dale prayed in his mind.

And he pulled the trigger.

Faraday screamed as the bullet hit his elbow. He released his hold on Rowena and wrapped his fingers around his injured arm, like a tourniquet. Blood seeped from the torn sleeve of his threadbare shirt. Freed from the suffocating grip around her throat, Rowena hunched forward and hauled in deep gulps of air.

Which way was faster? Over the furniture? The back stairs? Dale chose to remain where he could see his wife. He took the bottom steps in two big leaps and jammed his boot between a wobbling chair and a desk propped on its side. From the corner of his eye, he could see Rowena straighten. One of her hands lifted high in the air. Her fingers were curled around some kind of silvery object, long and sharp. As Dale watched in stunned disbelief, Rowena swung her arm and buried that long silver implement into the side of Faraday's neck.

Faraday let out a terrified croak and staggered backward. His arms flailed in the air, spilling droplets of blood over Rowena's dress. With a heavy thud, he collided against the balustrade. For a moment, he hung over the railing, his back arched, shoulders tipping into the void.

Attempting to right himself, Faraday shoved hard against the balustrade. The timbers groaned and creaked beneath his weight, and with a sharp crack, a section of the railing gave way. Faraday tumbled over the edge. Spread-eagled, as if flying, he coasted downward on his back. The threadbare clothing flapped around his gaunt body. He seemed to float suspended in midair forever, even though it barely took a second.

When he hit the floor, the fragments of broken glass crunched beneath his weight. Pieces bounced into the air and rained back down on him. That long silver implement on the side of his neck fell off. It had been a fork, Dale realized. He didn't have to examine the body to know if the man was dead. The crack of Faraday's skull upon impact left no doubt.

Up and up he struggled, the furniture toppling and rolling beneath him. It felt like wading in snow full of knives. Splinters dug into his legs, piercing the leather of his boots and tearing open the scarred tissue. He ignored the pain. He was good at ignoring pain. What he couldn't ignore, could never ignore again, was the need that tightened like a fist around his heart—the need to get to his wife.

Up and up. A broken bureau, the skeleton of a bed. He leaped onto an armchair, felt his boot sink through the rotten padding. The rusty springs in the chair sang and moaned beneath his weight. He recovered his balance, yanked his boot free. Up and up, pain tearing at his shins, his body throbbing with a longing that filled him so completely he felt lightheaded with the emotion.

He jumped over the final obstacle, a bentwood hat stand that lay like a gate across the top of the stairs. Rowena. Rowena. He wanted to rush up to her. Bundle her into his arms. Make sure she was all right. Hold her, so he could feel the beat of her pulse, the rise and fall of her chest, the warmth of her skin, savor all that evidence that she was alive.

On the galleried landing, Rowena was on her hands and knees by the edge, peering down at Faraday's corpse. Dale halted. His focus had been so completely on getting to her, there had been no room for any other thoughts in his head. What had happened? His wife, his gentle, peace-loving wife, had stuck a fork in Faraday's neck. Would she be filled with remorse now, unable to accept her own capacity for violence?

He conquered the urge to rush to her. She was too close to the sheer drop. If her mind was fragile after the ordeal, a sudden approach might make her start, send her tumbling into the void. Forcing himself to remain calm, Dale studied his wife in the dim, shadowed evening light. Her blue cotton dress was wrinkled and disheveled, and the heavy bustle at the back hung askew, but he could see no rips, and no blood, apart from the spatter from Faraday.

Talking softly, he extended one hand toward her. "It's all right, darling. Come away from the railing. Come over to me."

"Is he dead?" The words came out hoarse, as if it hurt her throat to speak.

"Yes," Dale replied. "And he deserves to be."

The bustle on the back of Rowena's gown swayed, and then she was backing away from the broken balustrade and scrambling to her feet and rushing toward him. Relief poured over Dale, bright and golden, like the warmth of sunlight. He opened his arms, and Rowena barreled into him, so hard he had to take a few backward steps to maintain his balance.

He hugged her, cradling her close. He could feel the frantic drumming of her heartbeat, the restless tension in her body. She twisted and stirred in his embrace, unable to settle, unable to remain still. Dale recognized the ebbing of terror, the jittery sensation of too much energy that came from surviving a battle. He tried to soothe her by stroking her back, by crooning soft words, but Rowena wriggled against his hold and arched her back, her palms pressed to his chest to create a distance that allowed her to look at him.

"He killed my mother… It was not the Shoshone… It was him." Her eyes were wide, her speech a breathless stream. Dale did not interrupt. The aftermath of his first killing remained vivid in his memory. He'd eased his torment with whiskey, but for Rowena it would be better if she kept talking, purged her feelings with words.

"He said he had her earring…but he kept looking inside the box and it was her scalp… Oh, Dale, it was awful, awful. Her beautiful hair, all dried up and faded." Her expression grew defiant. "I'm glad he is dead."

Rowena stared up at him, her fingers fisted in his shirtfront, gripping tight. Her mouth quivered, and for a moment Dale thought she would burst into tears. He started to tell her that everything was all right, it was over, but Rowena cut him off with a quick shake of her head. Her gaze flickered over his face, tracing his features, studying them. Her voice, still raspy and hoarse, fell to a whisper.

"When I discovered about your outlaw past, it frightened me to think you were capable of killing without remorse. Capable of such boundless hate. But I felt it, too, Dale. When I stuck the fork in Faraday's neck, I felt the thrill of revenge. I watched him fall to the floor and I didn't care. I was glad to see him die. I'm no different from you. Just like you, I wanted to avenge the love that was taken from me. And I feel no remorse."

You will, later, Dale thought grimly. *When you come down from the euphoria of having vanquished your enemy, you'll see the blood on your hands and wish you could wash it away.*

However, if Rowena's claim that Faraday had killed her mother was true, he could ease her conscience. "You did Faraday a favor. Even if he didn't hang for murder, he would have lost his honor. His sons would have disowned him. More than likely, he would have been declared insane and locked up in an asylum. This way is better."

Rowena closed her eyes and expelled a small sigh, her shoulders sagging. Her expression grew pinched, a battle of emotions reflected on her face. Finally, she opened her eyes, looked up at him and forced a shaky smile. "At least no one can call me a coward now."

"No." He cupped her chin and stroked her trembling

mouth with the pad of his thumb. "You are a woman of courage. Have always been."

Their gazes locked and held. The wariness that had come into Rowena's eyes after she learned the truth about him was gone. Completely gone. In its place Dale could see trust and understanding. He wanted to tell her a million things. That he was sorry for having left her alone, undefended. That he was sorry for having allowed her to be exposed to danger.

More than anything he wanted to tell her that he loved her, but it was not the right time. Not with the aura of death and violence thick in the air around them. He swept his thumb over her lower lip once more and gave a sigh of frustration. It was only three small words, but at this rate they might grow old before he could get them said.

Her body hummed like the strings of a violin, like the lilting tune of a flute. She could almost hear the music. Her limbs refused to remain still. Nervous energy thrummed through her veins, twitched in her muscles, tingled on her skin. Her throat ached from the crush of Faraday's thumbs but she hauled in deep breaths, savoring the air, despite the musty smells that filled the house. It hurt to speak, but the words had kept pouring out of her from the moment she found herself safe in Dale's arms.

And yet, behind the euphoria of survival, dark thoughts loomed like storm clouds. Already, Rowena could feel guilt and horror and remorse scurrying around her mind, like rodents digging beneath a fence, looking for a way to break through.

Bravery was not just the ability to respond to a threat,

she realized. That had come easy. Survival instinct had taken over, removing the need to think. The true test of courage would come in the aftermath, when the fighting spirit ebbed and she would have to come to terms with the fact that she had killed a man.

But when that time came, when this glorious feeling of being alive no longer buzzed within her, like the finest of champagne, she'd have Dale to turn to. He'd help her dispel the nightmares. Just as she had done for him. In every way, they were equals now. The idea gave Rowena a tiny shudder, the first of those dark rays of remorse.

Dale eased his hold around her. For a while, they had been standing still, arms wrapped around each other, her face pressed to the crook of his neck. Inside the house, the shadows were deepening, the dusk slowly giving way to darkness outside.

"We'd best get going," Dale said. "Night is falling."

"What about…?" She twisted to stare at the broken railing.

"I'll ride out to Clayton tomorrow, fetch the sheriff." Dale lifted one hand and brushed a lock of hair away from her face in a soothing gesture. "I could tell him that Faraday invited you to supper. That he was hurrying to fetch his silver cutlery from upstairs. On his way back he stumbled, and a rotten piece of railing gave way."

"I don't wish to lie to protect myself."

"You wouldn't be lying to protect yourself. You'd be doing it for Faraday. Allowing him to die with honor."

A sigh whooshed out of Rowena's chest. It was the first tiny step of accepting what she had done, of moving on from the ordeal. She had spared Faraday from shame, from a prison sentence, perhaps from a death by hanging. She might have deprived him of his final years on earth, but he might have preferred his life to end this way.

"What you said is true, in a fashion." She considered, arranging the facts to suit her conscience. "He came to find me in town and told me he had my mother's earring. He said he had found it on the riverbank, buried in the sand." She paused and took another step of dealing with the situation. "I'd like to find the earring. It fell on the bedroom floor."

They fetched a lamp and candles, lit them and searched the floor in the big bedroom until they found the earring. Rowena couldn't bear the thought of touching her mother's scalp, but she steeled herself and packed it away in a square of linen cloth Dale cut from the bedding with his knife. Indians believed in making a body complete for the afterlife. Perhaps one day she might wish to bury that last piece of her mother with the rest of her.

On the way home, she sat on the dun gelding in front of Dale, across his lap, the way a Southern gentleman would rescue a lady. He kept the pace to an easy lope. Night had fallen, but a three-quarter moon hung in the sky, casting a pale glow over the landscape.

As Rowena leaned against Dale's chest, his arm anchoring her into place, a new confidence settled over her. They were a good match. Dale was hard and tough, tempered by his past, but he longed for a peaceful life. She was gentle, but she was learning to act with courage. Together, they completed each other. She was the sunshine in his darkness. He was her shelter in a storm. Whatever he had been, whatever he had done, it no longer frightened her. She might not condone the way he had sought revenge, but she understood and would not judge.

At Twin Springs, light spilled out through the windows. Puzzled, Rowena shot a glance up at Dale. He smiled back at her, green eyes full of mischief. "I have a surprise for you."

"I hope it's not a housekeeper."

Dale tipped his head back and burst into a roar of laughter. "No. That I can promise. My mother has no personal acquaintance with a cleaning cloth or a scrubbing brush."

"Your mother?"

He brought the horse to a halt and slid Rowena down to the ground. "That's right. I wired her that I'm married. She derailed a dozen trains and messed up the entire transcontinental railroad timetable to get here."

Rowena shielded behind the horse, keeping out of sight. Memories of Freddy Livingston's mother buzzed like insects in her mind, stinging and biting, just like Mrs. Livingston's cruel comments had done. If Dale's mother disliked her with equal fervor, would she at least be polite enough to hide her hatred behind formal manners?

Dale clucked his tongue at Louis and the horse set off toward the stable. Exposed to sight, Rowena remained frozen to the spot. She could see a woman standing on the doorstep, silhouetted in the light. Small and slender, she wore a dark blue silk gown. Her hair, as black as Dale's but with a few gray strands in it, was set in intricate twists.

At the thought of her own appearance, Rowena

closed her eyes and stifled a groan. Her bustle hung askew, making her look like a lopsided hen. Her dress was stained with blood and spittle and dirt, not to mention that she had slept wearing the garment. Her hair must look like a bird's nest, and no doubt she had streaks of dust on her skin.

I'm not a coward, she told herself.

She pasted a smile on her face and marched up to the door. "Hello, Mrs. Hunter. I'm sorry I wasn't here to welcome you. I hope you had a good journey."

The woman's slim eyebrows rose. "Mrs. Hunter? Is that what you plan to call me?"

Dear Lord. Did she have a title? Your Grace? Milady?

Rowena curled her fingers into the crumpled fabric of her skirts to steady her hands. "What would you like me to call you?"

"I was hoping you might call me Mad. It's short for Madeline. The abbreviation is Dale's little joke, from when he was a boy." She spread her arms. "Come here. Let me hug you. I've been worried out of my mind."

Stunned, Rowena stepped into the older woman's embrace. Slender arms wrapped around her. A faint scent of perfume, light and floral, floated on the night air. A gentle voice whispered in her ear. "A long time ago, I lost a daughter. Now Dale has given me another one, and I can't thank him enough."

Closing her eyes, Rowena basked in the glow of acceptance. She had done nothing to earn it, except take a few steps and speak a few words. She had not proved her worth in any way. And yet Madeline Hunter was prepared to love her, accept her, with the greatest love and acceptance of all, one that did not need to be earned in any way but came as a right. Because they were family.

Exhuming a body was never an easy business. They had done it right, Dale thought. They owned Faraday's land now, had bought it from his surviving sons, who had given their permission without hesitation. Spencer had been harder to convince. In the end, it had been Dale's mother's Southern charm that brought the man around.

Spencer's ranch hands had helped Dale with the digging. They had found Edward Faraday's handsome oak coffin still solid, resisting the decay of nature. They had lifted the coffin onto a wagon bed and transported it over to Spencer's land, where Rowena and Spencer stood waiting beside a newly dug grave.

Spencer was gone now, back into his house to mourn his lost daughter. The sun was sinking in the west, the low rays falling on the pair of memorials in front of Dale and Rowena. They had left Lucille Spencer's headstone in place and transported Edward Faraday's to stand next to it. Behind the two gray granite headstones, they had placed a third one. It only had three words: *Together in eternity.*

Rowena had wanted to burn Faraday's house to the ground, but Dale had persuaded her to let it stand and fix it up. When they got more sheep, they might want to employ a foreman, and by offering accommodation they might attract a man who had a family.

Beside Dale, Rowena was patting the corners of her eyes. She had been getting more and more emotional recently. And her constant bouts of nausea couldn't be due to her cooking. Soon they'd have to visit the doctor in town. Dale couldn't wait to have the news confirmed, but he had preferred to wait until his mother had returned to New York. If she discovered there was a grandchild on the way, she would never have left.

"They must have loved each other very much," Rowena said.

Now, Dale told himself. *You can say it now.* But the words didn't come. This was the moment to remember. The moment of Edward and Lucille. Lovers who had lost their chance of a life together.

"I know how he felt," Dale said, his eyes on the headstones. "Every morning when he woke up, she was his first thought. Every night when he went to sleep, she was his last. And everything he did in between was for her. Without her, nothing mattered. Without her, there was no future. No light. No laughter. No love."

"And I know how *she* felt. Every time she heard an approaching rider, her heart beat wildly, in case it might be him. And every time he rode away, it felt as if the daylight had dimmed and a chill wind swept in." Shifting beside him, Rowena wrapped her hands around Dale's arm and leaned against his side. "Will it last? Will it always feel like this?"

Dale thought of his parents, the hardships they had faced when the war broke out and she was from the South and he was from the North. He thought of all the losses and disasters, how they had consoled each other, until Madeline Hunter found herself widowed and alone.

"It will last," he said. "It may not always feel the same, but a love that matures is no less powerful." He nodded toward the graves. "And one day we'll rest like this, side by side, together in eternity. But before then, we'll have a long and happy life. And I hope that when we are gone, there'll be children and grandchildren to stand at our grave and remember us."

Rowena looked up at him, that impish humor he loved so much lurking in her eyes. "On the topic of children…you may not need to wait very long."

Dale bundled her into his embrace and held her tight. And the words came, after all. Three small words. "I love you."

Epilogue

"I hear riders."

"Are you sure it's not a buggy or a wagon?" Dale bent to set the cup of coffee down on the table beside his wife who lay curled up in their big double bed.

"I can only make out the clip of hooves. Several horses."

The accuracy of his wife's hearing never ceased to amaze Dale. The April sun was bright outside, the snow already melted, but they kept the windows shut to retain the heat indoors. Even through the glass, Rowena could hear what went on out in the yard. All those hours she spent practicing on the piano he'd ordered from Steinway & Sons in New York City must serve to sharpen her ears.

"Maybe Mama is bringing a nursemaid and servants with her," Dale suggested. "She knows how to delegate. I'll go downstairs and welcome her."

Rowena stirred beneath the covers. "I must get up, get dressed."

"You stay in bed," Dale ordered, mock severity in his tone. It had been a difficult labor, two weeks premature. Although the doctor had pronounced Rowena fit and well, and she had resumed sleeping beside him, Dale wanted her to get plenty of rest.

When he got to the vestibule, a formal knock on the front door startled him. Surely, his mother considered herself family, allowed to come and go at will, and Rowena's friends from town who'd come to help had already returned to their homes. Dale took his gun belt down from a hook on the wall and buckled it on before he opened the door.

He came face-to-face with Major Parks. Standing ramrod straight, the brass buttons on his uniform polished to a high gloss, the major greeted him with the solemnity of a soldier bearing dispatches. From the twitch of the major's right arm, Dale guessed the man had barely conquered the impulse to perform a salute, although he had not been able to stop his heels clicking together, and his posture snapped even more erect.

Behind the major, in the yard, Dale could see two saddle horses and a string of packhorses carrying parcels wrapped in oilcloth. His mother stood by the saddle horses, attempting to look demure.

"May I come in?" the major asked.

"Of course." *And leave my mother to take care of the horses?* Baffled, Dale stepped aside.

In the parlor, the major took down his hat and tucked it under his arm. With a ceremonial air, he settled to stand in front of Dale. "A year ago, I was in a position to grant you a favor. I told you that I hoped you'd remember the occasion and let it count to my benefit if we ever met under more familiar circumstances. That time has come now. I am here to ask for your mother's hand in marriage."

So, that was it. Suddenly, the major's display of nerves, Mama's attempt to look innocent, it all made perfect sense. Dale suppressed his smile. "Surely, my mother is old enough to make up her own mind."

"She says she spent so many years without her son, she is not going to do anything that might risk losing you again." The major's ramrod posture eased. "I need your blessing, Hunter. Do I have it?"

"I'm too old to need a stepfather." The major stiffened, denting the hat tucked beneath his arm, and Dale hurried to complete his response. "But I could use a friend, and there is no one I'd rather have than you, Major Parks. Welcome to the family. And now, perhaps you can fetch my mother before she gets bored with the waiting and decides to reorganize the stable yard."

But, true to form, his mother had been eavesdropping, and now she edged into the parlor. Skirts swishing, she hurried over to the major, and the two of them linked hands and faced Dale, like young lovers seeking parental approval.

Dale smiled at them. "Congratulations, Mama."

"You don't mind another man taking your father's place?"

"I have fond memories of my father, but that's all they are. Memories. I'm sure he wouldn't have wanted you to spend the rest of your life alone, and neither do I. And I think it is high time you two made it legal. I have an inkling you have been living in sin."

His mother blushed. "That is the one good aspect of widowhood. One is allowed the occasional moral lapse."

"No more moral lapses now. You are grandparents."

"Grandparents? But I intended…? Oh, no!"

Dale grinned. "Yes, Mama. My offspring defied you by arriving early."

"Is Rowena all right? Is the baby all right? Where are they? Can I see them?" Barely able to contain her excitement, Madeline Hunter was bouncing on her toes, eyes shining, her hands flapping in the air.

"Rowena is resting upstairs. Follow me."

Dale knew his wife considered his sense of humor wicked, but he could not resist the temptation. He had chosen his words carefully to maintain the element of surprise, and when they entered the bedroom, he positioned himself to block the cribs from view. Rowena was sitting up in bed, dressed in a lace-trimmed robe, her hair neatly braided.

After the flurry of greetings had died down, Dale went to the cribs, picked up a baby and placed it in his mother's arms. "One for you." He went back to pick up the second baby and proffered it at Major Parks. "One for you."

Gingerly, the major took the infant.

"Twins." Madeline Hunter had been admiring the baby she was holding, and now she craned over to see the other child. "Like peas in a pod."

"I know how highly you value manufacturing efficiency, Mama. I hope you are impressed." Dale went to the bedside and helped Rowena up to her feet. "Now, if you don't mind, my wife has been looking forward to a bath, and I have water heating on the stove."

"We have decided to name the girls Holly and Heather," Rowena cut in, beaming with pride. "We thought of Laurel, and Isla after my mother, but decided not to look into the past."

The major held the infant away from his pristine uniform. "I think this one is leaking."

"Splendid timing." Dale ushered Rowena toward the door. "Mother will teach you how to change a baby. There is water in the washbowl and clean diapers in the armoire."

In the corridor, Rowena tugged Dale to a halt. "Can we just leave them?"

"Of course we can. Mother is the only one of us who has experience with babies." He scooped Rowena into his arms and carried her down the stairs. "You can have your bath, I'll deal with the horses, and then we'll go back upstairs and see how they are doing."

When Dale unloaded the packhorses, he spotted a book on veterinary science he had asked his mother to purchase. He paused to leaf through the pages. A newspaper cutting fell out. *The mention of Pinares might interest Rowena* was written on top in his mother's neat handwriting.

Curious, Dale skimmed through the text. And burst into a roar of laughter.

Quickly, he finished taking care of the horses and hurried into the bathing room. Rowena was immersed in the tub, her baby bump still evident. Her breasts were full and heavy, but Dale did not allow the sight to distract him from the news.

"You won't believe this," he said, waving the newspaper clipping in the air. "Those mining shares your friends were peddling, it appears they were not worthless, after all."

With a slosh of water, Rowena sat straighter in the

big steel tub. "Don't tell me they have struck a lode of copper?"

"No. But the Phelps Dodge mining company has merged with the Copper Queen, and they want to build a new smelter and a warehouse. That parcel of land is the most convenient location. They have acquired the claims, six of them in all, giving a windfall to six different towns, one of which is Pinares." Dale lifted his brows. "You wrote to your former employer, didn't you, and gave your address here? And you let the post office in Pinares know?"

Rowena stared back at him. "Yes…yes, I did."

"This newspaper article is dated three months ago, and not one person has written to you, offering to reimburse your fine. Not one." Dale slipped the clipping in his pocket and knelt beside the bathtub. "If you've been harboring any guilt over how you betrayed the people in Pinares, you can forget it now. They have paid you back, with interest."

While Dale helped Rowena rinse and dry her skin, she kept telling him there must be some delay. People were busy. The post office was slow. *You fool*, he thought tenderly. But he wouldn't have it any other way. He never wanted her to lose that sense of loyalty, her faith in people she considered her friends.

They returned upstairs to find Dale's mother bundling away dirty diapers. The major was in his shirt-sleeves, his hair mussed, a suspicious-looking brown stain decorating his chest like a medal. He cradled a sleeping infant in the crook of each arm, and he smiled the blissful smile of someone who has just discovered his calling in life.

"I had lost all hope of ever having a family. And now

I have a wife, a son, a daughter-in-law and two grand-children. I must be the luckiest man on earth."

"No," Dale said. He pulled Rowena to his side and kissed her in front of his mother and Major Parks. "I am."

* * * * *

If you enjoyed this story check out
The Fairfax Brides miniseries
by Tatiana March

His Mail-Order Bride
The Bride Lottery
From Runaway to Pregnant Bride

And don't miss

The Outlaw and the Runaway

2018 CHRISTMAS ROMANCE COLLECTION!

You'll get TWO FREE GIFTS & TWO FREE BOOKS in your first shipment, plus a trade paperback by *New York Times* **bestselling author RaeAnne Thayne!**

This collection is packed with holiday romances by internationally famous *USA TODAY* and *New York Times* bestselling authors!

Get 4 FREE REWARDS!

We'll send you 2 FREE Books plus 2 FREE Mystery Gifts.

Harlequin Presents® books feature a sensational and sophisticated world of international romance where sinfully tempting heroes ignite passion.

FREE Value Over **$20**

YES! Please send me 2 FREE Harlequin Presents® novels and my 2 FREE gifts (gifts are worth about $10 retail). After receiving them, if I don't wish to receive any more books, I can return the shipping statement marked "cancel." If I don't cancel, I will receive 6 brand-new novels every month and be billed just $4.55 each for the regular-print edition or $5.55 each for the larger-print edition in the U.S., or $5.49 each for the regular-print edition or $5.99 each for the larger-print edition in Canada. That's a savings of at least 11% off the cover price! It's quite a bargain! Shipping and handling is just 50¢ per book in the U.S. and 75¢ per book in Canada.* I understand that accepting the 2 free books and gifts places me under no obligation to buy anything. I can always return a shipment and cancel at any time. The free books and gifts are mine to keep no matter what I decide.

Choose one: ☐ **Harlequin Presents®**
Regular-Print
(106/306 HDN GMYX)

☐ **Harlequin Presents®**
Larger-Print
(176/376 HDN GMYX)

Name (please print)

Address   Apt. #

City   State/Province   Zip/Postal Code

Mail to the **Reader Service:**
IN U.S.A.: P.O. Box 1341, Buffalo, NY 14240-8531
IN CANADA: P.O. Box 603, Fort Erie, Ontario L2A 5X3

Want to try 2 free books from another series? Call 1-800-873-8635 or visit www.ReaderService.com.

*Terms and prices subject to change without notice. Prices do not include sales taxes, which will be charged (if applicable) based on your state or country of residence. Canadian residents will be charged applicable taxes. Offer not valid in Quebec. This offer is limited to one order per household. Books received may not be as shown. Not valid for current subscribers to Harlequin Presents books. All orders subject to approval. Credit or debit balances in a customer's account(s) may be offset by any other outstanding balance owed by or to the customer. Please allow 4 to 6 weeks for delivery. Offer available while quantities last.

Your Privacy—The Reader Service is committed to protecting your privacy. Our Privacy Policy is available online at www.ReaderService.com or upon request from the Reader Service. We make a portion of our mailing list available to reputable third parties that offer products we believe may interest you. If you prefer that we not exchange your name with third parties, or if you wish to clarify or modify your communication preferences, please visit us at www.ReaderService.com/consumerschoice or write to us at Reader Service Preference Service, P.O. Box 9062, Buffalo, NY 14240-9062. Include your complete name and address.

HP19R